THE LAST
CABIN

BOOKS BY JOHN DEAL

CJ O'Hara Crime Thrillers

All the Natural Beauties

Under a Blood Moon

Beautiful Death

The Last Cabin

THE LAST
CABIN

JOHN DEAL

THE LAST CABIN
ISBN-13: 978-1-7375382-6-4 (paperback)
ISBN-13: 978-1-7375382-7-1 (eBook)

Dedicated to the people of Alaska, The Last Frontier, a place with breathtaking beauty, rugged terrain, lots of water, and the two littlest men in my life.

Why does God allow evil people to exist in the world?

Standing on the second floor of a vacant warehouse in South Boston, he gazed at the lights twinkling against the dark sky. A fog, coming in from the harbor, crawled toward him as the same old haunting question cluttered his mind.

His grandmother had told him wickedness was often because of a person's surroundings, friends, or circumstances. But she said for some it was the way they were born. He'd never understood this last part. *What does this mean?* In his experience, babies weren't wicked. They cried a lot, but that was because they were hungry, tired, sick, or had filled their diaper. *The old woman was clueless.*

A movement below distracted him, and his eyes caught an oversized rat scurrying along a row of trash cans in the alley. *Disgusting creatures.* Every few feet, the furry rodent stopped and popped upright as its nose twitched, sniffing the air. The billboard for a movie on the building's wall above the rummaging varmint reminded him of a film from his past.

What is the name of the movie? He couldn't recall the title, but it had a guy named Hannibal and a deranged man who skinned young women in it. Buffalo somebody. *Are these men molded into wickedness, or are they born this way?*

His mother had spoiled the ending when she shooed him from his comfy spot on the couch in the living room saying, "Your dad is gonna bust your ass if he catches you watching those kinds of movies!" If she let him stay, perhaps he would have understood these men's motivation. *Jeez.* The film was a product of imagination, or so he thought. Why did it matter that he was only ten? But he was lucky she didn't snitch on him, or he would have been sore for a week. His father, who ran a butcher shop, was a mean cuss. He ignored him unless he made a mistake, and when he noticed him there was lots of pain. His fingers probed under his shirt and traced the line on his lower back. *I don't need to worry about my mother harassing me or my father's abuse anymore—they're gone for good.*

Now that he was older, he pondered morality more. *How can some people appear good on the outside and mask their true self, like that prissy girl from high school?* She wasn't a saint, but adept at hiding her wicked ways. But he knew about her nastiness with the boys in dark backseats and how she'd manipulated his friend, Miles.

Miles wasn't wary like he was, and was the best student in their class. Poor Miles didn't deserve what she did to him. Miss Perfect offered him her attention if she could borrow his paper for ideas on hers. Then, she submitted it to the teacher as her own. She lied when he presented the same paper and said Miles stole it. Miss Perfect got an A, and his only friend got suspended.

His keen eyes always uncovered the truth about people. *I don't miss her either.* He lacked answers to many questions, but was confident his wicked ways weren't his fault. All those faults belonged to the monster within that shared his birthday. His name was Jeffrey.

PART ONE

THE WARNING

ONE

Saturday, September 6
Boston, Massachusetts

He peered through the narrow crack, his eyes sparkling in anticipation. His tongue crawled across his lower lip as he wiped his sweaty palms on his jeans.

As the familiar sensation crept in, his breathing increased, and he envisioned what he would do to her. She was scared now, but soon her face would show panic before terror consumed her. What thrilled him more—the build-up or the act itself?

His memory took him back to high school and to a young woman with long blond hair and green eyes who'd returned home from college. She thought being a cheer-leader made her hot shit, but he showed her. At first, he only wanted to scare her and make her notice him. Then Jeffrey whispered in his ear and took control.

He spent three years locked away in the psychiatric hospital afterward. Over the first two years, he tried to explain he wasn't the guilty party, and it was the wicked one inside him. The doctors started referring to him as Doctor Jekyll and Mr. Hyde.

So, he gave up trying to explain and outsmarted them. After all, the tests showed he had an IQ of over one hundred and fifty. He was much more intelligent than the buffoons who treated him. He tricked them into thinking they were miracle workers and his mind was sound. They wished him luck and let him go.

He was a model citizen for a time, but then his inner demon resurfaced. This time, it wouldn't leave, and the battle for control continued to rage.

A gray rat, plump from feasting on Boston's garbage, quivered one last time before becoming dead still. The metal jaws had slammed shut and ended its existence.

Marilyn stared at him from her own trap across the room, shivering from the chilling temperature. Would she be dead soon, too? *Don't cry. Don't cry, damn it!*

Marilyn's tears rolled down her face as she recalled how she'd wound up in this predicament. It started with her temper, which had landed her in real trouble this time. After her Friday evening hostess shift, she played catch-up, drinking too many margaritas in too short a time. It was stupid to storm out of the bar to walk home drunk and alone after getting pissed at her boyfriend.

As she wobbled along the sidewalk at 2:00 a.m., she veered into the alley to puke. After expelling her guts, she wiped her mouth, did her best to rub the vomit off her shoes, and turned to find a man with eyes devoid of life standing in front of her. *My self-defense class at the Y was a total fucking waste of time and money.*

She twisted her body and struggled hard again, but the plastic ties binding her to the cold metal chair only cut deeper into her wrists and ankles like razors. Her chin dropped to her chest as she fought to calm herself.

When her captor departed at dawn, he swore to return with the darkness. When the faint glow of a streetlight peeked through the lone window's grimy glass she knew he would appear soon. She needed a plan and a way to flee her musty prison.

Please help me! The duct tape over her mouth muffled her scream, only frustrating her. Angry, she jerked back and forth, hoping the bolts securing the chair to the floor would loosen. Nothing moved. She sat as the mixed odor of ammonia from her own urine, stale vomit, and sweat filled her nostrils.

Summoning one last round of energy, she yanked and twisted her arms and legs. The pain radiated throughout her body as physical and mental exhaustion consumed her. A crushing force suffocated her. Blood from her wrists and ankles dripped to the floor. Like the trapped rat, there was no escape. The room fell silent except for the sporadic dripping from a hole in the roof and her whimpers.

A rattling snapped her to attention. *Is someone there?* Her heart thumped against her chest, and she fought the urge to cry again. The door opened, the single hanging bulb above her flickered on, and the man stood in the doorway, squashing her brief glimmer of hope. True to his word, he'd returned to continue tormenting her.

"Hey, we got one of the little bastards," he said, pointing to the rat. "I hate those nasty things." He closed the door and slipped a padlock in place. "I trust he didn't nibble on you before his demise." He crossed the room and opened the top drawer in a tattered wooden cabinet. His lips curled as he selected the desired instrument—a twelve-inch black military knife.

Marilyn squeezed her lids shut, trying to take herself anywhere but here. The unmistakable scent of cheap whiskey caused her to open her eyes to find his face within inches of hers.

"There you are," he leered. "Did you miss me?" He waved his killing tool in front of her. "Whaddya think? This one's lovely, right?"

She twisted her head back as far as possible, but he moved in unison, staying close. Her eyes snapped closed again, and she jerked away when his fingers caressed her chin.

"Don't you wanna play with me?"

His vicious slap reverberated off the room's walls, and she moaned as he grabbed a handful of her sandy blond hair and forced her head back. "Have it your way. I don't mind playing rough. In fact, I prefer it. Last chance, bitch."

Her eyes fluttered open, and the man's face reappeared. "You're back. Good."

The glint of the blade flashed as he ran the tip of the blade along her cheek as she whimpered. "Where should I start? Maybe here. I have a better idea." He touched the knife to her exposed neck.

She flinched when he suddenly bolted upright, weapon in hand, waiting for the blow that would send her to join the rat.

Instead, he cocked his head and froze. "Shush, be quiet." Rain pecked at the window as the man remained rigid. He swung a quick, frantic fist up to shatter the overhead light, and the room dimmed. "Fuck," he hissed.

Marilyn's bleary eyes strained to follow him as he disappeared through a trapdoor in the corner. Once more, she sat alone with the furry creature as raindrops pounded on the glass.

Out of nowhere, the sound of footsteps echoed outside the room. Her heart raced as she struggled to listen, praying for someone to be her savior. The steps grew closer and stopped right at the door.

An explosion erupted when the door splintered and two police officers entered. The beams from their Maglites crisscrossed the floor until hitting her in the face, blinding her.

"We have a young woman," one officer yelled.

The other hurried to her and leaned close. "You're safe now. I got you. I'm Detective Harry O'Hara, but you can call me Harry." As he took the tape from her mouth, he told his partner to call for a bus and backup. "We need to find his ass this time!" He started cutting the ties from her wrists. "Miss, did he hurt you?"

"No," Marilyn said, her voice gravelly. "He got scared and left."

Harry thumbed through the photos on his cell phone. "Is this the man who took you?"

She nodded.

"When was he last here?"

"Umm, I'm not sure. Just a few minutes ago." With her right hand now free, she pointed to the corner. "He crawled through that little door in the floor."

Harry wrapped her in his jacket after he helped her up from the chair. He held her trembling body until the paramedics arrived and loaded her for transport to the hospital. Multiple officers searched the building and surrounding area, but Marilyn's captor had vanished into the dark, rainy Boston night.

When the forensics team started collecting evidence, Harry stepped outside and made a phone call. "Hey, Cap. The tip paid off, and we got here before he killed another young woman. She's gonna have a black eye and a bunch of nasty abrasions, but we expect her to be okay, physically at least. We sent her over to General. The bad news is we can't find him." Harry's fingers rubbed a knot in his neck. He exhaled and whispered, "The Butcher's gone."

TWO

Three Years Later
Tuesday, September 6
Downtown Charleston, South Carolina

Detective CJ O'Hara approached the familiar door and stood frozen. She fixed her emerald green eyes on the shiny nameplate. No matter how often she came here, she always felt pure dread. It was less enjoyable for her than her annual gynecological exam and far more uncomfortable.

CJ reminded herself of how far she had come in her therapy. *Face it,* she told herself, *you were a train wreck and spent your sessions hiding your true feelings.* Now she was more open. *Sometimes.* She blew out a long breath she'd been holding and knocked.

Doctor Charles Greedsy swung the door open, and CJ found herself focused on his piercing chocolate-brown eyes hidden behind his wire-framed glasses. Upon meeting him for the first time over a year ago, she'd noticed his hair was salt and pepper. Now, only a few white hairs clung on for dear life to his shiny scalp.

He was always professional and polite, but he analyzed every word and every move of her body—probing, questioning, and judging. She was certain he would even scrutinize her answer about her breakfast.

"Detective O'Hara." He stepped back and motioned her into his office. "Please come in and have a seat. You're right on time."

CJ followed him into his spacious office and took her usual dark brown leather recliner across from his mahogany desk that was so big it was suitable for landing planes. She squirmed, the chair squeaking at her every move until she finally surrendered and sat with both feet flat on the floor and hands in her lap.

Before dropping into his black leather high-back chair, he stepped over to a mini-fridge in a cabinet filled with psychological books of all sizes. "The Battery was lovely this morning on my run, but I need another bottle of water. Would you care for one?"

"No, thank you," she said, "I'm fine."

His desk was pristine except for a Montblanc pen, a clean white legal pad, and one yellow manilla folder about a half-inch thick. Once he settled in his chair, his eyes locked on her. "Okay, let's start." He picked up the folder, pulled out a lone sheet, and scanned it. "Based on your email, I understand you're requesting an end to our sessions." His chocolate browns trained back on her.

She shifted—*squeak.* "Uh, yes. You've done wonders for me, but there's not much else we need to cover. I'm all good to go now." *Please confirm I'm right.*

The ordinarily stoic man in his mid-sixties cracked a smile. "Well, I appreciate your positive attitude toward my psychiatry prowess. However, I'll defer my sign-off for the brass until we complete today's session. Fair?"

Her head bobbed. *He's not gonna go down without a fight.* "Okay."

He went back to the folder, flipping through the pages.

CJ's thoughts wandered to what he had written in his notes. The two had discussed the three men she killed in the line of duty ad nauseam. She was confident—or hoped—that he felt satisfied with their position on that issue. Their deaths haunted her, but her actions were unavoidable. Her past would not interfere with her doing her job.

"Let's talk a bit more about your challenges with guilt," he said. "I'm curious about where you are with this."

CJ gazed out the window at the growing dark clouds. A bluish-gray pigeon stared at her from its perch on the window-sill. "I'll be honest. Occasionally, I still struggle with my role in my parents' and sister's deaths, and I'd give anything to bring Paul back." She nibbled her lip and locked eyes with him.

"And?"

"With your help, I've evolved to feeling regret now instead of guilt. I regret losing my family and losing my predecessor and friend, but my actions didn't cause their deaths. I'm not to blame. A drunk driver killed my parents and sister, and a tormented young man murdered Lieutenant Paul Grimes."

"How about your call to come home from the sleepover? Is it still your belief this led to your parents being on the road and their fatal accident?" His left hand rested on the folder, and his pointer finger lightly tapped it as his eyes bore into hers.

CJ let out a slow breath. *This question is fucking hard to answer,* her mind screamed. "I guess the best way to explain it is I regret not sucking it up and staying."

He nodded with understanding and jotted a note down on his pad. "How often do you think of them?"

She shrugged. "Quite often, I guess. The holidays are the hardest times concerning my family. As for Paul, I sometimes catch myself going to his office to discuss a case. Every time I flash my lieutenant's badge, I'm reminded it's his spot I'm now filling."

"How do you cope?"

"I focus on the positives, the happy memories, and surround myself with my new family."

"New family?"

She chuckled and said, "The family I've built here in Charleston. I have my two uncles, Ben, and his brother and father. And, of course, I have Sam and her parents. Her friendship is a rare treasure. She's more like a sister to me than a friend and co-worker."

CJ's thoughts went to the man who raised her, Uncle Harry, and how she'd almost lost him in May, twice. First, when a blockage in his heart nearly killed him, and then again, when the first surgery failed. A lump caught in her throat.

Doctor Greedsy made more notes and rubbed his chin. "What about the excesses you've used in the past as an escape, alcohol and sex?"

A clap of thunder rumbled in the distance, and the blinds vibrated, causing the pigeon to flee from its perch.

"I've stopped drinking altogether after I hit rock bottom following Paul's death." She paused before she said, "Well, full disclosure. I had a glass of champagne at Sam's wedding, but only a couple of sips during the toasts."

"And the random sex?" he asked, narrowing his eyes.

"The only person I've slept with since arriving here is Ben. The bottom line is leaving Boston was refreshing for me. I no longer consider going to bars alone to drink or pick anyone up." Sensing where he would go next, she said, "As for my overall physical health, my doctor is pleased with where I am now. I'm eating better, drinking lots of water, and taking my vitamins."

"Do you still have nightmares? The ones where you see the faces of victims."

She adjusted in her chair. "Not so much. I'm not sure what's changed exactly, but perhaps having Ben with me has made a difference. We either spend the night at my apartment or at his house."

"And you're in love with him?"

She nodded. "I am. Very much so. Ben returns today after helping his dad with a charter. It's only been three days since I've seen him, but it seems like a month."

"You two will marry soon, as I understand."

Her face lit up. "We will. We don't have a firm date yet, but we're thinking by the end of the year. Something small by the water." She laughed. "Sam, of course, wants to invite all of Charleston. She keeps telling me anything less than three hundred at a wedding is a travesty."

He stood and went to the window. With his back to her, he said, "You're in a good spot now, CJ. You're happy, and the stress in your life is low." He turned to face her. "What happens when your job goes awry, things turn rough with Ben, and those self-doubts resurface?"

"Doc, none of us can predict the future. All I can tell you is I'm better equipped to handle it. I finally have a support system, something I've never had before."

His eyes narrowed, and he opened his mouth to speak, but offered no words. He moved back to his desk and dropped into his chair. "I tell you what. How about we set our next appointment for two months from now?"

Her nose and forehead scrunched up before she realized what he was saying. "Does this mean you won't sign off?"

"Yes. I'm not convinced it would be in your best interest. We're close, but not quite there."

Heat flushed through her body, and her pulse raced. She fought to control herself and said, "I don't agree with you. Isn't being sure I'm fit for duty the primary aim of this whole damn exercise? You've informed my captain in your progress report that I'm cleared to work."

He leaned forward, resting his folded hands on the desk. "You're correct on both counts. I signed off on you being fit for duty and stand by my decision. There is no doubt in my mind that you acted responsibly and as you should have based on the facts when you took three lives. The man you shot in Boston had a gun to your partner's head, and he would have killed him and maybe you.

"The serial killer here in Charleston severely wounded you and the man trying to save you. He would have finished the job without your quick action. The troubled poor soul you shot in Beaufort left you with no choice. He would have buried his knife in your friend Sam."

He stood, rounded the desk, and took her hand. "Look, I'm sure you're disappointed, but let's give it a little longer to get there. I want to do everything in my power to ensure you have the foundation to succeed in life, not just at your job."

CJ wiped her eyes and sniffed. She nodded and stood. "I'll see you in two months."

Wheeling around, she left his office and pushed through the double glass doors of Charles Greedsy's office building into the steamy morning. She unlocked her black Ford Explorer and leaned in front of the vent, waiting for the cool air to arrive. The voice on the radio announced the temperature would reach ninety degrees by late afternoon. Resting her forehead on the steering wheel, she cried.

I wanted to have good news for Ben. "Hey, I'm no longer a nut job and in danger of falling into the abyss." How can I marry someone if I can't take care of myself?

She glanced at the time—11:10 a.m. Digging in her purse, she found a Kleenex and did her best to wipe the streaks of tears away. She wasn't a fan of makeup, but tried to touch up what little she wore. Using her fingertips, she brushed her shoulder-length auburn hair back in place. *I wanna at least look half decent when Ben sees me.*

***

CJ steered onto the ramp and sped up as she climbed the Arthur Ravenel Jr. bridge. The late morning rays of the sun glistened on the white-capping surface of the Cooper River.

She checked the time and realized Ben would dock with his dad and their guests within minutes. The whole day had been a rollercoaster with ups and downs. She'd been certain Greedsy would release her—*up*—but he didn't—*down*—and Ben is coming home—*up*.

As she crossed the Shem Creek bridge, she turned right and drove to the back of the parking lot. She jumped out and raced down the wooden walkway. In the distance, Ben waved to her from the deck of the fifty-foot fishing boat. She returned the wave as she admired his six-foot-four frame clad in tan khaki shorts and a white T-shirt with *Parrish Charters* printed in bold navy lettering. The boat drifted to a stop, and the bumpers kissed the dock.

"I stink like a fish," Ben yelled.

"I don't care, Mr. Parrish. Get your butt off the boat and kiss me."

He hopped over the railing and lifted her off the ground, pressing his lips to hers. "I missed you so much."

She playfully pushed him away and pinched her nostrils together with her fingers. "Ooh. You stink." Then she grabbed him and whispered, "Let's go home so I can give you a bath and put you to bed."

"I love the sound of that. Let me check with Dad and see if I need to help him clean up." He climbed back on the boat before reappearing minutes later. "Pop told me to get the hell out of here." He laced his fingers with hers and led her toward the truck.

THREE

Wednesday, September 7
St. Helena Island, South Carolina

CJ answered the knock to find her best friend Sam on her landing in a canary yellow sundress and white flats. She was two inches shorter than CJ's five-eight, and her baby-blue eyes contrasted with her golden-brown hair.

"I bring gifts," Sam said, holding a tray with coffee and a bag.

"Ah, you brought me some goodies from Sal's. Thank you. Come on in," CJ said, waving Sam into her one-bedroom apartment above the Watkins Clothing Shop in the French Quarter. "I'm almost ready." She placed the tray on the counter, separating the kitchen from the den, and returned to the neighboring bedroom.

"I figured you could use some coffee and a blueberry muffin," Sam called to her. "Sal's niece, Gia, made them. She's here from Italy and helping for a couple of weeks." She walked to the picture window that provided a view of the rooftops and a slice of the Charleston harbor. "It's gonna be another hot one today. By the way, where's Ben?"

"He left an hour ago to pick up a few things before our trip." CJ slipped on her wedge sandals and glanced in the mirror mounted on the back of her bedroom door—a navy sundress with scattered yellow flowers and a string of her mother's pearls met her gaze. She stepped back into the den. "Well, I think I'm ready. Is this all right? I don't wear dresses much, and I'm still learning Southern fashion."

"You look gorgeous."

"Thanks. Now let's go surprise Grannie." CJ dropped her credentials into her purse, grabbed a vividly wrapped box, and they hurried down the steps into Sam's new white BMW 328i. "I sure do love this car," CJ said.

"Yeah, me too. I still can't believe Will bought this for me as a wedding present."

CJ grinned at her and asked. "How is the husband and married life?"

"I'm so happy I could burst. It's only been a few months, but every minute has been bliss." The younger woman poked her. "And just think. Soon, you'll join me."

"I'm thrilled with Ben, but I'm not sure I'd go that far," CJ said, laughing.

Over the two-hour drive to St. Helena Island, they talked more about Sam's married life, CJ's pending wedding, and her upcoming trip to Alaska with Ben. Sam tried to convince her she should marry in a church with a huge reception.

"No, thank you. We want a small, quaint ceremony with our family and closest friends. And no fancy."

"Okay, suit yourself. My mom told me to tell you she's ready to jump into high gear if you change your mind."

"How is your mom?"

"She's fantastic, and both my parents love Will. Their only issue is when they can expect grandchildren. Speaking of my parents, I think they've filed papers to adopt you."

"They are wonderful, and they've treated me like a daughter," CJ said. "Hey, do you realize we'll officially be sisters-in-law when Ben and I marry?"

Sam raised her eyebrows. "That's right. You and I marrying the Parrish brothers is better than I thought."

They sat silent for several minutes before CJ broke it. "I can't believe this isn't a surprise party."

Sam chuckled as she dismissed the idea. "That would never work. Grannie only leaves her house to attend church nowadays. But most importantly, she would see a surprise party coming, and you more than anyone should know that."

"Ah, yes. Grannie has the gift of sight."

CJ gazed out the window at a herd of cows and recalled meeting this unique old woman who initially resisted wanting anything to do with her. CJ was an outsider to Grannie's world on the island … and she was White. Over time, and with the help of those close to her, Grannie had warmed up to CJ and wound up helping her save Sam.

Most people would say Grannie's gift of sight was nothing more than her being a highly perceptive individual. A few, especially those who descended from slaves, the Gullah, believed she was a psychic and able to see things before they happened.

CJ couldn't put her finger on the special bond she shared with the old woman. Grannie now treated her as though they were kindred spirits. All she knew for sure was that Grannie had a special gift, and Sam wouldn't be sitting beside her without it.

"Do you think she always shares her visions with others?" CJ asked.

Sam shrugged. "I'm not sure, but I doubt it."

"It must be hard for her to always have visions in your head. Some of them awful."

"Yeah. It's gotta be difficult."

"I wonder if any other Gullah people possess this ability?"

"From what I've heard, she's the only one, and when she's gone, I guess it'll end with her. Unless ..."

"Unless what?"

Sam glanced over at her. "I kinda think you might have the gift. You possess something, although not to the same extent as Grannie."

"You're nuts." CJ focused back on the window as they passed a red barn. "Why do you think that?"

"I'm not sure. Perhaps it's the way you work cases. It's almost like you visualize what's happened. As someone who works with you, I've seen it myself."

"Crazy talk! That's just intuition and experience."

"Okay, if you say so," Sam said as she pulled her car onto the shoulder of the road and stopped the engine.

CJ pointed to the rows of cars parked along both sides of a dirt driveway leading to a single-story white house with black shutters. "Wow. This is an enormous crowd."

Sam smiled and said, "Everyone on the island loves Grannie, and it's not every day someone turns a hundred. The funny thing is she didn't know when she was born until the pastor researched it and found an old Bible with her birth date." They exited the car, and Sam moved to the rear. "I hope Grannie likes what I made for her," she said as she lifted a box wrapped in paper with flowers and a yellow bow out of the trunk.

CJ closed the lid. "Wait. You made her a gift? What is it?"

"I did, and I'm not telling you. It's a surprise," Sam said, grinning.

They started up the gravel driveway toward the tent on the side of the house near the marsh.

"You better not show me up, Samantha Ravenel Parrish."

She and Sam were the only White people among over a hundred individuals of various ages and sizes. CJ recalled the same situation when she'd attended the nearby Brick Baptist Church with Grannie on two prior occasions. She recognized numerous people who welcomed her.

Making their way through the masses, they found the guest of honor—Grannie. She sat in a wicker chair with a dark red cushion, individually acknowledging the partygo-ers. They joined the line and waited their turn. The older woman wore a burnt orange dress and matching hat and took each person's hand. Her face lit up when her green cat eyes found Sam's. "Oh. My baby girl has come to visit."

"Happy birthday." Sam leaned down and kissed her on the cheek.

Grannie's frail arms wrapped around her, squeezing her tight.

"I brought you something." Sam turned, picked up the box, and placed it in front of her. "I hope you like it."

Grannie's eyes sparkled. "Thank you, baby." Her gnarled fingers worked to remove the paper and open the lid. She leaned over and peeked inside. "Oh, my."

Sam reached in and removed a patchwork quilt. "My mother helped me make it. Do you like it?"

"I love it," she said. "It's the most beautiful thing I've ever seen." She traced her fingers along the delicate stitching.

CJ stood behind her, waiting her turn. Her stomach grew tight. *Jeez, that'll be hard to top.*

Sam turned and motioned her forward. "Grannie, look who else is here."

The older woman clapped her hands and extended her arms. "Come here, child. I wanna look at you, and my eyesight ain't much anymore."

CJ stepped closer, leaned in, and hugged her. "Happy birthday."

Grannie's fingertips rubbed the engagement ring on her finger. "Marrying such an angel makes Ben a lucky man."

How did she know? I haven't told her yet. "Oh. You've heard about me getting married?"

A smile grew on the older woman's wrinkled face. "No, child. I saw it in one of my visions. It was sweet how your beau proposed, and this ring means a lot to him. I'm so pleased."

The night on the dock after Sam's wedding, Ben had surprised her with his mother's wedding ring. "It was. Ben is a wonderful man, and I hope you can meet him soon. I'd love to have you at the wedding."

The old woman patted her hand. "Grannie's too old to leave the island, but I'll be there in spirit." Suddenly, the smile left her, and she dropped CJ's hand. Her face went dark as she struggled to her feet. "Help me to the sittin' tree, child."

Sam stepped forward and took her arm. "I can help you."

Grannie snatched her arm away. "No, baby. Not you. I want CJ to do it. I wanna speak to her ... alone."

"Uh, okay," Sam said, frowning. "Let me know if you need me."

Grannie told the guests waiting to meet her she'd return, wrapped her arm around CJ, and wobbled toward a massive southern live oak tree on the marsh's edge. After they arrived, she settled into a wrought-iron chair and gestured for CJ to sit on the matching table in front of her. "Sit there, close to me."

CJ's heart thumped and sweat formed on her forehead. She trembled as she carried out the instructions. She sat silent as the old woman's eyes shut, and she rocked back and forth. "Grannie, what's wrong? You're scaring me."

A single tear ran down Grannie's cheek. "I'm afraid for you. You're in danger. Your trip to Alaska ain't a good idea."

CJ shook her head. "I don't understand. What do you mean?"

Grannie opened her eyes. "Take hold of my hands, child."

No. No. No, CJ thought as she recalled the last time she'd done this. The visions she'd witnessed through Grannie were horrific.

"Come on, child. Take my hands and close your eyes."

As if touching a hot stove, CJ took Grannie's hands. The old woman's fingers squeezed, and her eyes closed again. The rocking back and forth resumed. CJ moaned as the scene flickered through her mind like an old black-and-white movie. Nothing was clear, only distorted flashes of images. Waves … an overturned boat … Ben struggling in the water … a dead body—

"No!" CJ jerked her hands away. "I can't …" Tears erupted, and she pleaded. "Please don't make me do this." She dropped to her knees and fell into the old woman's lap. "Pleeease."

Grannie patted her back and exhaled. "Okay, child. Grannie won't make you." She lifted CJ's chin. "You best be careful, though. He's dangerous."

"Who? Who's dangerous?"

"The man with the scar. You be mindful of him."

FOUR

Thursday, September 8
The French Quarter, Charleston, South Carolina

C J gave up on sleeping and slipped from the bedroom barefoot to the comfy chair by her picture window. The flashbacks of Grannie's warning kept cluttering her mind. Little prickling sensations tickled her arms as she wondered how often the unique old woman was mistaken.

A detective's job naturally heightened one's sense of paranoia, or maybe it was Grannie. Who the hell knew? Spending a significant portion of her life dealing with scumbags, the lowest of the low, made typical day-to-day situations send off alarm bells in her head.

She'd see a young woman jogging along the Battery, not a care in the world. Wires hung from her ears as music blasted away, and she'd think, *How the hell is she gonna hear anyone sneak up from behind?* And then there was the young woman she'd seen wandering alone down the shadowy sidewalk on Market Street after a night out drinking. Those damn dark hidey holes were mere feet away. Her first thought was, *What the hell is she thinking?*

CJ climbed out of the chair, peering out the window as the Charleston day began. Willing her thoughts away from the raspy words of warning, she concentrated on a seagull floating on the breeze—a fluffy, light gray ball of carefree feathers.

A wisp of white in the harbor caught her attention. A row of white caps danced across the water's surface, and her chest grew tight as if someone reached in and wrapped their fingers around her heart.

Waves.

Shivering, the voice of Doctor Greedsy replayed his question in her head. "What happens when things go awry?" She frowned. What did he know she didn't? Was she so broken that she'd never recover? Never have a normal life? Maybe she could if people quit planting ideas in her head she was about to have a catastrophe or go down a dark rabbit hole. She chewed on her bottom lip and refocused out the window and the coming of the bright day.

She watched as her favorite paper boy hustled along the sidewalk below, shoving copies of the *Post & Courier* in holders. He was an ambitious fourteen-year-old. When he saw her in the window, he stopped and waved, as was his custom.

CJ returned his greeting before realizing she only wore a T-shirt and panties. *Great, now I've flashed a teenager.* Thankfully, he was too far away to catch a peek or see her crimson cheeks as she stepped back.

Dropping back into her chair, she resumed her fight with her fears over her and Ben's pending trip to Alaska. She'd been so excited when she booked the remote lodge midway between Ketchikan and Sitka. Ben loved the water and fishing. She loved the idea of seeing the unbelievable beauty of nature and being away in the middle of nowhere with him.

The Paradise Cove Lodge website showed that only twenty-four other guests and a crew of twelve would be with them. They'd have their own cabin, a full-sized bathroom, and their own boat. As Ben was an expert boatman, there was no need to attempt to hire a guide.

Boat.

The black and white flash of an overturned boat raced in her thoughts. Damnit! She worked to slow her escalating breathing and bumping pulse. *Is this crap gonna keep happening? How can I enjoy a dream vacation if I can't control my paranoia?*

She fought to stop it, but the vision crept in … *Ben in the water.* After jumping up and going to the kitchen, she poured herself another cup of coffee. As her hands trembled, she drew the mug to her lips and sipped. She had to talk to Ben again about these feelings.

Believing Ben's response the night before had proved challenging for her. He thought Grannie's concerns were only about their safety of being out in the boat. But CJ knew Grannie's visions foretold danger. The trip concerned both her and the old woman and it wasn't just about boating. Her mind raced, and she worried she was losing herself—again.

Waves ... an overturned boat ... Ben struggling in the water ... a dead body ... a man with a scar. I wanna go spend a week with the man I love ... but I'm freaked out about this trip.

The bedroom door creaked and startled her. Her head snapped up to find her six-foot-four fiancé in his red checkered boxers.

"Have you been up all this time?" he asked as he approached her, running his fingers through his messy, dark brown hair. He wrapped his arms around her, kissed the top of her head, and stroked her back. "Something bothering you?" he said as he pulled her to the couch and brushed her auburn hair from her face.

"I'm nervous," she said as her voice cracked. "Maybe I'm just being silly."

"No, you're not. You can't help how you feel, so let's talk about it."

She described her vision to him again. They were just flashes of scenes, as if she had been watching an old-fashioned projector. The confusion and lack of coherence, coupled with Grannie's fearful words and behavior, unnerved her.

Ben listened as she talked. "So, are you saying you wanna stay here and not go?"

"No, I don't want that," CJ said as she buried her face in his bare chest. "Neither of us has had a chance to get away and go somewhere like Alaska together, and it's not fair."

"I'm sure it'll be fine," he said. "We'll be in a remote location with only a few people, so there's not much to worry about."

She remained silent as her heart thumped.

"But if you don't wanna go, we can still take the week off and drive somewhere together. That's the primary aim here, right?"

"Yes, but I want to go to Alaska. Plus, we'd lose a bunch of money canceling this late."

He kissed her again and said, "I'm not worried about the money." He caressed her cheek. "You decide. Whether we go or stay, I'm happy as long as I'm with you. If we go, I promise we'll wear our life jackets on the boat, and if one cloud pops up, we'll head for the lodge. Like I told you last night, I'm sure Grannie was only concerned about us being out on the boat."

She shook her head and asked, "You don't believe in her visions, do you?"

"I do, but as you've said yourself, she's told you that some things she sees don't come to pass." He squeezed her tight. "As for being out on the water, we'll be careful."

He doesn't understand what I do about Grannie, but maybe I'm just acting like a child afraid of the dark.

After several minutes of silence, she sucked in a deep breath as her stomach fluttered. "Okay. We're going."

"Are you sure?" he said, as he lifted her chin and stared into her eyes.

"Yes, we've been looking forward to this trip. Let's shower, finish packing, and head to Charlotte."

They ate lunch at Henry's on Market Street before driving north. Four hours later, they checked in at the Sheraton near the airport. CJ fought her sense of panic from Grannie's ominous words that pushed her to tell Ben to turn around. She kept telling herself Ben was probably right about the trip. At least, she hoped he was right.

Friday, September 9
Ketchikan, Alaska

He stood under the shade of a blue awning of one of the many jewelry stores littering Front Street. Watching. Tourists from the cruise ships wandered about, snapping photos, gawking at God knows what, and buying junk.

Ketchikan's temperature was unusually high this time of year, which irritated him. He pulled off his rain jacket and flung it over his shoulder. *Ah, who's this?*

A college-age woman with blond hair pulled into a ponytail high on her head crossed the street. Her golden mane bounced as she rushed to beat the flashing light and headed straight toward him. He liked this. She waved and smiled as she reached the sidewalk in front of him. He leaned forward, and his eyes trailed her as she walked away. She reminded him of someone. His first.

She left the pool on a Saturday afternoon in her tiny white shorts, a pale blue bikini top, and flip-flops. Her body was toned and golden brown from the sun's rays. Every boy wanted her, and she teased them all except him. She never paid him any attention. Until ...

He followed her to her cherry red Toyota Celica. In contrast to his dilapidated pickup, she had a brand-new vehicle equipped with all the features. He snuck up from behind to scare her, but Jeffrey made an appearance, provoking him to hit the young woman square in the jaw. Once she went down, dazed and confused, he grabbed her wrists, and dragged her into the trees and ...

Breathing hard, with his fists clenched, he struggled to calm himself. He'd maintained control for three years, except for that one slip-up last year. One person had noticed, but they'd kept their big mouth shut. He had become adept at appearing normal on the outside—average, quiet, and unassuming. On the inside, where the monster lived, he was a mess. There lurked pure chaos, rage, and a yearning to break free of his control.

He leaned back against the wall. *I do like it here.* Blending in with the crowd was easy, as no one paid much attention to others. Like him, Alaska had many souls who didn't fit into society or desire to. He'd always loved to play hide and seek, and this was a perfect place to hide.

Maybe he'd head over to the Sourdough Bar and grab a drink and a bottle to take with him. The problem was that if he started sipping the brown liquid, he might overdo it. That meant a tougher time controlling the monster. Jeffrey, his inner demon, was sneaky and conniving and always searched for ways to gain the upper hand. He'd tempt him, whispering evil words into his ear. The bastard always had a better chance to come out when he was drunk.

Blowing out a long breath, he decided to pass on the drink. *Maybe I'll just grab a magnum of whiskey to sneak back with me.* He wiped his forehead. *Damnit! Why is it so damn hot today? It's September, for Christ's sake.* Hopefully, it'd be cooler when the rest of his group arrived, and he made it to the lodge.

His eyes tracked a floatplane on the Tongass Narrows until he caught the perky blond coming back in his direction out of the corner of his eye. Given more time, he might ask her for a drink or indulge her in his true expertise, slitting her throat.

SIX

Friday, September 9
Ketchikan

CJ's fingers squeezed the armrest as the Alaskan Air Boeing 737-900 jet swayed and landed—the overheads rattled from the jolt when the wheels bounced on the runway. "Well, that was fun," she said sarcastically. "I'm ready to get off."

Ben took her hand and pressed it to his lips. "Me too. I'm used to flying into Alaska and the crosswinds with planes, but that was rougher than normal. Are you hungry?"

"Starved. The snack the airline gave us didn't help much."

The plane taxied to a stop, and everyone popped out of their seats. Bins opened, and hands eagerly grabbed roller bags, jackets, and various belongings.

"I never understand why everyone always jumps up so quick," CJ said. "We're not going anywhere soon."

Ben laughed and patted her leg. "Nope. We're stuck." He glanced at his Hook + Gaff King Tide watch. "It's four-thirty in the afternoon local time, but eight-thirty for my stomach. How 'bout we grab dinner at Annabelle's after we check in? I've been there a couple times and it's excellent."

"Sounds wonderful. Where's our hotel?"

"Not far, just up the hill from town. Once we pick up our checked bags, we'll need to take the ferry across the Narrows, and a hotel shuttle will pick us up. I'll call them as soon as we get off. We can walk to the restaurant."

They pulled their backpacks from under the seat, stood, and shuffled off. Inside the terminal, their two checked bags slid through the flaps and onto the carousel. In less than a hundred yards, they stepped onto the ferry and the spray from the Tongass Narrows caressed their faces as the craft made its quick journey to the other side. The salty air, mixed with a fishy odor, filled their nostrils.

A passenger van painted red with a totem pole and the words "Ketchikan" waited near the top of the ramp where they disembarked. Fifteen minutes later, it pulled in by the Cape Fox Lodge lobby, where a stuffed black bear greeted them.

After they checked in, Ben unlocked their door with a card key and entered a room with a king-sized bed. The room overlooked the town and water, which sparkled in the fading daylight. Two enormous cruise ships sat docked— *Royal Caribbean* and *Holland America*. "Those guys will pull out soon, and they'll roll up the sidewalks," he said. "The whole town caters to the tourists."

"How many ships come in each day?" she asked.

"In the summer, probably four or five. Each one is loaded to the brim with potential shoppers and sightseers. It's why the city's businesses revolve around them."

She hugged him, took his hand, and led him toward the door. "As long as they don't close the restaurants, I'm happy."

CJ and Ben entered one of Ketchikan's most popular eateries where a young woman with curly dark brown hair smiled and said, "Welcome to Annabelle's."

"Do you have room for two?" Ben asked.

"Are you okay with sitting in the bar area? The menu is identical to the dining area, and I have a window table."

Ben nodded, and they followed the hostess to a two-top. She handed them a menu and informed them a server would be with them soon.

"The food smells delicious," CJ said. "Now, I'm famished." Her eyes scanned the entrée choices.

"I'm sure we'll eat lots of seafood this week, but I'm getting the Dungeness crab anyway," Ben said. "Whatcha gettin'?"

"I'm gonna try the clam chowder as an appetizer and grilled halibut for dinner."

They ordered after the waiter arrived, and CJ scanned the restaurant. The dark wood tables and chairs contrasted with the light-colored floor. A massive carved wooden bar with a brass rail covered most of one wall with an extensive selection of tap beers and alcohol. She opted for water while Ben ordered an Alaskan Amber. Both dug into their food when it arrived, as if they hadn't eaten in a week.

"How's the halibut?" Ben asked.

"It's yummy."

"The crab's tasty. Here, have a bite." He held his fork up to her.

"It reminds me a bit like lobster, but slightly sweet." She snatched a fry from his plate and shoved it in her mouth.

"Hey!"

Grinning, she said, "Soon, we'll be married, and what's yours is mine." She was grateful to be spending time with him away and how he looked forward to showing her around and teaching her to fish.

Ben finished his crab and stretched his arms over his head. He pulled a folded sheet of paper from his jacket. "According to this, we're on the third plane out tomorrow. We meet the Island Air van at 7:00 a.m. It'll take us and six others to the airport to catch our floatplane."

"Does it show who else is on our plane?"

"It lists the names—two men plus two other couples. At least you won't be the only woman in the group."

She frowned, teasing him. "Aww, I was hoping I'd be the center of attention."

He rolled his eyes and chuckled. "Oh, yeah. Coming from the woman who finds a corner at every gathering." His fingers brushed her hand, and they stared at each other until their waiter returned and topped up her water.

"Can I bring you anything else?" he asked them.

Ben glanced at her, and she shrugged. "Not right now."

"Okay, I'll check back later."

After he left them, CJ asked, "Will we ride the ferry again?"

"We will, but in the van. Our plane will take off from the runway and land on the water. It's probably only a forty-five-minute flight."

Her insides quivered. "I hope it'll be okay if the weather's bad."

Ben leaned forward and rubbed her arm. "The Cessna Caravan is safe and the instrumentation's reliable, so there's no need to worry."

She smiled. "I would worry less if we shared a slice of three-layer carrot cake."

After finishing dessert and paying the bill, they walked around downtown before returning up the hill. They sat in two Adirondack chairs on the patio overlooking the city's twinkling lights below.

"Are you cold?" Ben asked.

"A little. But I don't wanna go in yet."

He pulled her into his lap and wrapped his arms around her. "Is that better?"

"Uh-huh," she said. Her body melted against his chest. She couldn't recall when she had been happier than she was now. Coming on this trip was what they needed, away from their everyday life of fighting crime and the evil in the world.

I'm glad I didn't let my paranoia stop me from this.

SEVEN

Saturday, September 10
Paradise Cove, Alaska

The Cessna Caravan glided toward the water and smoothly touched the surface. After four hundred yards, it pulled alongside a dock in front of the Paradise Cove Lodge, near the Sumner Straight and the northern end of the Prince of Wales Island.

The floating lodge sat nestled in the back of the cove and consisted of a large two-story structure separating rows of connected cabins on either side: six cabins on the right and seven on the left. The trees, in various shades of green on the mountain behind the lodge, provided a breathtaking backdrop. Two otters floated on their backs behind the plane, busily crunching on oyster shells.

The buildings were painted dark brown or light green with forest green roofs. An expansive wooden platform extended in front of the main structure, connecting the cabins with wooden walkways. A boat floated in a slip in front of each cabin.

Ben leaned over to CJ and whispered, "You made a good choice. This place is nice."

She smiled. "It is. I like that it's smaller and not one of those large impersonal lodges. I wanted to go to the Sea Otter Sound Lodge, which is spectacular, but the owner informed me they were booked through next year."

Two young men grabbed the ropes hanging from the plane's wings and tugged until the pontoon thumped against the bumpers. The pilot, a man in his early forties, removed his headphones, turned, and smiled at the eight passengers. "Welcome to your new home for the week."

He climbed out and opened the side door, guiding each of them onto the wooden platform filled with people. One by one, they stepped down and met Alan and Debra Satterfield, the owners of the lodge.

Alan was in his late forties, and his wavy black hair showed gray flecks. He beamed, hugged returning guests, and shook the newbie's hands. His wife, ten years his younger, stood six inches shorter than his six feet. She had sandy blond hair and close-set green eyes.

Debra snapped a photo of each twosome as they stood on the corner of the dock. When Ben and CJ's turn came, she greeted them, saying, "You two must be the newly engaged couple from Charleston. Congratulations. Can I see your ring?"

"Sure." CJ held out her hand. "It was Ben's mothers."

"It's lovely."

Her husband approached and said, "We're so happy you've joined us. Fortunately, we can accommodate you this year. You booked the last cabin."

"We're thrilled to be here," CJ said. "It's so beautiful, and I think I saw a whale as we landed."

"Oh, yes. We have lots of those hanging around, as well as eagles, otters, moose, and bears. I hope you brought your camera so you can capture some memories."

Ben laughed. "She's been snapping away since we landed in Ketchikan."

CJ glanced at the lodge's staff lined along the walkway. "You have a big crew."

Alan turned and said, "We have ten, not counting Debra and I. We're short one for our inside crew as we had a young woman who didn't return this year. Chantelle would have given us a little more wiggle room to give folks a break, but we're fine with what we have."

After Debra had everyone's images, she directed them into the lodge's common area—a massive space serving as the den and dining area. The interior décor emanated an Alaska vibe. Mounted photos of fish, fishermen, and wildlife adorned the walls. Soft leather couches and recliners filled the den. The adjacent dining area had three large dark cherry tables and matching chairs. One table was large enough to seat a dozen people.

A counter ran the length of the back wall, separating the common area and providing two gas stove tops for cooking. A broad picture window provided a view of the back area with buildings of various sizes for the crew, storage, and maintenance.

After settling into their seats, Alan briefed the twenty-six guests, introduced the other ten crew members lined up along the wall, and showed a fifteen-minute video.

"We've assigned one of the crew to be responsible for each cabin," Alan said. "They'll ensure your room is cleaned daily and help with whatever you need while you're here with us. We've also assigned someone to each boat." He began reading the cabin and crew assignments, ending with Ben and CJ. "You two are in cabin and boat thirteen. Stephanie and Simon will take care of you."

After answering a few questions, Alan informed everyone they could grab a bite of breakfast, settle into their cabins, and fish for the rest of the day. They would serve dinner at 6:00 p.m. every evening.

A college-age woman with braided black hair and a bad case of acne approached Ben and CJ. "I'm Stephanie, but everyone calls me Steph. I'll be helping in the dining room and taking care of your cabin." She spent a few minutes completing a form and showed them to their room. The common area divided the cabins into two groups on either side, and all faced Paradise Cove. Cabin thirteen was at the end of the row.

Red cedar paneling adorned the walls and ceiling, with dark brown carpeting covering the floor. The room had a queen-sized black spindle bed, a dark brown dresser, and a matching mirror. A four-foot round glass table with two chairs sat in front of a picture window facing the water. A bathroom with a shower, a pedestal sink, and a toilet was at the back of the room.

"Well, it's nice to know we won't be roughing it," CJ said.

"No, we want everyone to be comfortable," Stephanie said, grinning.

As she finished the tour, Stephanie said, "There's a safe on the dresser if you want to lock up valuables. Our guest room doors don't have locks, but we've had no issues. Once you're settled, Simon will meet you at your boat right out front. He'll help you with whatever you need for fishing and rain gear."

Ben glanced out the window. "Perfect. The only thing we'll need are rubber boots and float coats."

The young woman smiled and exited.

"Do you wanna unpack now or wait until after dinner?" Ben asked.

"Let's wait," CJ said. "I'm eager to get on the water." She ran her hands down her side. "I'm already wearing my new fishing pants and shirt."

"You're ready then. We'll swap our boots for the rubber ones so we don't ruin them."

Simon, a man in his late twenties with curly blond hair protruding from under a camo-colored baseball hat, met them at their nineteen-foot Jetcraft boat. He reviewed the instrumentation, radio, fishing tackle, and gear and left to grab their lunch.

"Hey, guys. I'm Anita." A perky college-age woman, much shorter than CJ, approached them with her sandy blond hair in a ponytail. Her tan khaki pants were wet from the knees down, and her boots squeaked as she walked. Her sweatshirt was too big, engulfing her thin frame.

"I work with Simon and the outside crew in the back. As you can see, I've been washing the boats and had a battle with the hose." She climbed into the craft. "Simon asked me to put some more bait in your boat." She used a knife to open the packages and then dropped smelly silver minnows in the white bucket. "This should be plenty for the day." She tossed the empties in the trash bag. Her hazel eyes sparkled as she looked up at Ben. "You need anything else?"

"I think we're good," he said, smiling.

Anita climbed back on the dock and said, "Have fun and bring back a boatload. It's my first year here and the boys are teaching me to clean fish."

After she'd left, Ben said, "Boy, she's a firecracker of energy."

"Yes, she is, and she's smitten with you."

His brow furrowed. "She's only being nice. The crew makes most of their money from tips."

"Yeah, okay," CJ said as she grinned and rolled her eyes. "I'm not sure she even realized I was in the boat."

Simon returned and handed Ben a red and white Igloo cooler, rain boots, and two float coats. Once they were set, he untied them and pushed them out of the boat slip. "Have a spectacular day, guys."

"You should have told him you're an experienced boatman," CJ said as Ben pushed the throttle forward after they left the no-wake area.

"And miss his speech," he said, chuckling. "No way. Speaking of that, are we gonna tell people what we do for a living?"

CJ furrowed her brow. "Hmm, what do you think?"

"I'd opt to keep it to ourselves. Let's put our jobs out of our minds while we're here. If everyone knows what we do, they'll question us all week."

"That makes sense, and I agree, no work talk on this trip."

He glanced at her and asked, "So, what do we do?"

She rubbed her chin. "I'll be a receptionist at a law firm, and you run the family auto mechanic's shop."

He grinned at her and shook his head. "Those jobs should be boring enough. No one will ask us much. Are you warm enough?"

"Yes, this jacket is thick and warmer than I expected."

"Before we fish, we'll put on our rain pants to keep the blood and slime off our clothes. I brought each of us a rain suit in my backpack, and I have a pullover for you if you get cold."

CJ fixed her eyes on him as he concentrated on where they were going and smiled.

EIGHT

Saturday, September 10
Paradise Cove

After catching their daily limit of silver salmon and riding around sightseeing, Ben and CJ returned to the lodge and cleaned up for dinner. At 6:00 p.m., the clanging of the dinner bell summoned them to the dining area.

They joined the two couples they met on their float-plane and a man and his eight-year-old son at a table for eight. Platters of grilled salmon, dirty rice, and green beans graced the table as they settled into their chairs.

Noah and Jamie sat to their left. Like Ben and CJ, they were in their early thirties. Noah had a nerdy look about him thanks to the black-rimmed glasses he wore. His hair was a curly medium brown, the same color as his eyes, and shaved close on the sides.

Over dinner, Jamie told them she taught preschool in Denver and loved her kids. She hoped that one day they'd have some of their own. Her husband seconded that idea and laughed about the many babysitters they'd have from their school.

It was the couple's first time in Alaska. Jamie said the scenery was breathtaking, and she was having fun, but being out on the boat made her nervous. "I keep telling Noah not to go out too far from shore. Every time we rock back and forth from the waves, it scares me."

"She's afraid we'll flip over," Noah said as he rubbed her back. "I keep telling her it's tough to capsize a boat."

"Well, I'm still gonna wear my life jacket the whole time," Jamie said as she rubbed a cross dangling from her neck between her thumb and pointer finger. She tugged at her long dark brown hair and added, "We were supposed to have a guide."

Noah explained they could not book one as none were available this late in the season. With some pause, he said he was comfortable maneuvering the boat. Jamie remained quiet and seemed to retreat to some place else.

"And what do you do for a living, Noah?" CJ asked.

"I also teach the sixth grade. That's how we met."

CJ glanced at the man with his son sitting to her right—Rory and Luka. The son was a mirror image of his father with close-cropped brown hair and eyes the color of walnuts. Both wore Texas Rangers baseball caps. Luka, who appeared small for his age, had his hat adorably turned around backward.

"What about you, Rory?" she asked.

"I'm a civil engineer with a fifty-person design firm in Houston," he replied. "I primarily work on road and bridge projects."

"Is this your first time here?" she asked.

"No. This is my third straight trip to the lodge, and I plan to keep coming every year. I've been coming with a buddy from work, but promised to bring Luka this year."

"I got to come, and my little sister had to stay home," Luka chimed in as he smiled proudly, exposing a gap in his front teeth. "She's only six." His eyes sparkled as he peered up at CJ. "You're really pretty."

"Son, let's not bother the poor lady," his father said. He looked at CJ and shrugged. "Sorry. He says whatever is on his mind."

She smiled warmly at the boy and, leaning down, whispered, "Thank you very much."

The last of the group, Evan and Olivia, sat across the table. Their preppy attire seemed to overdo it for a remote fishing lodge. Olivia was extremely thin, almost anorexic, and CJ wondered if she had an eating disorder based on how little she ate.

The thirtysomethings had been uncomfortably quiet throughout dinner, so CJ drew them into the conversation. "Evan, what do you do for a living?"

"I'm an investment banker in Atlanta," he said as he slid his arm around Olivia. "My wife doesn't work. She takes care of the house. Right, honey?"

"Uh, right. I always wanted to be an interior designer—"

"But now she's busy taking care of me," Evan said, cutting her off.

CJ nodded at her, ignoring Evan's dismissive tone. "That sounds like fun, Olivia. Do you have any children?"

Olivia opened her mouth to speak, but her husband cut her off again. "Not yet. I've been telling my lovely wife that we need to have some soon. Of course, she'll need to keep up her fantastic figure."

The rail-thin woman frowned.

CJ told the group what she and Ben did, the lie they'd agreed upon, and that they were newly engaged. As they expected, no one asked for any details.

After the main course, Stephanie returned and placed dessert plates with warm cherry cobbler and a scoop of vanilla ice cream on the table. Everyone but Olivia dug in.

"Can I bring anyone anything else?" Stephanie asked. Everyone shook their heads. "I wanted to remind you we have beer, sodas, and water in the refrigerator and wine on the shelf. There's a variety of snacks in the bins. Everything's free except for alcohol. For that, please mark down what you drink under your cabin number on the clipboard."

"Are the snacks really free?" Luka asked, his eyes wide.

"Absolutely," Stephanie said as she poked at him. "I love the Oreo cookies myself."

The boy hopped from his chair and held out his hand to CJ. "Will you help me pick out my midnight snack?"

"Son."

CJ grabbed the boy's hand and winked at his dad. "I'd love to." She stood, told Ben she'd meet him on the deck, and left the table, never noticing the man's stare from across the room.

NINE

Sunday, September 11
Paradise Cove

CJ peered at the glowing hands of the old-fashioned wind-up clock on the nightstand.

Ben stirred beside her, rolled over, and pulled her to him. He nibbled her ear. "What time is it?"

"It's a few minutes before five." She squirmed and pushed herself tighter against him. "You know, breakfast isn't until six. You wanna—"

He pressed his lips to hers and then began kissing her neck.

She pulled the long T-shirt over her head and dropped it on the floor. "I'll take that as a yes."

"Uh-huh," he said as he continued to work his way down.

When the bell rang at 6:00 a.m., Ben and CJ entered the dining room and joined the table with the familiar group from the previous evening. Everyone listened to Luka's story about how he caught "the biggest bass ever" when Alan tapped on a glass for their attention.

"Good morning," he said. "I trust you slept well and are prepared for another fantastic day on the water. Today, our chef, Bev, has prepared a delicious breakfast for you—French toast with powdered sugar and cinnamon, link sausages, and a fresh fruit medley."

Everyone clapped and helped themselves from the platters placed on the tables by the kitchen crew.

While they ate, Alan covered the day's fishing report, what spots were hottest for which species, and reminded them to grab their lunch before they departed. His gaze flitted around the room until it became fixed on the back wall. "I need to alert you about something. I always track the weather, and a storm initially moving north has changed its course. It may impact us."

"You mean some rain or wind?" a man named Harley in his mid-fifties asked at the neighboring table. "A little wind and rain ain't no problem for us experienced folks."

Alan cleared his throat and drew his eyebrows together. "This storm would bring us heavy rain and high winds." He strained to smile. "But don't worry. I'll monitor it and alert everyone over the radio if it continues to move our way."

"Well, I for one, am gettin' a full day of fishing in. I didn't spend all this money to sit on my ass here—"

"Harley, please," Alan said with irritation. "Everyone wants to catch fish, but safety is always the top priority for our guests."

Red-faced, the heavyset man with suspenders struggling to hold up his tan pants against his pot-belly glared at Alan, still mumbling under his breath.

CJ glanced out the plate-glass window at the bright sunshine and calm water's surface—her heart rate bumped as her thoughts went to Grannie's warning. She leaned over and whispered to Ben. "What does this mean?"

He put his arm around her and said, "We'll be fine. We can keep an eye out and make sure we listen to the radio. As our loud-mouthed friend mentioned, rain is aggravating, but any high winds could pose problems. The waves increase as it picks up."

As she stared out the window and chewed on her lip, she said, "It's perfect weather now."

Ben gazed out at the early morning rays, causing the flat surface of the water to sparkle. "We'll be fine." He glanced at her plate and asked, "Aren't you gonna finish eating?"

"I've had plenty." A touch on her arm caused her to turn to her newest friend.

"Miss CJ, are you taking snacks on the boat?" Luka said, his eyes gleaming.

She nodded and leaned to him, smiling. "I am. Wanna help me pick them out?"

Before she finished her response, he was out of his chair, grasping her hand and leading her across the room.

"You think we'll be okay to go out, Ben?" Rory asked. "I'm not concerned for myself since I've fished here the last three years and have been in bumpy water, but it's Luka's first time. I'd hate to scar him for life."

"I'm in the same position. CJ's been on the water a bunch of times, but I can tell she's nervous." Ben turned to find her laughing with Luka as they grabbed goodies from the bins. "I'd recommend we not take any chances and fish closer to the lodge in case we need to hightail it back. I'm thinking Port Lucy."

"Are you experienced if it gets rough?" Rory asked.

Ben sighed. "I am. My dad was a commercial fisherman, now turned to charters, and I grew up on boats. I've been out in deep water when it took everything you had not to go overboard."

"Luka and I are gonna fish near you," Rory said.

"Yeah. I think we will, too," Noah said. "Being first timers to Alaska, this is sorta overwhelming."

"Can we join you guys?" Evan, who appeared to be auditioning for GQ with his freshly gelled black hair, chimed in from across the table. "We're in the same situation as everyone else."

"Fine by me," Ben said as he scanned their eager faces. "I'm not claiming to be an expert, but I've spent plenty of time on the ocean, and numbers are helpful in case of a problem. There's plenty of room for us to troll for salmon at Port Lucy, and I marked a couple of nearby spots where we can bottom fish for bass and perhaps catch a ling cod. If the weather holds, we can fish for halibut by Stump Island when the tide turns around noon."

CJ returned with her hands full of various packages of snacks. She slid into her chair and kissed Ben on the cheek. "Did you miss us?" She held up her hands. "Look what we found."

"We did," Ben said. "Listen, the table decided we're gonna start at Port Lucy today, where we caught five of our salmon yesterday."

CJ furrowed her brow and shrugged. "Sure, the more the merrier."

Ben stood and motioned toward the door. "I'm gonna check out our boat with Simon and make sure we're ready to roll. How 'bout we all leave in, say, twenty minutes?"

Heads nodded around the table.

He leaned down, kissed CJ, and told her he'd meet her in the cabin.

Ben checked the safety gear in the boat—life jackets, emergency horn, and flares. Simon provided the radio channel with local weather information. After staring out at the horizon, he thumbed through the apps on his cell phone until he found the closest weather report. He frowned when he pulled up the radar. A red and purple mass lay in the distance, meaning heavy rain, strong winds, or severe thunderstorms. *I hope this storm will stay north of us.*

His thoughts wandered to when he and his dad were fishing the Charleston Bump some fifty miles offshore in the Atlantic Ocean, and their radar erroneously predicted how fast the storm was moving. Before they could return to shore, it hit them, hard. He exhaled and peered at their boat.

I don't wanna be in this thing if the winds hit. We were in a forty-eight-footer that day, and if the Coast Guard wasn't close ... well ... He shivered and turned for the cabin.

TEN

Sunday, September 11
Paradise Cove

Ben led four Jetcrafts to Port Lucy under a clear blue sky. Eagles soared overhead, and several sat perched in the tall trees on the rocky cliffs. The water shimmered under the sunshine as ripples crawled across the surface. By 8:15 a.m., the vessels moved back and forth along the shoreline, trolling for salmon.

CJ jumped from her seat when her line yanked. "I've got one."

Ben cut the engine and reeled in his line, coaching her to be patient and keep her rod tip up. The fish turned and ran when it got near the boat.

"Oh, no! Where's he going?"

"You're all good. Don't let him get slack in your line, but don't horse him."

She glanced at him and returned her concentration to landing whatever she'd hooked. "What do you mean?"

Ben laughed. "Don't pull too hard and break your line. Let him wear himself out."

Once the fish stopped fighting, she began cranking him back toward them. "He's heavier than the others. Come here, fish!" Her lips pressed together, and she set her jaw with pure determination.

"I think you have a king," he said, pulling the net from its holder. "They're bigger and stronger than the silvers ... they're a top-of-the-line salmon." In one smooth swipe, he brought the fish into the boat. "Yep, that's a nice one." He dropped to a knee and busied himself, pulling the hook out.

"Can we keep him?"

"Yes, we can each keep one for the week as long as they're over thirty inches." She joined him on a knee as he slid the fish over to the ruler glued to the floor. "Thirty-eight inches. He'll weigh over twenty pounds." He kissed her. "Way to go, partner. Grab your camera so we can take your picture."

As he snapped a photo, Rory and Luka cheered as they passed.

Over the next three hours, they caught six more silver salmon, bringing their total to twelve, and Ben lost a second king.

CJ teased him. "You horsed him. If you hook another one, how 'bout I show you how it's done?"

He smiled and shook his head. "My dad's gonna be so proud. I've created a fishing monster." Gazing toward the horizon, he noticed dark clouds. "We have our limit of silvers, so let's catch some bass. Unclip your hoochie and put on the jig you used yesterday."

She laughed as her fingers worked to swap her tackle. "I love the name hoochie."

Ben called the others on the radio and told them he and CJ were going around the point to bottom fish. He pushed the throttle forward and said, "We're gonna try a rocky pinnacle on the map. Bass love to hang around them." He also wanted to move closer to the lodge without telling her as the swells loomed larger. Focused on fishing, CJ failed to notice until she saw the boat swaying.

"Ben, we're rocking."

"Yeah, there's a few rollers coming in." His eyes peered at the depth chart as he eased them to a stop.

"What's a roller?" she asked, furrowing her brow.

"I also call 'em swells. They're surface waves not caused by the local wind." Clearing his throat, he added, "Winds in the distance cause them, usually from a storm. We'll be fine. I'm keeping a close eye out." As he picked up his rod, he said, "Okay, fish away." As he turned the crank on his reel, he kept glancing at the distant horizon and wisps of whitecaps on the water's surface beginning to form.

"Damn it!" CJ mumbled. "I'm hung on the bottom. No, wait, maybe not."

Cranking his reel, Ben peered over the side of the railing. "Did you come loose?"

"I think so, but I have something heavy."

"Keep reeling. Maybe you have a fish." He jammed his rod in the holder and waited until a dark image appeared below the surface. "You have a ling. Take your time bringing him up and keep his head underwater so I can use the gaff without hurting him." Seconds later, a brown creature with a large head and mouth, teeth like razors, and copper-colored blotches lay on the deck.

"He's scary looking," CJ said as she kneeled closer.

Ben grunted as he twisted the pliers to remove the treble hook lodged in the fish's jaw. "We need to measure him. Damn, you're kicking my butt today." The fish wiggled as he slid over to the tape. "Forty-three inches. He's a keeper." He high-fived her.

They had added six black bass and the ling cod to the cooler when a sudden gust of wind swung the boat's bow around.

"Ben!" CJ stumbled backward, and he grabbed her.

"I got you."

She dropped back into her seat, trembling.

Ben took her rod, removed the tackle, and placed it in the holder. "Let's call it a day. I wanna get our catch in so the crew can clean it." He alerted the others they were returning to the lodge.

The radio crackled, and Evan told them they would join them as he and Olivia were seasick. The two boats neared the cove when a drizzling rain started and the breeze picked up. Ben glanced over his shoulder at the horizon as he slowed—the distant sky was now black as coal.

Simon met them at their slip, wound the ropes around the cleats, and secured their vessel. "How'd you do today?"

"I caught a king and a ling cod," CJ blurted out.

"Wow. What a great morning. We've not seen many kings come in this late in the season." Simon stepped into the boat and opened the cooler. "You guys caught a bunch of fish."

"Unless I miss counted, we have our limit of silvers and a half dozen black bass," Ben said, slipping his arm around CJ. "And, of course, my lovely fiancée's two whoppers."

Simon busied himself tossing their catch into a rolling cart. "I'll take these 'round back so we can process them. Are you going back out?"

"Uh, what's the latest on the weather?" Ben asked.

"Alan says he thinks the storm may miss us, but we'll get some pretty good wind and rain. It should blow past us tonight."

Ben glanced at CJ, who'd climbed out and moved under an awning, fidgeting with the zipper on her coat. "You know what? We're done for today."

"Okay. Alan wants us to bring the boats 'round back and tie them up in case of high winds later." He lifted the handles of the cart and wheeled it down the walkway. "You wanna watch us clean your king, CJ?"

"Sure," she said, glancing at Ben and shrugging. "You wanna come too?"

"I'll be back there soon. I wanna talk to Alan about the weather." Frowning as he thumbed his cell phone, he said, "I'm not able to pull up the app from this morning. My phone signal doesn't have any bars, and the lodge's Wi-Fi is spotty at best."

CJ trailed Simon between the row of cabins and the main lodge to the area where the crew handled everyone's catches. The processing area contained three large tables covered by two brown canopies secured to the wooden deck. Buildings of various sizes stood beyond the processing area.

———

CJ stared as Victor and Cal used sharp knives to slice up their fish and slide the fillets into a plastic bin—quick, efficient, and effective. Their hands flew while the music blared with the song *Journey*. Her memories recalled the raised hand of a killer from her past, and a shiver ran down her spine.

He became calm. His body was rigid as his eyes bore through her. His fingers tightened on the knife, and he smirked. "Fuck you!" The blade flashed up.

Victor, a forty-year-old man with shaggy black hair and a matching beard, broke her trance. "You caught a nice king," he said, grinning.

Something about him made her skin crawl. The way he brandished the blade, and the unsightly chipped front tooth and tobacco stains on his teeth contributed to the impression.

Once they'd finished, they moved the bins to another table, vacuum-packed the fillets, and stored them in a massive walk-in freezer. "You wanna see where we store 'em?" Victor asked.

"Uh, sure." She stepped forward, stuck her head in the frosty cavern, and scanned the metal shelves with boxes labeled with the cabin numbers. She flinched when he put his hand on her back.

"When you leave us, we'll label them and add bands so you can check them at the airport." He wiped his hands on a dingy white towel and winked. "They will freeze rock hard within a few hours."

Unbelievable. I think this asshole is flirting with me.

CHAPTER

ELEVEN

Sunday, September 11
Paradise Cove

Evan's boat had trailed behind Ben's as they returned to the lodge. Simon secured it in the slip and took the five silver salmon he and Olivia caught back for processing. Evan followed his wife into their cabin, yanked the window curtains closed, and exploded. "How in the hell could you embarrass me?"

Olivia's eyes watered and her bottom lip trembled. "Honey, I'm not sure I understand."

Tossing his rain jacket on the bed, he glared at her. "You know damn well what I'm talking about!"

Wetness crept down Olivia's cheeks. "No, honey. I don't."

He stepped close and jabbed his finger in her face. "I told everyone on the radio we both were seasick, and you blabbed to CJ that you felt fine when we returned. It made me seem weak."

Swallowing hard, she mumbled. "I ... I'm sorry. I didn't mean to." She reached for him, and he jerked away. "I'll do better. I promise."

"You damn well better," he said, turning for the bathroom. "By the way, the blond color you dyed your hair looks like shit. You need to change it when we get home."

She dropped onto the double bed nearest the door. Her shaking hands picked up one of her most prized possessions, a new black Olympus E-5 digital camera. She scrolled through the photos she'd captured on the boat— the sparkling water set against the lush greenery on the mountains, the tail of a humpback whale, and numerous eagles swooping down for their breakfast.

Her marriage was a disaster. Evan had been kind, caring, and loving when they dated, but he changed within months of their wedding. She worked hard to please him, giving up her career, hoping to get pregnant, and staying at home taking care of things. Nothing helped. After five years, things had only become worse.

The unmistakable sound of him losing what was left in his stomach caused her to stand and creep toward the closed bathroom door. "Sweetheart, are you okay?"

"Hell, no! I'm puking my guts out."

"Can I get you anything? Perhaps ginger ale would—"

"No! Leave me alone."

Wiping her puffy brown eyes, she asked, "Do you mind if I go take some more pictures? If you need me to—"

The door flung open, and he stared at her. "You don't give a shit about me, do you?"

"Sweetheart, I love—"

"Get the fuck out of here," he spat. "Go take your sorry pictures. That's the only reason you wanted to come here. I should have never let you talk me into it." His face twisted. "I wanted to go on a cruise, but as always, you got your way."

Her mouth dropped open, but no words came out. At least, none that Evan would accept, so she remained silent, alone with her thoughts. *You're the one who wanted to come here. I'm the one who suggested a cruise.*

He grabbed her arms, spun her, and pushed her toward the door. "Go. I'm gonna take a nap."

Grabbing her camera from the edge of the bed, she left. She couldn't be sure, but she assumed Ben and CJ had heard the argument in the cabin beside them. Well, it wasn't an argument, but her on the receiving end of Evan's verbal abuse, as usual. *Why am I so weak?* She lowered her head and hurried down the walkway, praying for invisibility.

A voice startled her as she made her way behind the guest cabins. "Can I help you with something?" a college-age man named Kenny asked. His small stature and soft features made him appear younger than his age.

"Uh, I'm sorry," she said. "I guess I'm not supposed to be back here." She flinched. *Why am I always apologizing for myself to men?*

"Oh, it's fine," he said, smiling. "I thought you were looking for someone or needed help."

"I ... I wanted to take a few photos since the rain has stopped." She thrust her camera forward, hoping he wouldn't notice her trembling hands. "I'm a wannabe photographer," she said, weakly laughing as her eyes searched for an exit.

"I love snapping pictures too, and this is where to do it." He glanced back over his shoulder. "I tell you what. Guests really aren't supposed to be back here, but how 'bout I show you how to get to the shore? There's a path you can take for a spectacular view of the cove."

"Umm, I don't wanna get you in trouble," she said as her tension eased.

"You won't. As long as I take you back and make sure you don't slip, it'll be cool." He motioned for her to follow. "Watch your step and don't trip over any hoses or cables."

As he walked ahead of her, he pointed out the various buildings hidden from the guest area—the crew quarters, complete with cabins, a kitchen, and a den. According to him, they used several other buildings for storage, maintenance, and what he referred to as junk.

An older man with graying dark brown hair and a scruffy beard tipped his head to her as she passed. Oil and grease stained his coveralls, and his baseball cap had seen better days.

"Who's he?" she asked Kenny.

"Oh, that's Walter. He's been here a while and handles the maintenance. Nice guy, but keeps to himself." As they stood at the end of the dock, he took her arm and pointed ahead. "I'll go first, but we need to take the narrow footbridge from here to the shore. Hold on to the rope handrail and go slow."

They crossed the thirty feet of wooden boards until they reached the shore. The purring of a boat motor grew louder.

"I hear someone coming in," he said. "I'm on boat cleanup duty today, so I gotta hurry back. Are you okay to go alone? The path is well marked."

"Yes, I think so," she said, nodding. "How far is the spot where I can take photos?"

He furrowed his brow. "Hmm, not far. Maybe a couple hundred yards, but you can't miss it. There's a bench on the edge of the path. Alan built it so he and Debra could sit and enjoy the view. Don't go any further, though, 'cause the trail gets harder to find."

"Okay, that's easy enough. Thank you."

"Have fun, and don't forget dinner is at six." He turned and hustled back, leaving her alone. She chewed on her lip, second-guessed whether she should go alone, exhaled, and stepped off the walkway.

Olivia started up the path, careful to miss the slick, muddy spots. After slipping once or twice, her body relaxed as she adjusted to the terrain and the separation from her husband. The crisp air invigorated her, and a sense of calm washed over her. *I think it's time I left Evan.*

After traveling a hundred yards, her way became dim as the sun's rays were broken by the passing clouds, and the trees were lush overhead. She paused as she went to snap photos to add to her shots of whales, otters, and eagles—the trees, a raven, and the red, yellow, and purple wildflowers.

A sudden movement in the bushes behind her caused her to hold her breath while her heart raced. She stood frozen as her eyes scanned to find nothing. *What do I do if I run across a bear or a wolf?* After her heart slowed, she mumbled, "Jeez, relax." Shaking her head, she turned and quickened her pace while her thoughts raced about potential dangers lurking around her. *Maybe it wasn't such a good idea to be out here alone in the middle of nowhere.*

The man crouching behind the bushes stood and followed her.

———

Darkness. Olivia struggled to focus and find light, but her eyes saw nothing. A musty, fishy odor almost suffocated her, and a loud scratching sounded behind her. Her head throbbed, and her shoulders ached. She willed herself to move, but her hands were locked behind her back. Numbness gripped her fingers and toes as she struggled to breathe.

Her mind raced, and she tried to make sense of her situation. *She was inside, but where?* Her mind replayed what she could remember. *I was sitting on a bench, staring at the most beautiful scene. I turned at the sound of rustling and a man swiftly punched me, leaving a metallic taste in my mouth. Something's wrong here!* She tried to scream, but something coarse, tasting like gas, filled her mouth.

Her vision failed her, but she was being watched, she sensed it. Creaking and ominous whispers joined the scraping noise outside before a hoarse male voice said, "Hush, no one's going to hear you. It's just you and me now." A hot, whiskey-laced breath bathed her face. She moaned for the last time as a cold metal edge drew a stinging line of pain across her throat.

TWELVE

Sunday, September 11
Paradise Cove

The clanging bell signaled dinner time just before the sky opened, and raindrops pelted the metal roof of the lodge. The winds also increased, and the adjacent shore's tall pines thrashed from side to side. Rollers from the cove plowed into the floating lodge, rocking it violently.

Ben and CJ raced under the walkway awning to avoid the deluge.

Alan swung the door open as they approached. "Watch your step, and don't slip," he said.

After entering, they removed their rain jackets and hung them on the back of their chairs to dry. Noah, Jamie, Rory, and Luka sat in their usual spots.

"Where's Evan and Olivia?" CJ asked. Everyone shrugged. She glanced at Ben, who raised his eyebrows. *I hope they're not still arguing.*

Alan stood in the front and announced the night's dinner menu—baked halibut, scallop potatoes, green bean casserole, and homemade rolls. Stephanie took their drink orders as sleet bounced against the windows.

"It's nasty out there," Rory said. "Luka and I got drenched earlier, but it looked like the storm was gonna miss us. I'm sure Alan will update us after dinner."

"We thought the same," Noah commented. "I sure hope it'll move on through by morning. It got rough in the afternoon when the swells got bigger."

Ben stayed quiet, and CJ knew why. He'd told her the weather report he finally pulled up on his app showed a massive storm approaching, and it wouldn't leave anytime soon. No one would fish tomorrow or even the day after. Their relaxing getaway now verged on becoming a nightmare.

Alan moved to the front of the room as everyone finished their dessert of red velvet cake. His face was solemn as he cleared his throat. "I wanted to update everyone on the weather. Based on the latest, the storm will hit us."

The buzz of the room increased to a roar.

"We won't be able to fish tomorrow," Harley said in a raised voice. "So, when can we go out again?"

"I'm not sure. According to what they're saying, it may last several days."

"Several days!" Harley stood and poked his finger at the owner. "I came here to catch fish, not sit on my ass."

"I know it's disappointing for everyone, but until the winds subside, no one can leave the lodge. It's too dangerous to be out in a boat as you could capsize and drown." He told everyone good night and retreated for the stairs to the owner's apartment.

"Miss CJ, what's your last name?" Luka asked, smiling at her.

"It's O'Hara."

His small nose wrinkled. "That's a funny name. Are you from a different country?"

"Son!" Rory said. "That's not very nice, and stop asking so many questions."

"I'm sorry," Luka said as he dropped his head.

CJ nudged him with her shoulder, leaned over, and said, "It's okay. I'm from the United States. I was born and raised in Boston."

He glanced up and smiled. "Wanna play Go Fish?"

She returned his smile, though her heart wasn't in it, and nodded.

He jumped up, ran to the game corner, and returned with a deck of cards. "Okay, I'll shuffle and deal first."

For the next hour, she and the boy played. Ben left to talk to Alan.

———

He stood, leaning against the wall, and his ears perked up. *Hmm ... O'Hara ... Boston. No, it couldn't be.* He pushed away from the wall and left the room through a side door. The guests and most of the staff stayed behind in the dining room. The remaining staff were in the crew dining room eating dinner. His eyes scanned the dark hallway—it was empty.

He glanced over his shoulder and pushed the office door open. His fingers tapped on the keyboard, and the screen glowed. He scrolled down the page until he saw something that interested him.

The heading of the *Charleston Post & Courier* newspaper article read *Detective CJ O'Hara Stops The Lowcountry Killer*. His eyes flared as they scanned the photo underneath. *Well, whaddya know?*

Further down the page, he found an earlier article entitled *Charleston Hires First Female Detective*. His eyes narrowed at the photo of a man with salt and pepper hair pinning a gold badge on a female detective with auburn hair and unique emerald green eyes.

Well, well. We have someone in common.

His eyes closed as he remembered the day he'd last seen the older man.

He hid in a narrow, dark space between the walls of the warehouse that he knew like the back of his hand. The detective with salt and pepper hair comforted the slut he'd picked up puking in the alley after she left the bar. He shouted instructions, and his minions fanned out, searching for him. But he was too intelligent for them and too well hidden.

He opened his eyes, closed the search window, and crept away.

CJ glanced at the nautical clock on the wall—it was almost 9:00 p.m. She gazed around the room. Neither Evan nor Olivia were present. "Luka, I need to go check on something. I'll be back. How 'bout you start on this humpback whale puzzle?"

Clad in her rain jacket with the hood drawn tight, she raced down the walkway to cabin twelve. She braced herself on the door frame as the wind howled and knocked. The door cracked open, and she stared at Evan. He stood there shirtless, with his black hair matted. He rubbed his eyes.

"Hey, CJ." A massive gust of wind caused him to lose his grip, and the door slammed back against the wall.

"Shit!" CJ bolted in and helped him close the door.

Evan went to the bathroom and returned with two towels. He tossed one to her as he dried himself. "What's up?"

Her eyes scanned the mess, but his wife was nowhere to be found. "I wanted to come to check on you and Olivia since you missed dinner. Is she here?"

He blinked rapidly, and his expression went slack. "Uh, Olivia's not at dinner?"

"No, no one's seen her." She stared at him as her mind recalled the argument. Was he concerned?

As he ran his fingers through his hair, he told her his wife had left to take photos when he laid down for a nap. He'd been sleeping until CJ knocked.

She wanted to believe him, and it seemed he was telling the truth based on the pillow marks on his face. "Do you know where she went?"

Evan exhaled and rubbed the back of his neck. "No, and I didn't ask." He stepped to the window, pushed the curtains back, and stared into the darkness as rain streamed down the pane. "I think I fucked up. We had a disagreement and … oh, God, she's out in this storm." He wheeled around, and his eyes were wide. "I have to go find her."

"Okay, get dressed, and let's find Alan. We'll help you." CJ pulled her hood back over her head. "Meet me in the dining room. I'll get Ben and some of the others." She opened the door, forced it shut as the wind slammed against it, and ran back to the main lodge.

"Where's Ben?" she yelled as the buzzing room went silent.

"What's wrong, CJ?" Rory asked.

"Olivia's missing. She's not in her room."

Within minutes, Ben entered from the steps to the upstairs apartment, followed by Alan. She explained the situation as everyone gathered around. Evan burst through the front door, and everyone stared at him. Panic and guilt battled to replace his shock.

"Okay, everyone," Alan said. "She's probably here somewhere close, perhaps in one of the buildings, or she slipped …" He didn't finish his sentence when his eyes locked with Evan's. "We'll search the dock, buildings, and walkways."

"Uh, Alan," Kenny said as he stood in the back doorway. "We need to check out the path."

"The path? Why? I can't believe she'd know how to find her way to it."

"Well, umm, I showed her where it was and she—"

"Why in the hell would you do that?! I've told the crew no one is to leave the lodge area."

The young man stared at the floor. "I'm sorry. She wanted to take some pictures and, I thought—"

Alan's icy glare shut him down. "With that tidbit of information, we'll break up into three groups. One will search the buildings, one the surrounding water, and the third, the woods onshore."

Ben, Rory, and Noah offered to help, and Alan assigned them to search around the dock and walkways. Alan told everyone else to remain in the dining room until he returned. Jamie sat beside Evan, who was hunched over on the couch.

"Ben," CJ said, chewing on the inside of her cheek. "I think I should go help."

He stared at her before whispering, "We shouldn't be gone long, and it'd be good to keep an eye on Evan."

CJ frowned. "Please be careful."

"I will." He kissed her, tightened his raincoat, and left through the back door.

She stood and stared out the window, now bathed in a sheet of water. She wished she were out with Ben, searching for Olivia to chase Grannie's warning away. *Waves ... Ben in the water ...*

THIRTEEN

Monday, September 12
Paradise Cove

CJ stared at the hands on the nautical clock on the wall, which read 12:40 a.m. The search teams, including Ben, had been out for almost three hours. She paced in front of the window as the raindrops pounded on the glass and the wind whistled through cracks in the door. The lodge groaned as it rocked from the swells.

I wish Ben would come back. I can't push the image of him in the water out of my mind.

A soft voice behind her caused her to turn to find another guest, a woman in her late sixties. Her face had wrinkles, and her gray hair was in a bun. "Ben will be okay, dear. He's not alone."

CJ nodded, although the tightness in her chest remained. "Thank you," she said as she fought to contain tears and thought. *It's easy for you to say. The man you love isn't out there, and you don't have these images in your brain.*

"I'm Marie," said the older woman, offering CJ her petite hand, which matched her wrinkled face. Crow's feet radiated from the corners of her pale blue eyes. "My husband and I are in cabin one. Would you like to sit and talk?" she asked. "It'll take your mind off things while we wait."

"Sure, I'd like that."

Marie took her hand and led her to a brown leather loveseat in the corner, away from the other guests. Normally, CJ would rather be alone, but she found herself drawn to this woman. Perhaps it was because she was close to the age of her uncle, Harry, who she wished were here now.

The women sat and talked for the next hour—first superficial items, followed by more personal topics, like their relationships with the men they loved. For a reason she couldn't explain, CJ was at ease with her new friend.

"So, tell me about Ben," Marie said.

"Well, he grew up in Charleston and attended The Citadel, the military college there. Like me, he was an athlete. I played lacrosse at Boston College, and he was a football player. After graduating, he served in the Marines and then returned to Charleston."

"And that's where you two met?"

"Yes. I moved from Boston to Charleston a little over a year and a half ago."

"How did you two meet?"

"Oh, we work …" CJ caught herself, cleared her throat, and continued. "Uh, we met at a fundraiser."

Marie smiled. "Was it love at first sight?"

CJ shrugged. "I'm not sure, but we were comfortable with each other from the start. I suppose we were immediately close friends, and it grew." Her gaze shifted to the window as the rain splattered harder on the glass.

"Have you set a wedding date?"

"Not yet, but we're thinking sooner than later. We live together now, splitting time between Ben's house on John's Island and mine downtown. It's time to make it official." She smiled. "Plus, I don't wanna let my southern gentleman slip away. He's one of the best men I've ever met."

"Well, he certainly seems nice and you two look happy together."

CJ's thoughts went to how she and Ben had lost their mothers, both parents in her case, at an early age.

"Why did you move to Charleston?" Marie asked, as if reading her mind.

"I needed a change of scenery and wanted to be near my two uncles. My Uncle Harry raised me after my parents died when I was eleven. He moved to the Lowcountry to join my other uncle after he retired from the Boston PD. He was a detective there."

CJ waited for her new friend to question her about how her parents died, but instead Marie said, "My husband, Leo, swears he's seen you before. Have you ever spent any time in Houston?"

"No. In fact, I don't remember ever going there."

The back door sprang open, and Ben appeared, accompanied by a gust of wind and sheets of rain. His face was etched with exhaustion. CJ jumped up, raced across the room, and wrapped her arms around him.

"You've been gone for almost four hours. Jesus, you're a popsicle." She unzipped his float coat and pulled the soggy jacket off him.

"It's gotten so bad we had to come in and take a break," he said.

The remaining searchers barreled through the door and shed their rain gear no sooner than the words left his mouth. Some of the crew gathered the wet apparel, put it on hangers, and carried it to the mudroom.

"We've canvassed the water around the dock and walkways multiple times," Ben said. "With the waves, we haven't been able to use a boat to check behind some buildings." He shook his head. "Noah thought he saw her, but it was a tarp." He kicked off his boots and leaned on her as he tugged his rain pants down.

"Ben, your jeans and shirt are soaked," CJ said. "You need to change your clothes before you catch something." She led him to the crackling fire in the black stove in the corner. "Let's find you a spot before everyone else surrounds it. I'll go fetch you some dry clothes."

"No," he said, "I think I should go to the cabin, shower, and then put on something else. I wanna be warm when I go back out."

"It may be better to wait until the wind and rain subside or, at least, daylight," she said as she used a towel to dry him.

"It would help if the wind would die down a bit and stop churning the water up," he said. "It's slow going with all the trash floating around."

CJ leaned close and whispered, "I'm going back out with you. We need to drop the ruse with Olivia missing. Besides, Evan is just sitting on the couch with a stunned look."

"It's nasty outside and there's no need for both of us to get soaked," Ben said. "Tell you what. If we don't find her soon, we'll both search."

CJ opened her mouth to argue as Noah approached with Jamie, who, like CJ had with Ben, worked to dry him. Jamie shook her head and exhaled. "My dear husband here slipped and fell in the water."

"Honey, I'm fine. It was no big deal," her husband said as he glanced at Ben. "Thanks for fishing me out."

"No problem. You need to check out your ankle," said Ben.

"You hurt yourself too?" Jamie said, as her eyes went wide. "Come sit down and let me see." She dragged him by the hand to a folding metal chair and rolled up his pants leg to find a red, swollen ankle. "That's it! You're done. No more searching for you."

"I don't want you going back out tonight either," CJ said to Ben. "It's too dangerous."

Ben sighed and tilted his head toward Evan, who sat motionless on a dark brown leather couch. Alan and Debra flanked him as he gazed emptily at the floor. "Honey, I have to go back out. What if it were you?"

Her mind screamed. *But it's not me. It's someone we hardly know.* CJ sniffed and patted her eyes with the damp towel. She was sure there was no way Ben would stay inside. He wasn't wired that way. Truth be told, she understood. *We make our living helping strangers.* "Can you guys at least wait until daylight?"

Alan's voice provided the answer. He stood on a chair and announced, apart from Noah, that the groups would resume their search at 4:30 a.m. Everyone had three hours to get some rest and dry out.

Marie handed CJ a mug of hot tea and rejoined her on the loveseat. "It's 5:40 a.m. The sun will come up soon." She gazed at the long plate-glass window. "The wind and rain appear to be dissipating a bit. Leo heard on the radio that there was supposed to be a lull in the storm before another powerful surge."

Numb. Dazed. Between her irritation of not being out searching, worrying about Ben and only a couple hours of sleep, CJ was a shell. She had ingested enough caffeine to sustain her for a week, but now it only caused her stomach to burn. "I hope they find Olivia soon and she's okay." She said the words but knew the answer deep down. The only way the young woman could be alive was if she was onshore, hunkered down somewhere.

A ray of light appeared. It came from the window and snaked its way across the floor. CJ stood and went to the window. "The wind isn't blowing as hard. It's still raining, but nothing like before." She turned to Marie. "Wanna stretch our legs and get some fresh air before round two hits, and we're trapped again? We can walk down to my room so I can grab some aspirin."

The older woman stood and approached her. "Sure. Leo's asleep, so I can sneak out." She pointed toward a brown recliner where Leo was snoring peacefully. "Besides, I'm not letting you go alone."

CJ glanced at her husband. He was sprawled out and his oddly shaped body reminded her of a praying mantis— heavy at the bottom, elongated torso, and short, skinny arms.

They donned their raincoats, pulled their hoods tight, and slipped out the front door. A cool blast of wind and stinging drops of rain hit them. They turned their backs to it and side-stepped down the walkway, careful not to trip on part of the awning, ripped down by the wind.

After covering forty yards, they stood safe and sound inside cabin thirteen. CJ went to the bathroom and grabbed a bottle of aspirin and some Tums. She wasn't sure which hurt more, her head or her stomach.

"Debra said they'd have breakfast soon," Marie said. "You need to eat something. That'll make you feel better." As CJ returned, the older woman pointed out the window. "A boat got loose from the back."

CJ peered out and said, "It's banging against the dock pretty hard." She pulled her hood back in place. "I'll try to tie it up, and the crew can handle it. When the wind ramps back up, it may smash the walkway. I'd hate to be unable to reach our cabin."

"How 'bout you crawl out?" Marie asked. "I don't want you falling into the water."

CJ opened the door, dropped to her knees, and crawled to the edge on all fours. She couldn't quite reach the boat, so she laid flat, bobbing up and down with the walkway.

Marie grabbed her around the ankles. "I'm gonna hang on to you just in case. If you can't reach it, leave the dang thing."

CJ's eyes focused on the rope dangling from the eyelet on the front of the bow. "I can almost reach it. The damn wind keeps whipping it around." She glanced back over her shoulder. "Hang on tight to my feet."

Sucking in a deep breath, CJ stretched as far as she could. She finally hooked the rope with her fingers before the walkway dipped, and she lost her grip, causing her arm to go under the water up to her elbow. As she regained her balance, something soft and cold touched her hand. She gasped and jerked her hand away as Olivia's chalk-white face and glassy eyes popped to the surface.

"Shit!" She scrambled backward, slamming into Marie.

"What? What's wrong?"

"I … I found Olivia. She's dead. Stay here." CJ jumped to her feet and raced down the walkway toward the main lodge. She slipped and fell twice, driving her knee into the unforgiving wooden boards. She burst through the front door and screamed, "I need to find Alan!"

Debra ran to the counter, rummaged through a drawer, and handed her an orange pistol with a black handle. "Here, use this."

CJ raced back out on the front deck, cocked the hammer back, pointed the gun up, and squeezed the trigger. The muzzle flashed and a bright red line traced upward against the dark gray sky.

FOURTEEN

Monday, September 12
Paradise Cove

Ben and CJ stood near the end of the walkway as Victor, Cal, and Kenny worked together to retrieve Olivia. While Victor stood on the dock and held a rope to the boat, the other two men pulled the body toward it. As they rolled the body over, Kenny's eyes went wide.

"Oh my God, what happened to her neck?" he said as his head snapped back.

Alan stepped closer and peered down. "The poor thing must have gotten tangled in one of the wire cables under the dock. Okay, everyone. Let's go back inside."

Ignoring him, CJ squatted and scanned the dark red and purple gash along Olivia's throat. *No cable would cause that,* she thought as she glanced up at Ben, who shook his head.

Alan touched her shoulder. "CJ, how 'bout you guys head in? We wanna give the young woman some respect."

She stood and moved back, still staring at the body.

After two more failed attempts at retrieving the body, where Kenny's hands trembled too much to maintain his grip, Simon replaced him. Kenny climbed out and vomited off the deck. Several others who had stayed decided they were satisfied with their curiosity and departed.

The weather cooperated long enough for them to drive the boat to the back and secure Olivia's body in a storage shed. The wind and rain increased no sooner than the task was complete.

CJ suggested they use rubber gloves when handling the body in the event an autopsy was required, drawing strange looks from several people.

Harley, who needed to run his mouth about everything, asked her if she was a big fan of *Forensic Files*. "The damn woman drowned, and you're talking like you're a damn expert or something. Probably never seen a dead body."

She glared at him but held her tongue. *If you only knew.*

Rory stepped forward and snapped, "How 'bout you shut the hell up, asshole?"

Ben stepped between them, and, at six-foot-four, both men backed down.

Alan used this as an opportunity to herd the few remaining guests and crew back into the main lodge. Ben and CJ trailed the group, and she pulled him close as they entered the building.

"We need to tell Alan who we really are and examine her. The wound on her neck looks suspicious."

He nodded. "Yeah. We don't have jurisdiction, but it shouldn't matter to him. Help is help."

She scanned the room of somber faces, except for Harley, who scrolled on his cell phone. *Someone wasn't on the dock or in here.* She walked over to the corkboard, which showcased photos of every guest and staff member labeled with their names. As she nibbled her thumb, she realized who wasn't present—Walter, who handled maintenance.

"Okay," Alan said, "I know we're all upset over poor Olivia's death and wish Evan our condolences. This is a terrible accident ... the worst thing to ever happen here." He asked the group to bow their heads and then said a prayer.

"Considering this unfortunate occurrence, it would be best if everyone returns to their cabins, since everyone grieves differently. You're welcome to stay here if you choose." He glanced at the clock. "We'll serve dinner, but have it at 5:00 p.m." He stepped over to the couch and patted Evan's shoulder. "We're all sorry for your loss."

CJ's jaw and facial muscles were so tight it hurt. The unmoving owner's speech and use of the words "accident" and "unfortunate occurrence" didn't fit the situation. At least, she didn't think so. Her eyes narrowed as they bore into the man in his late forties, who stood smiling and chatting with Harley. *Rory's wrong. We have two assholes, not just the one.*

She turned to Ben, and he nodded. They crossed the room to where Alan stood.

"You got a minute?" Ben asked.

"Uh, sure. What's up?"

"We'd like to speak with you in private," Ben said.

"Let's go back to my office." They followed Alan into a room no larger than a medium-sized bedroom. A desk with a computer monitor and keyboard sat against one wall. The walls were littered with calendars, fishing charts, and various photos of guests with fish. A three-drawer file cabinet sat beside the desk.

"I'd invite you to sit, but I'm a little cramped for space."

"No problem," Ben said as he closed the door. "This won't take long." He glanced at CJ, and his eyes locked with hers. "You wanna do the honors, sweetheart?"

"First, Ben and I need to inform you he doesn't run an auto mechanic's shop, and I'm not a receptionist at a law firm. We're both officers with the Charleston Police Department. To be accurate, Ben's an investigator, and I'm a detective. We work on major crimes, including murder."

Alan's eyes blinked rapidly, and he struggled to find words. After a long pause, he said, "Your instructions when we collected the body make more sense now." He licked his lips and frowned. "Why are you telling me this?"

"We want to examine Olivia," CJ said in a steady, low-pitched voice.

His eyes narrowed. "I'm not sure why that's needed. It's clear—"

CJ closed the short distance between them. "She didn't drown."

He leaned back. "I can't believe you can reach that conclusion with what little you saw."

"Can't hurt, right?" Ben asked. "Think about it. If we look and confirm she drowned, you'll have two qualified people share your opinion."

"Well, that makes sense."

"Plus, think how that will help you with insurance," CJ said. "The company can't hold you responsible for an accident by a guest who broke the rules." *I'm lying, but he seems to be buying it.*

Alan's fingers tugged at his lip, and he nodded. "Okay, fine with me." He dug into his pocket. "I put a padlock on the storage room door, but this'll get you in." He placed his hand on CJ's arm. "Please do it quietly. I don't want to scare the guests and crew by having them think a murder is possible here at the lodge."

They nodded.

"One last item," CJ said. "Can I assume you've alerted the authorities?"

"Uh, no. I haven't yet. With this weather, no one will be coming here anytime soon."

"Call them, or better yet, I'll do it."

Alan groaned. "It would be best if it came from me. I know the Ketchikan PD folks. I'll do it now."

They left his office, clad themselves in rain gear, and jogged to the storage area. Neither paid any mind to the man who stood in the hallway outside the office.

———

Ben flipped the light switch, and the overhead lights sputtered to life. The storage area had a long metal rack with shelves containing cardboard boxes of various sizes. Half the room was empty except for Olivia's body, wrapped in a blue plastic tarp.

CJ stood frozen as her eyes grew wet. *The poor girl didn't deserve this.*

Ben dropped to a knee, slipped off the rope wound around the tarp, and his fingers worked to peel off the clear tape used to seal the bundle. He glanced up. "Are you ready?"

She handed him a pair of plastic gloves she'd taken from a drawer in the kitchen and joined him on her knees. "I'll take notes as you provide details, and I brought my camera to take photos." *These will suck next to my picture of the whales.*

Ben laid the flaps back, and the faint light made Olivia's face appear even paler than before. "I'll unzip her jacket and open her blouse." He turned to CJ. "I'd rather not unclothe her unless we need to, so forensics can check for any trace."

"I think that's fine," she said, "although I'm not optimistic anything useful will remain after the body was in the water for so long." She pulled several baggies from her jacket pocket. "I brought bags if we want to collect anything."

Both jumped back when a crab scurried away when Ben opened Olivia's jacket. "I'm gaining a new respect for the tech guys," he said.

CJ recalled the many times she'd been present when the Charleston County Medical Examiner performed an autopsy. *How could anyone want that job?*

"Aw, shit," he said when he opened the long-sleeve denim shirt the young woman wore. A dark reddish-black line ran from one side of Olivia's throat to the other.

She placed her pad on a box, clicked on a flashlight, and snapped several photos of the wound. "Someone sliced her throat," she whispered.

As his eyes scanned, Ben recited his findings for the next ten minutes, and CJ jotted down notes. More than once, she scolded him for talking too fast. He opened his mouth to respond, but let it go.

"Jeez, Ben. I'm sorry. The last thing I expected us to do on this trip was examine a dead woman."

"Not what either of us wanted," he said, caressing her cheek with the back of his hand.

She exhaled and added a list of the pictures she'd taken. "I think we have what we need."

"Any doubts about what happened?" he asked.

"No. Someone murdered Olivia. This was no accident, and Alan's bullshit story about a cable causing the damage is a crock."

"Agreed. The wound is open, but the edges of the laceration are too clean, precise, and perfect. Whoever killed her is skilled with a knife. No way a cable did this damage."

The vision of the crew gutting their catch flashed through CJ's mind and how quickly they'd completed their work with their razor-sharp fillet knives. A shiver ran through her, and it wasn't from the icy winds penetrating the cracks around the door.

"I'm so sorry, Olivia," she whispered. "Let's finish up and head back before the storm gets worse. I wanna take a shower and wash this odor off."

After they wrapped the body back up, they snapped the padlock closed and hustled back to the lodge. Alan swung the door open, and the looks on their faces told him all he needed to know. The Paradise Cove Lodge had a murderer.

FIFTEEN

Monday, September 12
Paradise Cove

"Can you guys agree to keep this quiet?" Alan asked, his voice shaking. His pleading eyes darted back and forth between Ben and CJ.

"The number one thing is to ensure no one else gets hurt," Ben said, "or worse."

Alan dropped into his rolling chair at the desk in his office, rubbing his face. "We have over three dozen people here, and if we tell them someone was murdered, it will only freak them out," he said.

"And if we don't, they won't be alert and watchful," CJ said.

His nostrils flared, and his face turned beet red. "We can't be certain it was a murder," Alan said in a harsh tone. "Everyone believes the woman drowned. Why not leave it at that? The three of us—"

"Three people can't keep an eye on nearly forty people," CJ said, her voice tight. "Especially if they're not all kept together." She stared at him as he slumped over, his hands clasped behind his head.

He exhaled and hopped up. "I'm in charge here," he said sternly. "I say we only tell a few of my most trusted staff ... have them be watchful." He glared at CJ. "If either of you open your mouth about this, I'm suing you for endangering my business and scaring my customers with your hunch. You best remember you aren't cops here in Alaska."

CJ stepped toward him with her teeth clenched. Before she tore into him, Ben grabbed her arm. "Come on, let's go."

She yanked away from him. "Ben, it's ridiculous not to inform everyone."

"I agree this is foolish, but it's Alan's responsibility." He turned to the owner. "I assume you've called the authorities by now."

The owner's lips twitched. "Uh, yeah. They'll be here as soon as the weather breaks."

After Ben and CJ left his office, Alan closed the door and landed hard in his chair. His fingers massaged his forehead. *This is a fucking disaster.* He organized his thoughts on updating the guests and crew about the storm, while avoiding revealing the manner of Olivia's demise and addressing the "issue" of last year.

He knew Ben and CJ would be a problem. *What luck! I wound up with two law enforcement officers, and one is a damn detective.* At least, he hoped he was the only person aware of this. If anyone else found out, he'd have a more challenging time arguing that Olivia had drowned.

Alan rested his forehead on the edge of the desk. His insides quivered. *Think, damn it!* He sat up, grabbed a pad and pencil, and jotted down a few bullet points. After erasing and rewriting his notes twice, he smiled. *Yes, this will work.*

His lips moved as he practiced his speech and facial expressions until he satisfied himself the story he crafted was perfect. *Now, let's hope everyone else will believe this bullshit.* He picked up his handheld radio and summoned Victor to his office.

———

Ben and CJ returned to their cabin and closed the door. He dropped to the foot of the bed while CJ went to the bathroom. When she returned, he said, "I know you're pissed off at me, but I'm not sure how we can force Alan to tell everyone about how Olivia died."

"So, your defense is it's not our job?" she asked, her tone sharp. Ben reached for her hand, but she pulled away and sat by the table in front of the window with her back to him. Without turning, she asked, "Just because we aren't cops here in Alaska and don't have jurisdiction, how am I supposed to turn off what I've spent my whole life doing?"

"Look at me, CJ." When she refused, he stood, walked over to her, and put his hands on her shoulders. "Okay, don't. This isn't easy for me either. Like you, I took an oath to protect and serve."

She glanced back at him. "Then do it."

"Do you wanna wind up in the middle of all this?"

"We already are, and I don't understand why we won't tell everyone about the murder."

He turned and went to the bathroom, leaving her alone. Five minutes later, he returned and sat in the chair across from her. "Okay, okay, you're right. How 'bout we give Alan a chance to inform people over dinner? He told us he'd arrange a way to protect everyone and if he's called the local authorities we may see help soon."

"And if his plan is crap, what then?"

Ben shrugged. "We provide a new plan. One that advises everyone to be watchful, stay in groups, and avoid concealed areas." He blew out a long breath, causing his lips to putter. "My hope is this doesn't bite us in the ass somehow."

She stared at him without speaking.

"Happy now," he said, spreading his arms. "You win."

Her lips quivered before she said, "Thank you."

She left her chair, sat in his lap, and put her arms around him. "Neither of us imagined our trip would turn out like this. It sucks, but I'm happy you're here with me." She kissed him and ran her fingers through his dark brown hair. "You'll protect me."

"No sense in laying it on thick now. You already got your way. And since when have you needed someone to protect you?"

They sat in silence for several minutes before CJ asked, "Do you think Alan called the authorities like he told us?"

"Um, I dunno. I hope so, but his face screamed *liar*."

She scrolled through the contacts on her cell phone, found what she was looking for, and held the screen up to Ben. It was the name of the FBI Special Agent Wally Gauge who she'd met the prior year when she traveled to Sitka to help the agency in a case at their request.

"You're gonna call him, aren't you?" Ben asked.

"If the stupid Wi-Fi calling works. I don't have any service without it." Her fingers pressed the send button again. "Damn it!" After she failed a third time, Ben told her moving closer to the office might help provide a better connection.

They donned their rain gear and splashed down the walkway until they neared the front door. CJ found a spot where some remaining awning obstructed the rain and tried her call again. "It's connecting," she said.

CJ provided FBI Special Agent Gauge details of their location, the storm, and Olivia's suspected murder. She asked for his help to make sure the local authorities were notified. After she ended the call, she told Ben her friend knew where they were and about the storm. CJ rubbed her eyes, and said, "I also learned from him we haven't seen the worst yet, but you already know that, don't you?"

Ben nodded. "Yeah. I hoped I read the radar wrong, but that's dreaming. Maybe we'll get lucky, and it won't hit us square and be gone soon."

CJ checked the time. "It's after four. Let's head to the dining room."

SIXTEEN

Monday, September 12
Paradise Cove

Ben and CJ entered the den and dining room to the sporadic chatter of guests. The group had reassembled after the break in their cabins. Of those talking, two topics dominated the conversations: the storm and the tragedy of Olivia's death.

Alan announced dinner was ready, and the staff would start service if everyone took their seats. Stephanie placed bowls of spaghetti, Caesar salad, and garlic bread on their table. Except for Evan, who remained in his room, Ben and CJ's tablemates were the same. No one talked much between the storm and the two empty chairs at their table.

The meal was one of CJ's favorites, but she absent-mindedly toyed with it on her plate without eating much. She should have been starving after not eating since last evening, but she wasn't. She glanced around the table and saw she wasn't the only one picking at her food.

"Miss CJ, don't you like spaghetti?" Luka asked, his eyes red and puffy.

"I do, but I had a late lunch, so I'm not hungry," she lied. She couldn't force Olivia's vacant, lifeless eyes out of her mind.

"Will you play cards with me again after dinner?" he asked.

"Uh, yeah. I will."

"Son, eat your food," Rory said.

CJ's mind wandered back to when she was in elementary school at Saint Catherine's. She had been fortunate to get a scholarship for tuition at the private Catholic school. The nuns labeled her a chatterbox, so she always ended up at the designated quiet table for those who talked in class. She hated it then, but now, not so much. She was afraid she might blurt out how Olivia died if she talked.

"Excuse me," Alan said to the room, interrupting her thoughts. "We'll be serving dessert, and I thought I'd update you all on a couple of things."

CJ's eyes cut to Ben. *Here we go.*

"I regret to inform you that the storm is projected to intensify and—"

"When will it pass so we can fish?" Harley interrupted.

Alan's eyes flashed at him. "I'll inform you, if you'd be so kind." He cleared his throat. "According to the National Weather Service, the storm will be with us for at least two or three more days."

"What the fuck!" Harley screamed. "We won't get no fishing in at all."

"I'd appreciate it if you watch your language," Rory said. "I have my son here."

"I have mine here too, and I'll—"

"Your son is thirty-five. Mine is eight."

"Guys, let's calm down, please," Alan interrupted. "As I mentioned, we expect the storm's intensity to increase and last several days. No one is happy about it, but we must make the best of it."

Harley erupted into another tirade. He'd never come back and shouldn't have let Alan talk him into coming for the last week of the season instead of his usual late July slot. By now, almost everyone was sick of his mouth and shouted at him to shut up. He jumped up, knocking his chair over, and stormed out the back door.

Alan continued with his update on the storm. He explained that the generators, which provided power for the lodge, would run twenty-four hours per day instead of the usual from 5:00 a.m. to 10:00 p.m. Food wouldn't be an issue since they always planned their menus for the entire week.

"Considering our poor Olivia's unfortunate accident and this nasty storm, I'm asking all guests to restrict their movements to their cabins, the front walkway, and this room. We don't want another person to slip and fall."

Ben squeezed CJ's fingers as she glared at Alan, shaking her head.

"As an extra precaution, Victor or Simon will patrol the front. In the event you're tempted to wander off, Cal and Kenny will patrol the back. The safety of our guests is our—"

He paused when the back door opened and slammed against the wall, and Harley reappeared. His face was pale and his eyes bulged.

"Why haven't you told us that Olivia was murdered?!" Harley screamed.

Alan's face instantly matched Harley's, and the whole room was stunned. Some yelled questions, some cried, while others were angry at being kept in the dark. Alan waved his hands and tried to quiet the crowd. Rory wrapped his arms around Luka, who pressed his hands over his ears, tears dripping from his chin.

"Please, everyone. Please." After the noise dropped, Alan said, "I'm not sure where my friend Harley here is getting his information, but—"

"Ask her!" Harley yelled as he pointed directly at CJ. "She knows. I was just told by one of the crew she and her boyfriend were in the storage room investigating."

Leo jumped to his feet. "Wait! That's where I know you from. You're the detective from Charleston who caught that serial killer. I remember now. I read an article about you."

The room erupted again, except everyone now focused their questions on CJ.

Ben and CJ stood. "It's true," he said. "CJ is a detective in the Charleston PD's Central Investigation Division. I'm an investigator in a different department."

"So, you lied to us about what you do?" Rory asked.

Ben glanced at him and then back at the group. "Yes, we lied. We came here to escape our daily grind of dealing with vile humans. If we told you what we did for a living, we'd spend all week talking about it. It was my idea, but we never intended to hurt anyone."

"And what about Olivia?" Harley asked. "Was she murdered, or are you lying about that, too?"

CJ said, "Based on how she died, we believe someone murdered her." She glanced down at Rory rocking Luka. "The details aren't important, but based on the evidence, it would appear she didn't die by a fall or drowning."

The room erupted for a third time back at Alan, trapped like a caged animal in the corner.

Marie crossed the room and pried Luka away from Rory. She led him back to the kitchen. "Come on, Luka. All this noise is hurting my ears. Let's have some ice cream."

Rory followed and stood in the doorway, keeping Luka in sight.

For the next ten minutes, the group grilled Alan with questions. Some offered ideas on how they could stay safe in their cabins, or they could all stay together in this room, or have someone take the largest boat and go for help. People who barely knew each other engaged in shouting matches.

"Excuse me!" Rory yelled from the back. "I have an idea." He pointed at CJ. "Let's put her in charge. If she caught a serial killer, she could catch whoever killed Olivia, and Ben can help her."

Before CJ could respond, Rory called for a vote. She won an election she didn't want to run for, getting everyone's vote except three—Ben, Alan, and Evan, who wasn't present.

Ben warned me and here I am, right in the fucking middle of this.

PART TWO

THE STORM

SEVENTEEN

Tuesday, September 13
Paradise Cove

CJ gave up on sleep and sat on the edge of the bed as the wind howled outside and the window rattled. A heaviness engulfed her as her mind raced. What she'd hoped would be a wonderful experience was now anything but an idyllic sojourn with the man she loved. However, using the word nightmare didn't fit her situation either. It was a worst-case situation—trapped and isolated with a murderer and everyone looking to her to solve the problem.

"Ben, do you think we made the right decision allowing everyone to stay in their cabins?"

He left the chair by the table, dropped beside her, took her hand, and squeezed. "I think so. Almost everyone preferred this over sitting in a cramped room staring at each other, wondering who killed Olivia."

She rubbed her eyes. "I wish these damn doors at least had locks on them."

"I'm sure everyone will push the dressers against their doors and take turns sleeping."

Her fingers pinched the bridge of her nose. "Let's hope so. Of course, I'm not sure what anyone can do if someone breaks into their room. No one has a weapon, including us."

She refused to accept Alan's statement that there were no weapons on the premises. This was Alaska, and everyone had a gun. In fact, she believed little the owner told her. After over ten years in law enforcement, she could read people. The movement of their eyes and head, forced smiles, clenched jaws, hand gestures, and the distance they tried to stay away told her a lot. Alan kept a lot hidden.

CJ stood and paced like a caged tiger. "We gotta decide between two options. We either focus on keeping everyone safe until the weather breaks, help arrives, and let the local authorities solve what happened to Olivia, or try to solve it ourselves." She pulled the curtain back and stared into the blackness as sheets of rain trickled down the pane. *When is this fucking storm gonna end?*

She wheeled around and grabbed her camera. Her fingers scrolled through the photos of Olivia's body. "Are we wrong? Is Alan's theory, right? Did a cable cut her neck?"

Her gaze fixed on the image of the wound on Olivia's neck. It was wishful thinking, and she knew it.

"A cable didn't slice her neck that cleanly," Ben said as he stood and stared at the photo along with her. The tip of his finger traced the stark white image. "The edges of the wound are too smooth. A knife caused this, and it was a sharp one."

The vision of the crew cleaning fish popped into her mind again. They were quick and skilled and knew exactly how to peel the meat away from the bone. A chill ran through her. She peered up at Ben. "So, what do we do? Wait or try to solve it?"

He rubbed his chin. "As much as I'd like to hunker down and focus on keeping us safe, this storm isn't leaving anytime soon, and we have no way of knowing when help will arrive." He hugged her. "We're gonna need to protect ourselves and everyone else and find who's responsible."

He was right. They could opt to sit it out without the necessary jurisdiction, but the group expected them, specifically her, to take the lead. In their minds, a detective who'd caught a serial killer had the most experience. A vise squeezed her chest.

CJ crossed the room and rummaged through the night-stand drawer until she found a pad and pen. She drew a deep breath and turned to Ben. "Let's brainstorm what we have."

They spent the next hour going over information and who might be the individual most likely to commit a murder. Twenty-three guests needed to be considered, many they knew little or nothing about, and the ten-person crew, plus the two owners.

"Damn it!" CJ said sharply. "How can we narrow this list down? Some guests are much older, so perhaps we can assume they'd be a low priority. If we remove the women, assuming they wouldn't kill someone with a knife, we still have a long list." She handed Ben the pad with her scribbled notes. "I can't remember all their names. Writing down 'two men in cabin four' isn't helpful."

His eyes scanned the sheet, and he turned to the door. "I need to grab something." He dragged the dresser away. "I'll be right back."

She grabbed his arm. "Wait! Where are you going?"

"I'm gonna bring the chart here with everyone's photos and names from the den."

Her lips pursed. "We should both go. Remember, we told everyone to stay in groups."

Ben pulled on his rain gear. "It'll only take a minute, and it's pouring outside. I'll be careful." He leaned in and kissed her. "Push the dresser back." Before she could pull on her gear, he left.

Her heart pounded for fifteen minutes until she saw Ben returning as he passed the window. Seconds later, he handed her a board wrapped in plastic bags. "The damn rain is coming at us sideways right now, and I had to fight the wind the whole way. I hope I kept the chart dry."

"Did you see anyone?"

He shook his head. "Nope. All the lights were on, but no one was in the den or outside."

"How about Evan? Were his lights on in his room?" she asked as she pointed toward the wall between their cabin and his.

"No. It didn't appear so, but these curtains are thick, so it's difficult to tell."

She nodded. "I hoped Evan would stay with someone else or in the main lodge, but he's stubborn."

"He lost his wife," Ben said, "so I'm sure he wants to be alone."

"What's your take on him?" she asked.

"I'm not sure. Why?"

She frowned and said, "I keep thinking about how he yelled at Olivia the day they followed us in from fishing. I couldn't hear what he said, but he was pissed about something."

"I noticed how he talked about his job at dinner," Ben said. "He sure has a high opinion of himself."

CJ rubbed the back of her neck. "I don't like the way he treated Olivia. Both times we were around them, he did all the talking. When I tried to engage her, he cut in and answered for her."

"Yeah, I noticed that too. It's like she was a … uh …"

"A mouse. He was domineering. Poor thing was afraid to speak up around him. He's an asshole and is on my list."

"Makes sense. We've worked enough cases to know the spouse is always someone to consider," Ben said. He turned and gazed at the three-by-four-foot corkboard and the smiling faces with their names underneath. "How about we start fresh and work our way through all the folks one by one?"

"Okay, I'll make a list and circle those we believe have the potential to murder someone, and we can go from there." She circled Evan's name.

Two hours later, the black sky turned light gray as the sun fought to expel the darkness.

CJ stretched and held up a list of four names. "We have some others, but these are the top priority to evaluate," she said.

- *Evan, victim's asshole husband*
- *Alan, suspicious owner*
- *Walter, maintenance man who keeps to himself*
- *Kenny, last to see Olivia alive*

Ben glanced at the clock on the nightstand. "It's a little after six. We agreed everyone would eat breakfast together in the dining room at 7:00 a.m."

They pulled on their rain gear. As CJ opened the door, a blast of wind and pouring rain hit her.

"We can start interviewing people right after break-fast, starting with Evan," she said over her shoulder as she thumped down the walkway.

CHAPTER

EIGHTEEN

Tuesday, September 13
Paradise Cove

Evan pressed his ear against the wall but couldn't hear what the detective and her boyfriend were discussing. It was incredibly frustrating. He assumed they were talking about Olivia's murder and who might have committed it. More than once, he was sure they said his name.

He tiptoed back to his bed and propped himself against the headboard. His lips curled as he reflected on his life, and his insides vibrated. He was single again and only thirty-one years old. Prosperous, handsome, and free as a bird. And he had a bonus: people's pity over his beloved wife's tragic murder. *You poor guy.*

His mind wandered back to when he first met Olivia. They'd attended the University of Georgia together and found themselves in a psychology class study group at the library. He hadn't noticed her before from his seat in the back of the class of more than a hundred people, but she caught his eye that evening.

Olivia wore a yellow sundress with black splotches that reminded him of a sunflower. Her sandy blond shoulder-length hair, perfectly layered to suit her face, glistened under the overhead fluorescent lights. The same light made her brown eyes sparkle whenever she glanced at him. Throughout the study session, she furiously made notes in a spiral-bound notebook. He liked her quietness.

After the session ended, he asked if she wanted to grab a coffee. He waited until she whispered, "Yes, I'd like that." They sat for almost two hours as he explained his plan for his life. He told her he wanted to work in finance and make loads of money—have a big house, pricy cars, and take trips to exotic locations. To save his life, he couldn't remember if she said anything. She sat there, nodded, and listened to him. He'd loved that.

They dated over the rest of the school year, though her sorority sisters did everything they could to break them up, saying, "You shouldn't be with him. He's no good for you. He's a self-centered jerk. He cheats." *Blah-blah-blah. Stupid bitches. Who were they to say who was best for Olivia?*

After graduating with honors, he worked for his dad's investment firm with a hefty salary, a company car, a fancy office, and his own personal assistant. Olivia still had a year left before graduating, but he convinced her being an interior designer was a dumb idea.

She dropped out of school, moved in with him, and went to work part-time in a clothing store. He was okay with it as long as she kept their apartment clean, had dinner on the table when he got home from an actual job, fulfilled her duties in the bedroom, and dressed the part at his business parties.

He had to give her credit. The woman did a hell of a job keeping their home spotless and cooked some delicious meals—always his favorites. She wasn't gorgeous, but always tried to look her best for him. His business colleagues often commented on how lucky he was to have her by his side.

He smiled as he thought about their sex life. Olivia was a virgin when they met and had been awful in bed until he trained her in what he liked. After a couple of years, she was pretty good at pleasing him. Not as good as most of the others he slept with, but not bad. He promptly reminded her of her mother whenever she balked at one of his suggestions. Her father had left them for another woman. *That's what happens when a wife doesn't please her man.*

After stringing her along for another year, he proposed, and they married in front of over four hundred guests. His parents' money provided a high-class event and ensured all the right people attended.

All-in-all, he had been happy with their marriage. He told Olivia what to do, and she did it. She stayed home except for the two days he allowed her to work each week.

She played the adoring wife perfectly at business functions when they went out.

Evan sighed. Despite his overall satisfaction with Olivia, their relationship had encountered a few obstacles. Sometimes, when she found out about one of his indiscretions, she cried, he apologized, and she forgave him. "I'll never cheat on you again," he said. They both knew he would.

In recent times, though, the marriage had turned rocky because of her desire for children. Her begging made him so paranoid that he watched her take her birth control each day. Even when he was on the road, he Facetimed her and ensured she swallowed her multi-colored pills.

It wasn't a matter of disliking kids, but not being ready yet. Being repeatedly asked the same question every day about when they would have a baby was tiresome. She'd plead with him, he'd say no, and then she's sulk. He hated that.

Olivia's sulking was why he lost his temper more than once. He didn't enjoy slapping her, but she gave him no choice. She was to blame. He wasn't a violent person by nature, but she made him one. His father had always emphasized that discipline was crucial to a successful marriage.

Evan had hoped things would go smoothly on this trip. He'd wanted to come to the lodge to check it out as a potential place to take his clients. She agreed to join him and take those stupid pictures with her new camera, the one he bought her after she caught him in their bed with the trainer from the gym. He would have had a better time if he'd brought his new assistant, his latest treat.

He stood, went to the dresser, pulled open a drawer, and stared. *No need for this stuff now.* Searching through the cabinet by the bathroom, he found what he needed. He put Olivia's clothes in a black trash bag and hid it under the bed a few minutes later. When the time was right, he'd sneak the bag in the trash bin for the crew to burn. *Too bad her camera's gone. I know a young lady who would love it.*

Evan strolled to the bathroom and gazed intensely into the mirror, pulling at his black hair until it became disheveled. He splashed water on his face and used his fingertips to rub his eyes until they were red. Slipping on his rain jacket, he headed for the dining room. *Showtime!*

NINETEEN

Tuesday, September 13
Paradise Cove

Noah and Jamie were alone in their cabin—number eleven. "Sweetheart, we need to leave soon and go to breakfast," he said. "Everyone agreed to be there together." He leaned against the edge of the dresser they'd pushed against the door.

Jamie sat on the bed, huddled up against the headboard. She had her knees pulled up and her arms locked tight around them. "I wanna stay here. It's not safe outside," she said, wiping the wetness from her cheeks. "You go."

He approached, joined her on the bed, and wrapped his arms around her. "Honey, I'm not leaving you here alone." He kissed her forehead. "It's getting lighter outside, so we'll be okay going out."

Her body trembled, and she shook her head. "I'm staying here."

"We have to go meet everyone," he said as he kissed her forehead again. "I'm gonna take a quick shower, and then we'll go." He stepped into the bathroom.

The two of them had taken turns sleeping during the night. Jamie had watched Noah as he slept, her heart bumping with every floor creak, window rattle, and thump. *Were those footsteps outside the door?* She woke him up more than once. *"Noah, I heard someone."* He'd check, assure her it was nothing, and drift back asleep.

When her turn to sleep came, she lay awake, staring at the ceiling. She refused to turn the lights off, and there was no way she could close her eyes. What if Noah fell asleep, and the murderer came after them?

A thud from the bathroom caused Jamie to jump. She ran to the door. "Honey, are you okay?"

His head popped out from behind the curtain. "Sorry, I dropped the shampoo bottle. I didn't mean to scare you."

She turned and went back to her spot on the bed. No matter how much she told herself to relax and that Noah wouldn't let anyone hurt her, the tension in her body wouldn't release. Nor would the pounding of her heartbeat in her ears subside. Her lack of sleep had given her a throbbing headache to top things off.

As she waited for Noah, her thoughts drifted to her childhood. Like most ten-year-olds, she didn't have a care in the world until her best friend, Becky, who lived next door, went missing. At first, everyone assumed she went to another friend's house or was out somewhere playing. But law enforcement was called in when she wasn't found in a few hours.

The entire community turned out to help search and, with the help of the K9 unit, they found the young girl in the nearby woods. Someone had beaten and strangled her to death. The police apprehended the man responsible less than half a mile from the scene. He had a mental illness and used drugs. His arrest record included numerous assaults and robberies. *Why did he pick our small, quiet town to jump off the train?* Jamie wondered again.

The image of him on TV, as he laughed in court when pronounced guilty, was forever etched in her mind. The years of therapy had helped her cope with her anxiety, but she knew she'd never feel secure. *There are too many monsters out there.*

Jamie loved her husband, and he was always patient with her. He hid his frustration and never complained when she asked him to recheck the door locks, ensure the alarm was on, or go with her after dark. He'd smile and say, "No problem." But would he be able to protect her from someone like the person who killed her friend? Her friend's father was a cop, and he'd failed.

She blew out a long breath. *Let's get it together.* She went to the mirror on the wall where the dresser had been before they used it to block the door. Her trembling fingers worked to put her dark brown hair into a ponytail and rub her tired eyes. *I look like and I feel like shit.*

"Noah, I'm coming in to wash my face."

He peered at her from behind the curtain again as she entered. "Baby, you don't need to warn me you're coming in." He pushed the lever down and stopped the spray. After wrapping a towel around his waist, he stepped out and pulled her to him. "I've got you. You're okay."

All Jamie could do was bawl. Her tears dripped off her chin, and her whole body shook.

He cradled her and massaged her back. "Shh, you're safe."

After a long sniff and wipe of her nose with the back of her hand, she nodded. "All right. Let me do something with my face, and we'll go." She didn't want to leave the room, but they couldn't stay locked away until the storm broke. Besides, she knew Noah was hungry.

"That's my girl," he said.

While he put on his clothes, she washed her face, attempted to apply makeup to cover the dark circles and bags under her eyes, and threaded her ponytail through the gap in the back of a Colorado Rockies baseball cap.

Noah stood in front of the picture window as she entered the bedroom. He stared at the sky, which was still dark but not jet black. The rain was less intense, and the room wasn't shaking as violently from the wind and waves. "I think the storm is leaving," he said. "I'm sure Alan will give us an update at breakfast." He took over zipping up her raincoat when he noticed her hands shaking and pulled the hood over her head. "Are you ready?"

She wanted to say no and surrender to her fears that as soon as they stepped outside, whoever killed Olivia would grab them, but she didn't. "Uh, yeah. I think so."

He dragged the dresser back, reached out his hand, and she took it. "Hang on to me, and we'll run for it."

TWENTY

Tuesday, September 13
Paradise Cove

Ben and CJ entered the dining area to find about two-thirds of the guests were already there. Everyone except Harley sat somberly on the couches and chairs, waiting for the food to be served. He bitched about not being able to fish, being confined to his cabin, and when help was arriving.

CJ took her usual chair and mentally went through a checklist of who was present. She and Ben were the only ones at their table so far.

"Are you guys gonna do anything about who killed that girl or keep sitting on your asses?" Harley asked her angrily as he approached. He slurred his words, and a faint odor of alcohol wafted across the table.

"I'll give an update after breakfast," she said.

The front door swung open, slamming against the wall from a gust of wind, and Noah and Jamie entered. Rory and Luka hustled in behind them, and Rory wrestled the door closed. The four of them joined Ben and CJ at the table.

"Has anyone seen Evan?" Rory asked.

Everyone shook their heads.

He sighed. "I don't think that's healthy for him. Do you guys think it's safe?"

"He would be better off mentally if he wasn't alone, but all we can do is encourage and keep a close eye on him," Ben said. "I told him to let CJ or me know if he needed anything and to push his dresser against the door."

"Did you guys sleep much?" Jamie asked.

CJ shrugged. "Some. It wasn't easy with the wind rocking the cabin. Ben and I took turns, and each got a little rest. How 'bout you?"

Jamie's eyes watered, and CJ was afraid she was about to burst into tears. "Well, um, not really. Noah slept for a few hours, but I couldn't stop staring at the ceiling and thinking."

"She wanted to keep the bathroom light on, so that made it harder to fall asleep," Noah said, as he massaged his wife's shoulders. "We'll try to take a nap today. What about you Rory?"

"No." He patted his son on the back. "My little guy here slept like a baby. I didn't try since I wanted someone to be alert, just in case. Marie offered to take care of Luka today, and I'll grab some sleep then."

"Are you okay with Marie taking care of him?" Noah asked.

"Yeah, Marie's great," Rory said. "She and Leo have been coming here for a long time and I met them when I started coming. I've fished with them a couple of times and gotten to know them. In fact, one of the reasons I agreed to move to the last week of the season was because they changed their slot."

The bleary-eyed group continued to chat about the storm, when they expected it to break, and when help would arrive. Stephanie placed platters of scrambled eggs, bacon, and toast on the table. As they ate with little enthusiasm, Evan pushed through the door. Several guests hopped up to meet him.

Before Evan reached their table, Marie convinced him to join her and her husband. She slid her arm around him and led him to a chair. Several people surrounded him, all giving him kind words and expressions of sympathy. As Marie hugged him, his cold eyes met CJ's, and he smirked, causing a shiver to run down her.

CJ leaned over to Ben and whispered, "Did you see that?"

He furrowed his brow. "What?"

As Alan entered the room and asked for everyone's attention, she said, "Never mind. I'll tell you later."

"I hope everyone got some rest last night," Alan said with a forced smile. "I know the high winds made it tough."

He spent the next few minutes discussing the latest available weather information, saying the storm should subside over the next few hours before another surge in the early evening. However, the satellite had stopped working during the night, so the internet and Wi-Fi were down.

"Wait! So now you're telling us we're in the dark here?" Harley said. "That's just peachy. Damn! What else is gonna go wrong?"

"As soon as possible, we'll determine the issue and correct it," Alan said. "I'm sure it's only a glitch because of the weather."

Harley stood and jabbed his finger toward the owner. "I don't understand why someone can't take the bigger boat and go—"

"It's still too dangerous with the wind and waves." Alan raised his palms in a stop fashion.

The two men bickered back and forth for several minutes before Harley stomped out the front door without closing it behind him. Ben jumped up to close it as a powerful gust blew magazines and papers around the room, and rain soaked the floor.

"I'm sorry about him," Alan said, shaking his head. "I assure everyone we'll get the communications back up as soon as possible." He turned to CJ and asked her to provide any updates on Olivia's death.

"Ben and I plan to talk to people today in case anyone saw something that might be helpful," she said. "Often, someone's not aware they have important information." She gazed around the room at the slack expressions, grimaces, and raised eyebrows. "We'll also re-examine Olivia's body ..." She stopped as Evan's stare bore through her.

"That makes sense," Alan said. "I believe a second look at our poor Olivia may confirm my belief she drowned, and it was all a horrible accident."

CJ glared at him. "How 'bout you, Ben, and I meet in your office?"

He cleared his throat. "Umm, sure. I ... I'd be happy to help in any way possible." He motioned to his chef behind the counter. "Bev will have dinner ready at six, and we'll have cold cuts and fixings out at noon for lunch."

CJ and Ben trailed him down the short hallway and into his office. She closed the door. "Alan, you need to drop the 'it was an accident' bullshit."

"I'm still not convinced you're correct about Olivia being murdered, and I don't wanna scare the hell out of the guests," he said as he flopped into his chair. "It's my responsibility to—"

"What about your radios in the lodge and boats? Can't we use those to communicate?" Ben asked.

"Well, uh, the one in the lodge isn't working."

Ben raised his eyebrows and asked, "What's wrong with it?"

Alan shrugged. "I'm not sure. I'll have Walter take a look at it."

"And the ones in the boats?"

"I haven't checked those yet, but I'll do that as soon as we finish here. Anything else?"

"Are you sure you don't have a gun here?" Ben asked. "I find that hard to believe."

Alan crossed his arms. "As I've already told you, I don't allow weapons here as a safety precaution." His eyes narrowed and his jaw tightened.

While the two men exchanged stares, someone knocked. The door opened, and Anita appeared in the doorway. "Sorry to interrupt, but Kenny's gone," she said in a high-pitched voice. "He ran off up the path." She held up Ben and CJ's rain jackets she'd grabbed from the dining room.

Alan jumped up from his chair. "I'll go find—"

CJ grabbed his arm and stopped him. "No, you stay here. Ben and I will go." Before he could object, they were out the door, sloshing behind Anita down the walkway. They stopped when they reached the end of the wooden planks and stood under a covered area against the wall to avoid the wind.

Anita pointed at a narrow footbridge to the shore. "Kenny went across and ran up the path toward the woods."

"Do you know why?" CJ asked.

The young woman wiped the water from her face and shrugged. "Not really. He's been acting weird since we found Olivia and hasn't wanted to talk about it."

"Are you two close?"

"Yeah, I guess. It's not like the other guys are mean to me, but I'm new, and Kenny and Simon are the ones who always talk to me. Victor and Cal always hang around together. Walter's been here for years but doesn't associate much with anyone. He's always in his maintenance shop except to eat and sleep."

"All right. Ben and I will go find Kenny."

"I wanna go with you," Anita said. "I don't want Kenny to get in trouble, besides, I've been up there before, and the path is hard to follow in places."

CJ glanced at Ben and he nodded. "Okay, let's go."

Anita led them across the swaying footbridge, onto the muddy path, and toward the dense foliage. The sky, dark from the heavy clouds and rain, grew darker as they passed under the gnarled limbs overhanging the trail.

As they climbed, the scent of decaying leaves and moist soil filled CJ's nostrils. Her adrenaline increased, and a tightness gripped her stomach. One question ran through her mind. *Why did Kenny run?*

TWENTY-ONE

Tuesday, September 13
Paradise Cove

Walter stared at the three people as they started up the path through the foggy window of his shop. His eyes strained to follow them until the black forest engulfed them. He'd watched Kenny leave with his backpack earlier. The young man had at least a thirty-minute head start and knew the woods better than this group.

Why didn't Anita just let Kenny go? Walter rubbed his face with both hands and retreated into the dim light of the shed, where he spent almost all his time. His sanctuary. The place where he felt safe. It was not that he didn't like these people, he just didn't want to be around them. Well, that wasn't entirely true. He enjoyed being around Kenny.

He dropped onto an overturned five-gallon bucket and his mind drifted back to the past and the reason he was here—remote, isolated, and alone. Concealing his crime was now increasingly more complicated with the discovery of another dead body. *Maybe it's time I come clean and accept whatever happens to me.*

———

Ben and CJ followed Anita as they trekked deeper into the dense woods. They thought it might provide more protection, but the only benefit was that the wind was reduced along the forest floor. CJ kept her eyes focused ahead and avoided glancing up at the treetops, which appeared as though they would snap at any minute as they were swaying so violently.

"We'll reach the overlook area soon," Anita said, her voice loud over the roaring above. "I hope Kenny stopped there."

"Where does this path end?" CJ asked.

"I've never made it that far, but, supposedly, the trail will take you to a village with a few people on the other side of Port Protection. I understand they're indigenous Alaskans, and they don't care much for outsiders." Anita stopped and pointed toward a wooden bench on a rock patio a few feet ahead. "There's where folks can sit and look out across the water." She exhaled. "No Kenny."

CJ caught up to her and stood staring at the bench. Her rain jacket kept her dry from the pounding drops, but it trapped her sweat, causing her pants and shirt to cling to her. "Let's rest a minute."

They found a shielded location under a massive Sitka spruce and pressed themselves against the scaly, purplish bark. CJ peeled back her hood and released the trapped heat. After a few minutes, her gasps for air slowed, and her breathing returned to normal. "Whaddya think, Ben? Should we keep going?"

"It's up to you, but my vote would be to continue. We need to find Kenny ... he may be responsible for Olivia's death."

"No way!" Anita said as her eyes bulged. "He wouldn't hurt a fly."

"Why did he run then?" CJ asked.

The young woman shook her head. "I'm not sure, but I'd guess he's afraid of something. He's not been himself." Tears clouded her puffy hazel eyes. "I'm worried he's gonna get hurt out here. This isn't the safest place after dark."

Ben gazed through a narrow opening in the dense foliage. "Speaking of dark, we need to make sure we save enough time to get back ourselves. The storm has calmed a bit, but according to Alan, it's returning with a vengeance later. It's almost nine, so let's walk another two hours, and then we'll turn back for the lodge."

Anita nodded. "Okay, we may be able to reach the cabin by then."

"Wait! What cabin?" CJ asked as she pulled the soggy hood back over her head.

"Well, it's more of a shack hunters used in the past. It's in bad shape now, but Kenny may be hiding there."

The group had hiked for almost an hour and a half when an old, dilapidated structure appeared forty yards ahead. Anita stopped and turned back to CJ and Ben. "That's the shack." She picked up her pace, scrambling along the rocky path.

"Wait, Anita!" CJ said. "Let Ben and I go in first. In case—"

"Kenny won't attack me if that's what you mean," the young woman said.

CJ caught her and grabbed her arm. "Still. Let us go first."

Anita frowned, but let CJ and Ben pass her. As they approached the windowless building, a faint light shined through cracks in the walls.

Ben put his arm out to stop CJ. "There's someone in there." He motioned Anita forward and whispered in her ear. "Would Kenny have a weapon?"

She shook her head.

"Let me check it out first." He crept to the door, sucked in a deep breath, and pulled it open.

Kenny sat huddled in the dim corner of a single room no bigger than a bedroom. A small battery-powered lantern sat at his feet. He kept his head bowed until the door hinges creaked, and then his head snapped up. "Leave me alone!" He scrambled to his feet and held up a hunting knife. "I mean it. Get away from me."

Ben remained in the doorway and held up his palms. "Easy, Kenny. We're not here to hurt you. We're worried about you out in this storm."

Tears trickled down the young man's face. "I ain't going back."

"Kenny!" Anita yelled as she tried to squeeze past Ben. He grabbed her arm. "Hang on. Stay here."

"Damn it! Why did you bring them here?" Kenny said as his eyes flared at Anita. "All of you go away and leave me the hell alone!"

CJ tugged at Ben's jacket. "Let me talk to him."

He hesitated before stepping back and letting her go past him. "Be careful and don't get too close."

She nodded and said, "Okay, but step outside with Anita." She stood alone, staring at the young man still holding his weapon. "Kenny, please put the knife down. You're scaring me."

He shifted his weight back and forth, but refused her request.

"Tell me why you ran off. What's wrong?"

He wiped his eyes with his free hand and let out a loud sniff.

"Come on. Please put that down and talk to me," CJ said, pointing to the knife in his hand.

"Why?" he asked as his hand holding the knife trembled.

"Because whatever is going on, I'll help you."

He stared at her before he cautiously crouched, sat the knife on the floor, and stood.

"Thank you. Can we talk?"

He nodded. "I guess, but it's no use."

CJ eased closer and slid the knife away with her foot. "Now, tell me what's wrong."

"It's my fault a woman's dead. I caused it." He dropped his head.

She scrutinized him before she said, "I don't believe you. You didn't kill anyone or mean for her to get hurt." She motioned for him to sit and then joined him.

For several minutes, she coached him into telling her why he ran. It came down to something she knew well— guilt. Kenny told her he was the one who had shown Olivia the path and left her out there alone. If he hadn't done that, she'd be alive. She listened until he finished.

"I can understand why you want to assume the responsibility for her death, but the fact is her murder is not your fault. Who knows where someone killed her? It could have been somewhere on the lodge property instead of the woods, but either way, you didn't do it."

No matter how much she tried to convince him, he disagreed until she told him her story about when she was eleven and she called her parents, crying over the phone that she wanted to come home from a sleepover as she was homesick. A drunk driver hit her parents and older sister while they were on their way to pick her up, on a route they would never have taken otherwise.

Her parents died immediately, and her sister survived for five days until she passed away. After years of therapy, she could only now admit it wasn't her fault her family had died, and the responsibility lay with the drunken man and bad circumstances.

Kenny listened. When she finished, he said, "So maybe you do understand why I feel so damn guilty, but how do I get over this?"

CJ fought the urge to tell him, "You don't." She now handled it better, but still had dark days that haunted her. The same old question popped into her mind. *Why didn't I keep my damn mouth shut and stay put? My parents would have been safe at home instead of on the road that night.* "I tell you what. How 'bout you help me solve whoever committed this horrible crime?"

He looked blank but nodded. "I'm not sure that'll help, but I owe Olivia that much."

She patted his shoulder. "It's a deal. Now, let's get the hell off this mountain before the next wave of the storm hits us."

They stood, joined Ben and Anita outside, and hurried down the trail as the clouds darkened and the wind and rain picked up.

TWENTY-TWO

Tuesday, September 13
Paradise Cove

The rain pounded CJ, Ben, Anita, and Kenny as they crossed the footbridge, and the black clouds loomed overhead. Everyone was soaked as though they'd jumped in the cove with their clothes on. CJ had slipped and fallen on her butt twice on the steepest part of the path. Mud covered her pants, and she'd ripped her jacket. They stopped under an overhang, gasping for air.

"I'll grab you another rain suit and bring it to your cabin," Anita said. "We have some extras in the back." She grabbed Kenny's hand. "Come help me."

Before following Ben toward the main lodge, CJ stared at the two young people racing away. Her stomach fluttered as her mind screamed. *I know Kenny didn't kill Olivia, but . . .* She faced Ben. "Do you think it's okay for her to be alone with him?"

"Yeah. Like you, I don't believe he had anything to do with Olivia's murder. Plus, he'd never hurt Anita since we'd know it was him. Come on. Let's go change."

Reluctantly, she took his hand, and they ran for their cabin.

After peeling off their clothes, they jumped into the shower together. The hot spray stopped CJ's shivers. They scrubbed each other until they'd removed the residue from their mountain hike.

"Ouch!" CJ said when he accidentally rubbed a tender spot.

"Sorry." Ben kissed her. "You've got a lovely bruise on your right butt cheek."

"I'm not surprised. I landed hard. If you hadn't grabbed my collar, I would have slid all the way down the mountain on my ass." She turned, and they wrapped their arms around each other. "I'm sorry, this trip sucks. Next time, you pick where we go." A wave of frustration washed over her, adding to her exhaustion and helplessness.

Ben nuzzled her ear. "It's not your fault. I checked the weather before we left and saw a storm, but I never expected it to change direction and hit here. It's late in the season, and the weather's more unpredictable."

They stepped out of the shower, and Ben went to get dressed. CJ stood staring at herself in the mirror. Her eyes were puffy, and she was pale. *I look like crap.*

Her leg muscles ached from the climb up the mountain. She sighed as she traced her fingertips along the scar on her left shoulder, compliments of a robbery suspect in a Boston warehouse. Leaning down, she touched the two scars on her right side. One was from a broken bottle wielded by a wife beater. The second one came from a serial killer the press had dubbed The Lowcountry Killer. She lifted her left leg and frowned as she peered at her calf. Her fourth scar, a gift from a homeless man she'd tried to get out of the cold, was the one she hated the most. Anytime she wore a dress, she knew everyone wondered how she got it.

"You need to come get on some dry clothes," Ben said as he stuck his head in the bathroom.

She flinched and abruptly dropped her leg.

"What are you doing?" he asked.

Her heart rate increased. "Nothing." She couldn't tell him she was *admiring* her battle wounds. The fact was she wondered how much he noticed her blemishes—inside and out.

He pulled her to him and wrapped his arms around her, touching his forehead to hers. "I sure do love you, Cassandra Jane O'Hara."

She dropped her head on his shoulder. "I love you too, Benjamin Hunter Parrish."

A loud knock at the door startled her.

Ben released her and closed the bathroom door. "I'll get it while you finish drying your hair."

He returned a moment later and held up a forest green jacket. "Anita dropped off a new rain suit for you. She picked out this color to bring out your eyes," he said, grinning. "She brought me one too. It's an ugly gray color."

"Oh yeah, I'm all about fashion," she said with a weak smile. "By the way, did she say how Kenny was doing?"

"She told me he was in his cabin."

Once they were both dressed and clad in their new rain garb, they headed to the main lodge. They still needed to interview their other prime suspects—Evan, Alan, and Walter.

Debra, Bev, and Stephanie were prepping dinner when Cal pushed through the backdoor and entered the kitchen carrying a tub of frozen fish. His John Deere baseball hat covered his wavy, black hair and his matching beard was wet from the rain. He approached Debra and asked, "Where do you want this?"

"You can put it right there," Debra said, pointing to the counter. "If you don't mind, unwrap the fillets so we can thaw them."

"You got it." He opened a drawer and pulled out a knife. As he sliced each packet open, he asked, "Any word on when this storm is gonna break?"

"No. Unfortunately, we still can't get any reports on the weather." She stared at him as he spread the stark white fillets in a stainless-steel pan. "How's the crew holding up?"

He shrugged. "Fine, I guess. Most of us have been here and are used to the crazy weather." He tossed the empty packets into the trash can and added, "Everyone is upset about the murder. Who could do such an awful thing?"

Debra sighed. "I know. The young woman seemed so sweet. Alan still feels she drowned and was cut by a cable, but the two law enforcement officers here believe otherwise."

"Do they have any leads?"

"Not really, and there's not much for them to go on," Debra said. "It's hard to believe anyone could be so cruel."

"Some people are just mean, I guess," Cal said as his drab green eyes stared at her before he turned for the door. "See you ladies later."

It was 6:15 p.m. when the roomful of guests sat and ate the baked black bass, dirty rice, and carrots in hushed stillness. The lone exception was Harley, who mouthed off about the fact that the communications were still down. Alan explained that he and Walter had climbed to the roof, and the satellite receiving unit was missing. He told everyone the wind must have ripped it off, and it probably fell into the water.

"Can we call for help on the radios?" Leo asked.

Alan shook his head. "We can't get through with the weather."

"So, now we can't call anyone for help," Harley barked in irritation. "That's fucking splendid. We're stuck here with a murderer and have no idea when help will come."

"Damn it! I can't control the weather," Alan said, his face bright red.

CJ stopped pushing the food around her plate and gazed around the room at the tense, tired faces. Everyone's nerves were frayed, and it was apparent that no one had slept much. She knew the only way to address the situation was for her and Ben to find out who killed Olivia.

She stood and walked over to Alan. "What did the last weather update project about the length of the storm?" she asked.

"Uh, at least two more days."

"Are you sure there's no way to go for help?"

The owner shook his head. "No way. The wind and waves are coming straight into us, and our boats are too small. They'd capsize even if they could make it out of the cove."

"Anita mentioned a village on the other side of the island. Would they be able to help?"

He shook his head again. "No. Very few people live there, and they don't communicate with the outside world. The boats they have are smaller than ours. In fact, I think they only have canoes."

She told him she and Ben wanted to talk to him after dinner and returned to her chair.

Harley started complaining again, and several guests began yelling at him to shut up.

Rory, on CJ's right, jumped up and approached him. "You need to close your trap!" he said, wagging his finger at him. "Everyone is sick and tired of listening to you."

Within seconds, the two men were nose-to-nose, screaming at each other.

Ben ran over, grabbed Rory, and dragged him back to the table. "Come on, the guy's an asshole and won't listen to anyone. Besides, you're scaring Luka."

Rory dropped back in his chair and mumbled an apology for losing it. He pulled his tearful son into his lap, hugged him, and then they left. Several other guests stood, pulled on their rain gear, and returned to their cabins. Noah and Jamie, who hadn't touched her dinner or said a word, joined the parade.

After the staff cleared the tables and left, Alan sat with Ben and CJ. "You said you wanted to talk to me, so let's talk."

They spent the next thirty minutes asking him questions about his life. He told them he and his wife bought the place three and a half years ago after selling his construction business in North Carolina. He started it after he left the U.S. Army Special Forces, where he served as a combat diver.

"Wait. Aren't divers in the Navy?" CJ asked.

"The Army and Navy both have divers," he said. "I've always loved the sea. I guess that's why I wound up here," he added as he spread his arms.

They questioned him about past issues with law enforcement or crimes, to which he told them the only laws he'd ever broken were minor traffic offenses. He leaned close. "Look. I'm not your guy. I didn't hurt Olivia or anyone else."

CJ studied him attentively. He seemed convincing, but he was hiding something. His answers sounded too rehearsed. The question hung in her mind. *You're lying, but about what?*

After talking to him about himself, they covered the crew. How long had each one worked here? Had there been any past problems or known criminal acts? He defended every one of them and swore none of them would do such an awful thing.

"How did you get the scar?" CJ said as she noticed a jagged dark red line on his outer wrist protruding from under the sleeve.

Alan glanced down and said, "Oh, I cut my arm on a sharp piece of cable while diving."

CJ nodded as her thoughts went to Grannie's warning about "the man with the scar." She stared at the notes she'd jotted down on a yellow pad. There was no helpful information. Alan was mistaken about someone on the crew, lying to them, or one of the guests had committed the murder. After the owner left the table, she added a question mark beside Alan's name.

TWENTY-THREE

Tuesday, September 13
Paradise Cove

Ben and CJ pushed open the door of the crew den area and stood staring at nine Paradise Cove staff. Everyone was present except for Walter. The staff all stared back at them.

"Uh, can we help you?" Bev said. She was in her late thirties with short, dark brown hair and hazel eyes. She wore her white chef blouse with two rows of black buttons and the lodge insignia.

"We wanted to talk to Walter," CJ said. "Is he here?"

"No. He came and picked up his food, but he always eats by himself in the maintenance shop." She walked to the broad picture window and pointed to a building across the walkway. "He should still be there. He stays in there until he comes over to go to bed."

CJ nodded. "Okay, thanks." She and Ben turned to leave.

"You probably wanna knock," Bev said, stopping her. "He likes to be left alone and is a bit touchy about people coming in there."

"Um, okay," CJ said, frowning.

They crossed the wooden walkway as a gust of wind hit them, almost knocking them off their feet, and banged on a metal door. When there was no response, CJ opened it and stuck her head into the room. "Walter, are you here?" She jerked backward when he appeared from behind a metal cabinet a few feet away from her.

"What do you need?"

"Oh, there you are," CJ said. "Can Ben and I speak with you?"

"Uh, why?"

CJ scowled. "We want to ask you some questions." She cleared her throat. "It's raining hard out here, so please let us in."

Walter exhaled. "Fine, come in." They followed him into the thirty-foot square room, and he motioned to two folding metal chairs in the corner. "You can use those." He dropped onto an overturned five-gallon metal can.

"Thank you," she said as they took their seats.

Walter was in his mid-fifties, had graying dark brown hair, and a beard. He sat staring at her. CJ's gaze fell on a scar on the right side of his neck.

"What do you wanna talk about?" he asked, breaking her trance.

"Well, we're talking to everyone, hoping we can determine what happened to Olivia, and we—"

"Who else have you talked to?" he asked, narrowing his eyes.

"Uh, so far, Kenny, Anita, and Alan, but we're just getting started."

His head dipped, but he remained silent.

She and Ben asked Walter questions for thirty minutes, and he gave short, direct answers. Most of the time, they were only one word. He wasn't interested in talking to them, and no one would accuse him of being chatty.

Walter informed them he had been working here for ten years and the prior owner had hired him. Before then, he bounced around in various maintenance jobs—a cannery in Bristol Bay, a boat shop in Sitka, and an automobile shop in Ketchikan. He could fix anything and didn't mind dirty work as long as people left him alone.

When CJ asked him how long he'd been in Alaska, he hesitated, and his right eye twitched before he told her fifteen years. Before that, he'd lived in Houston and worked on oil rigs.

"Did you see Olivia the day she went missing?" CJ asked. "According to Kenny, she crossed the footbridge right outside your door."

"Nope. I only saw that lady when she arrived with her fancy husband. Alan makes the entire crew greet guests, but other than that, I mind my own damn business and keep to myself."

She nodded and jotted down a note. "Do you think Kenny would hurt her?"

"Hell no," he said, as his nostrils flared. "That boy's a good one and would never do such a thing. Leave him alone."

"How 'bout you? Have you ever committed a crime or had a run-in with law enforcement?" CJ asked.

"Uh, I ain't never been arrested or had scraps with the cops," he said, shaking his head.

She maintained eye contact with him until he looked down. "Are you sure?" she said as she leaned toward him.

"Yes!" he snapped at her.

"Okay." She made another note. "By the way, how'd you get the scar?"

His fingers touched his neck. "I cut it working."

"Here?"

He glared at her. "No. On a rig out in the gulf."

CJ stood and turned to Ben. "You have anything else?"

"Only one more question. What happened to the satellite receiver?"

Walter rubbed his face. "Didn't Alan tell you?"

"He did, but I'd like to hear your answer."

He shrugged. "I don't know. We went up to check it, and it wasn't there."

A driving downpour pelted Ben and CJ as they raced down the walkway to their cabin. Ben slipped as they rounded the corner and almost went for a swim. When they arrived, he pushed the door open and grabbed towels from the bathroom.

He handed her one and asked, "What do you think?"

As she dried her face, she said, "Neither of the men are telling us the truth. I'm not saying they killed someone, but they're hiding something."

"I agree. Alan has been acting squirrely ever since Olivia was murdered, and his special forces background shows he is well trained in how to take a life."

CJ sat at the table and went over her notes. "At this point, we can't rule either of them out." She pointed to Kenny's name. "Can we cross him off?"

Ben nodded. "I think so. I believe what he told you. He feels guilty over Olivia, but only because he showed her the path and left her out there alone."

She used the tips of her fingers to massage her forehead. Solving a crime without forensics, the ability to search or check databases, gather background information, and with so many possible culprits was a nightmare. "Well, we still need to interview Evan. Do you think he's awake?"

He glanced at the clock. "I'd think so. It's only 8:30 p.m." She stood, but he stopped her. "Instead of us going to him, how 'bout I bring him here? Save you from going back out in this mess."

"Works for me. Plus, we'll have him on our turf. Normally, I'd be more sympathetic toward a spouse that lost a loved one, but he rubs me the wrong way."

He yanked on his hood. "I'll run next door and be right back."

Five minutes passed before Ben returned empty-handed.

"What gives?" CJ asked.

Ben pulled off his jacket. "Either he was asleep or he told me he was. He answered the door barefoot in sweats and a UGA T-shirt." He hung his coat beside hers on a hook by the door. "I told him we'd talk tomorrow morning after breakfast." He stared at her as she pinched her lips together. "You don't like that, do you?"

"No." She exhaled. "I'm not a fan of letting a suspect dictate my investigation." She slipped her boots and rain pants off. "I suppose it's fine. He's not going anywhere, and if he murdered his wife, it's unlikely he'll kill again." A massive gust of wind rocked the cabin, and she walked to the window, watching ice pellets splatter on the glass. "None of us are going anywhere."

CHAPTER

TWENTY-FOUR

Tuesday, September 13
Paradise Cove

He believed people had urges—some good, some bad. Most people desired to be good, help others, and do the right thing. However, some couldn't care less about what happened to another human being or the resulting pain from their actions.

He was the latter. Well, that was a lie. Not only did he not care about anyone else except one other person, but he enjoyed it when others were in mental and physical pain. He sat in the dark corner of the storage shed, reflecting on the day. He spent it watching the chaos and the two law enforcement personnel running around searching for someone unknown.

His brow furrowed. *How do you find someone when you don't know what they look like?* They were trying to find him, but they had no idea he was right under their noses. It felt like trying to find something unfamiliar in a pitch-black room. Stumbling around in the blackness with no idea what you might grab.

When he killed the pretty little housewife, he sure set off a firestorm. He let a slow, long breath escape, and his lips curled. He loved it when people were questioning things. How they dealt with stress, fear, and the unknown.

He grunted. *The blame for her death falls on that woman, and poor Kenny deserves credit for helping. The young fool put her square in my sights. Offered her up. He practically walked up to me and said, "Here you go. Take her." She didn't have to go out alone and taunt me—stirring up Jeffrey's urges. None of this is my doing.*

He had no problem grabbing her, as years of practice had served him well. She was afraid, but he disarmed her with his charm. It was too late when she realized he wasn't the helpful sort. She was in his grasp and tied up. He loved it when they whimpered and smelt of fear. It would have been better to have kept her for a while. He could have toyed with her, turning her fear into unbridled terror, but time hadn't been on his side.

A warmth spread across his body as he recalled her last moments. How her muffled cries turned to loud moans. How her eyes darted erratically before slamming shut when he flipped on his flashlight and touched the tip of his blade on her cheek. He released a deep, gratifying sigh.

He cocked his head. If only her damn body hadn't broken loose and floated up so soon. It would have been easier to play it off as drowning after the body decayed some and creatures of the deep had their fill.

The metal door rattled as a massive gust of wind caused the shed to sway, distracting him from his thoughts. The rain, mixed with tiny particles of frozen droplets, tapped on the roof and walls. A loud scraping noise erupted as the steel posts rubbed the bumpers with every rocking of the building. He didn't mind the storm. In fact, it added to his glee, as those around him freaked out.

Everyone has two sides to them. There's the external one visible to all—the outer packaging. Then, there's the one buried deep within, hidden away. On the outside, he was normal. On the inside … well, Jeffrey lived there. He was an unimaginable evil.

His mind went back to when he was eight years old. His father had handed him an exquisitely wrapped Christmas gift. He eagerly anticipated opening his one and only present. His little fingers rapidly peeled away the red ribbon and gold paper when told he could open it. He tore open the box to find a gallon jar and popped open the lid.

He shuddered, remembering the stench of what was inside as his father roared with laughter. He was such a cruel bastard. *Who gives their child a slab of rotting meat for Christmas?*

"Do you like it, son?" asked his father, still laughing his ass off. It was worth the scar the old man gave him after he tossed his gift in his lap.

A rumble sounded in the distance, and a flash of light appeared in the window above his head. He chuckled. *This will add another thrill for the guests.* He pictured them in their cabins, terrified. *Stupid assholes.*

He needed to clear his mind and focus on his newest problem. The nosy little bitch had heard him. He was sure of it. Mumbling to himself had always been a part of his life. It started when he was a boy. He'd walk around in the woods conversing with his other half. He made it a point to be alone, but occasionally, he slipped up.

The rumbling grew closer, and another bolt of light flashed. He rolled his neck as his mind worked, stood, and stretched. Should he get a second opinion? *No. Fuck it. I have a plan.* All he needed was the right time and place, and Miss Nosy would join the pretty little housewife and the others before her. He crept to the door, pulled the hood up, and headed for his cabin.

CHAPTER

TWENTY-FIVE

Tuesday, September 13
Paradise Cove

Debra made her way along the walkway and into the crew
quarters. Alan had convinced her she needed to check on
the staff, especially with the young women, about Olivia's
death. She slipped off her raincoat and joined Anita on the
couch.

The women chatted for several minutes before Anita's
face turned serious. "Can I ask you something in private,
Debra?" she asked in a hushed voice as Bev and Stephanie
entered the den.

The older woman nodded and followed her to her cabin. They dropped onto the edge of the twin bed.

"What is it, sweetie?" Debra asked.

Anita ran her fingers through her hair. "Hmm, I saw someone on the shore the day the young woman went missing."

"You mean Olivia?"

"Yes." The young woman cleared her throat. "I was wondering if I should mention it to the detective. It's probably nothing, and I don't wanna get someone in trouble, but what do you think?"

"Who did you see?"

As Anita was about to answer, the door opened, and her roommate, Stephanie, entered so she leaned over and whispered the name in Debra's ear.

The older woman smiled and said, "I don't think you need to tell the detective, but if it makes you feel better, I'd do it first thing in the morning." Debra hugged her, told her she'd be up front if she needed her, and left.

Stephanie stood staring at Anita. "What's going on?"

"Nothing. I just wanted some advice," Anita said as she opened the dresser drawer and pulled out the sweats and T-shirt she slept in. "Am I still supposed to help with breakfast tomorrow?"

Stephanie nodded. "Yep. Bev figured you might as well help us in the kitchen, since there are no boats to clean."

"Sounds good," Anita said, as she searched the room, "I've been bored doing nothing."

"What are you looking for?" Stephanie asked as she yawned.

"My phone." She stood and pursed her lips. "I swear I had it here after I got back from up front." She took her rain jacket off the hook. "I'll be back."

As she passed Bev standing in the hallway, she told her she left her phone in the guest dining room but would be back.

"Okay, dear. I'm heading to bed and will see you bright and early for breakfast."

Anita walked into a dimly lit dining room and den. She flipped the overhead lights on and searched the counters, hoping to find her phone.

After searching for twenty minutes, she decided someone might have picked it up and would give it back to her in the morning. She turned the lights off and tightened her hood. As she exited the back door, the rain sprayed her face.

She was almost back to the staff cabins when someone stepped onto the walkway and blocked her. "Oh! You scared me. What are you doing out this—"

The man punched her, knocking her off her feet. She landed hard on the decking. Before she could scream, he was on top of her, slamming her head into the unforgiving wooden boards, and her body went limp.

He snatched her up, threw her over his shoulder, and disappeared into a metal shed. Within minutes, her wrists and ankles were tied to a chair with plastic zip-ties. He used duct tape to cover her mouth. He dropped onto a wooden bench and stared at her slumped body.

Fifteen minutes later, Anita's eyes fluttered, and she found him sitting across from her in the poorly lit room.

She squirmed and yanked to free herself, but the restraints held tight. *Why is he doing this?*

He leaned forward and closed the gap between them. "You're a snoop. Did you think I wasn't aware of you spying on me? And I know you heard me."

Her eyes darted, and her heart raced as she realized what had happened. *He killed Olivia.*

He stood, and she flinched. "I don't enjoy being the way I am." His nose was within inches of her face, and he was so close she could see the red veins in his eyes. "It's not my fault, ya know. I was born this way."

Her eyes followed him as he turned and went to a wooden table. An overwhelming wave of dread washed over her as he turned with a knife in his hand. He lifted the end of the bench, moved it closer to her, and sat.

"I never liked guns. They're dangerous." He held up his weapon of choice. "However, this works for me." His lips curled. "And I enjoy a personal touch." He stood. "I wish we could spend more time together, but we can't. I can't afford to get caught." He ran his hand behind her head and grabbed a handful of hair.

The last thing Anita saw was the twisted look on his face. She never heard the soft whirring sound following the low click, and faint flash of light.

TWENTY-SIX

Wednesday, September 14
Paradise Cove

Ben sat propped up on an elbow watching CJ sleep. They slept in shifts so someone could watch the door. For some reason, this situation and the fear he felt was the worst he'd ever experienced.

He wasn't afraid for himself, but for CJ. Throughout his life, he'd survived some terrible things—his mother leaving when he was young, a severe injury to his shoulder, being accused of a crime he didn't commit, and plenty of nasty storms out at sea. But now he had CJ and the thought of harm coming to her scared him.

The challenge wasn't protecting her from an attack. Ben knew he could do that or die trying. But now they were tasked with solving a murder and CJ was prone to take risks in her cases. He loved her strength and determination, but it terrified him when she went too far out on a limb—working alone.

CJ's eyes popped open, and she rubbed her eyes. "Jeez, I was out."

Ben pulled her to him and pressed his lips to hers. "I'm glad you got some rest."

"What time is it?"

"It's 5:35 a.m. How 'bout we shower, get dressed, and go grab some coffee?"

Forty minutes later, Ben and CJ entered the dining room to find only a handful of guests. Bev and the kitchen crew were setting up the tables for breakfast.

"Good morning," Bev said. "We have plenty of hot coffee ready and fresh baked cinnamon rolls if you'd like one."

Ben went to grab a coffee as CJ dropped into a chair at their usual table. Stephanie approached her. The young woman's eyes were red, and she was visibly upset.

"Are you okay, Steph?" CJ asked.

"I … I'm not sure." She leaned close and whispered, "Anita wasn't in our cabin when I woke up. She was supposed to help with breakfast, but I've not seen her."

CJ's heart rate picked up. "What do you mean?"

"Last night she told me she was coming here to grab her phone. She thought she'd left it here." She tugged on her black Paradise Cove Lodge T-shirt.

"What are you not telling me?"

"It may not be anything, but she was getting advice from Debra about something. She wouldn't tell me about what," Stephanie said, pursing her lips.

"Anything else you can think of?" CJ asked.

Stephanie glanced around before she said, "Um, she's been seeing Simon, a no-no for us as staff aren't supposed to date. When she wasn't in her bed, I assumed she'd stayed with him in his cabin."

"Have you checked with him?"

"No, not yet. I got dressed and came here. I expected her to be here, but she wasn't." Her eyes watered, and she swiped at them. "She's so responsible ..."

Ben returned with two white mugs of steaming black liquid.

"Anita may be missing," CJ said.

"What?"

She explained what Stephanie told her as Bev walked up.

"Bev, do you have any idea where Anita is?" CJ asked.

"Uh, no." She glanced at Stephanie. "I told Steph she probably overslept but would be here soon." She leaned closer. "I'm aware she stays with Simon a lot and didn't want Alan to find out. He doesn't want the staff dating."

CJ stood with her eyes fixed on her. "Normally, this would be no big deal, but this is a problem under the circumstances. Ben and I will go find her."

They zipped up their jackets and left through the back door. While heading toward the back walkway, they encountered Victor, Cal, and Simon standing under the covered fish processing area.

"Simon, have you seen Anita?" CJ asked.

"Uh, not this morning," he said, shaking his head. "We ate dinner together last night in the staff dining room. I think she's in the kitchen. She's helping—"

"She's not there, and no one's seen her."

He swallowed hard and grimaced. "What about her roommate?"

CJ shook her head.

"What do you want us to do?" Victor asked. "Want us to go find her?"

CJ had an empty feeling in the pit of her stomach. Knowing who she could trust was impossible, but they needed to find Anita. She and Ben would need help with so many places to search. "Okay, Victor, come with me, and we'll search the buildings on the left side of the walkway. Simon and Cal, go with Ben and search the right side."

Ben tugged on her arm and pulled her to the side. "It might be better if the two of us stayed together."

"Yeah, but we gotta split up. We know what to look for."

He rubbed his eyes. "You're right, but my first aim is to keep you safe." He reached and touched her arm. "How 'bout we swap so you're not alone with one person?"

She stared at him. "Okay, but I'm plenty capable." Her eyes caught Kenny jogging toward them, and she pointed to him. "Problem solved. Kenny! Come help Victor and I find Anita."

Walter glanced up when CJ opened the door to his maintenance shop. He was working on a boat motor at his workbench. "What's going on?" he asked, wiping grease off his hands with a blue towel.

"Have you seen Anita?" CJ asked, staring at him.

"Uh, no. Is she missing?"

Her brow furrowed. *He jumped there damn quick,* she thought. "No one's seen her since last night."

"Well, I ain't seen her."

CJ pushed past him as her eyes scanned the room. Victor and Kenny stood in the doorway. They appeared reluctant to enter Walter's domain without permission, as if they felt intimidated. She began opening the metal cabinets and peering under the various tables.

Walter twisted his lips. "I told you, she ain't here."

"Yeah, I heard you." She continued working her way around the room.

He exhaled. "Please don't mess anything up rummaging through my stuff."

Satisfied Anita wasn't in the maintenance shop, CJ waved her two helpers out the door. Walter slammed the door shut behind them.

CJ continued to the two storage rooms, the massive walk-in freezers, and the tackle room. Still no Anita. They stood under the canopy where they'd started when Ben and his team plodded up the walkway after searching the crew quarters. He shook his head as he drew near.

"Okay, guys. Let's search the water along the edge of the dock and walkways."

"Should we check the guest cabins?" Victor asked.

"Yeah. We need to search everywhere." She looked at Ben. "Wanna take your team and do that while we work back here?"

He nodded. "Come on, guys. Let's check the main building first, the owner's apartment, and then the guest cabins."

Cal raised his eyebrows. "Alan won't like us going into his place."

"Tough shit," CJ said. "In fact, start there first. He'd probably like to know that one of his employees is missing."

"Yes, ma'am," Cal said with a crooked grin.

CJ's frustration with Alan was turning to anger. She couldn't tolerate his reckless attitude any longer, and he was accountable for the crew's safety. *Where the hell is he, anyway?*

"Uh, CJ. Do you wanna start in the back by the footbridge and work our way back?" Kenny asked, breaking her trance.

"Sure, lead the way."

"Do you want us to go up the mountain?" Victor asked as he pointed to the dull gray sky. "The wind and rain aren't as bad right now, and we need to go before it gets too late."

She stared up at the dense trees, recalling her last trip on the path. Her legs still ached. "If we don't find her on the premises, yes."

They were almost back to where they started when Kenny called to her. Kneeling on the dock where the boats were kept, she joined him. He pointed to something protruding from under the back of one of the Jetcraft, moving up and down with each wave.

"What is that?" she asked.

"I'm not sure," Kenny said. "Maybe just some trash in the water. There's crap everywhere with the winds and waves pushing everything into the cove."

Victor crawled onto the boat's bow. Lying flat on his belly, he reached down. After a couple of failed attempts, he grabbed the object. "It's a piece of a rain ... aww, shit!" He turned to Kenny. "Go grab me a shark hook."

CJ stared as he retrieved his find. "Kenny, go get Ben and tell him to bring the camera off the table in my cabin."

Five minutes later, Anita's body lay face up on the dock. A deep purple and dark blackish-red gash across her throat contrasted with her milky white skin. One of her eyeballs was missing.

Ben squatted and said, "She's not been in the water long. I'd guess only a few hours."

"If she went missing well before midnight, as Steph suggested, it means whoever killed her held her a while," CJ said. "Let's get some clean plastic and wrap her up. I'd like to get her in the—"

"Oh my God, did poor Anita drown?" Alan said as he ran toward them. His head snapped back when CJ's slap landed square on his jaw.

TWENTY-SEVEN

Wednesday, September 14
Paradise Cove

"You okay?" Ben asked as he and CJ stood outside the back door of the dining room.

She shook her head. "No. This is maddening. What a fucking mess."

He hugged her. "We gotta regroup and let everyone know what's happening."

"Yeah, and we need to talk to Evan and sort out who else we need to interview. Let's go alert everyone."

They entered the dining room, and everyone turned. Alan trailed behind them, still rubbing his jaw.

CJ stood near the group and cleared her throat. "I'm sorry to tell you we have more bad news. We've had a second murder. Anita's dead."

The room erupted. Some guests cried while others yelled questions. Stephanie burst into tears and Bev consoled her.

Harley turned his anger on Alan. "When is help coming?! We're trapped here like sitting ducks."

"Uh, well. Nothing will happen until the weather clears. As I've told everyone, the communications are down, so there's nothing I can do."

Harley jumped up and marched toward CJ.

As he neared her, Ben stepped between them. "Calm down, Harley."

He stabbed his finger at CJ. "We elected you to find the murderer. Where's the progress?"

CJ's head was spinning, and guilt wrapped its fingers around her, even though she knew it wasn't her fault. "Ben and I will continue to work to keep everyone safe, but to do that, everyone has to do exactly what we ask." She turned to glare at Alan.

She scanned the room. "Under no circumstances is anyone, guest or crew, to be alone. It is imperative that no less than two people are always together. The only time we want you to leave your cabin is to come here to eat."

"Should everyone stay here together in this room?" Jamie asked, her voice cracking.

"I ain't doing that!" Harley screamed. "One of you may be the killer."

CJ glared at him as Rory yelled at him. She turned back to Jamie. "If folks wanna stay here, that would be fine. I'm sure we can clear some room and bring in mattresses. Everyone needs to think about it and decide."

Once the chaos died down, Ben and CJ grabbed coffees and dropped into chairs beside their usual table mates.

Several minutes passed before Rory spoke. "We talked and think the four of us are gonna move into the same room," he said. "Luka and I can take the bunk beds and let Noah and Jamie take the queen. That way, it'll be easier to keep an eye out."

CJ glanced across the room to Evan, sitting with Leo and Marie. "We need to convince Evan to move into a room with someone."

Rory shrugged. "I agree, but who will want him in their cabin? I mean, he's not real friendly and, well, face it. Who knows if he killed his wife?"

"Ben and I will talk to him and see what we can do," CJ said.

"CJ, is there any way we can call for help?" Jamie asked, her swollen eyes watery.

"Not until we can get a cell signal. As Alan said, the satellite is down."

"Isn't there another way to get a signal?"

"The only way is to get out beyond the cove into the Sumner Straight and hope you can pick up a cell tower," Ben said. "As long as the weather's this rough, that's impossible."

Tears ran down Jamie's cheeks as she trembled.

Noah stood and took her hand. "We're gonna go pack and get moved." He slid his arm around his wife and led her away.

"I guess Luka and I will head back to our cabin, too," Rory said. "We need to make room for Noah and Jamie." He took his son's hand, and they started for the door.

Luka pulled away and ran back to CJ and hugged her. She fought back tears.

"I'm gonna grab Evan and tell him we need to talk to him," Ben said.

"Yeah, okay," CJ said. "I need to ask Debra a quick question." CJ went to the kitchen and found Debra. "Do you have a minute?"

"Sure," the older woman said, wiping her hands on a dish towel. "What can I do for you?"

"I understand Anita talked to you last night looking for some advice. Can you tell me what she asked about?"

Debra cleared her throat. "Uh, it was nothing really. She was nervous about the storm."

CJ stared at her until the older woman dropped her eyes. "I heard she wanted to talk to me about it," she probed.

"Uh, well, she wanted your opinion on when help would come."

CJ stared at her before turning away. Her senses told her Debra was lying.

———

Evan followed Ben and CJ to their cabin and sat at the table across from them. He folded his hands in his lap and stared at them. "Well, I knew you'd want to talk to me at some point," he said, smirking. "Don't you cops always want to pin a spouse's murder on their partner?"

"Only when they're guilty," CJ said, her eyes locked on him. "But you're correct that a surviving spouse is always one of the first people considered, and often the one who committed the crime."

"I didn't hurt my wife, so ask what you want."

They spent several minutes talking about the night Olivia went missing. CJ asked him about their day, where he was, and why he let his wife go out alone. He reiterated his previous statement, emphasizing how he'd felt sick and gone to sleep.

"Can anyone verify that you never left the cabin?" she asked.

"No. I suppose not, but you're in the same position. You can't prove I went anywhere."

When asked about his marriage, he painted a rosy picture. He and Olivia were deeply in love and planning on having children soon. She stayed home and ran the household, even though he begged her to pursue her dream of being an interior decorator.

CJ jotted down notes and added the word 'lie' in the margin. It wasn't the first time she'd encountered a smooth liar—someone who could boldly assert that it was a bright sunny day even in the midst of a roaring hurricane. However, lying about your marriage didn't always mean someone was a cold-blooded killer.

She scanned her notes. "Are you a faithful husband?"

He flinched, and she knew he was processing his answer. "I've never slept with anyone else since we were married," he said.

She watched him squirm and asked, "Do you have life insurance on your wife?"

He cleared his throat. "Yes, of course I do. Any responsible couple would insure each other." He launched into the 'we were about to have kids' story again.

"How much is the policy, and who's the beneficiary?"

"Uh, one million dollars." He chewed on his lower lip. "I'm her beneficiary."

She nodded as she narrowed her eyes. "Hmm, okay."

Next, she asked him about his whereabouts when Anita went missing the previous evening. He told her he was in his cabin all afternoon and night. He didn't leave until coming down for breakfast this morning.

She knew she hadn't seen him at dinner and Rory told her Evan stayed in his room, but she asked, "Did you go to dinner?"

Again, he flinched. "Uh, no. I wasn't hungry after my poor Olivia's death." His effort to conjure up moisture failed.

"I understand." She watched him wipe his nonexistent tears. "I want to be certain I'm clear. So, you never ate after breakfast yesterday until this morning and stayed alone in your room?"

He dropped his eyes, picked at his fingernails, and in a hushed voice, said, "Well, I ate dinner in my cabin. They delivered it to me."

"Whose they?"

"Kayla. One of the kitchen staff."

"She's the one serving the table where you've been sitting, correct?"

"Yes, she's been very kind to me since Olivia's passing."

"What time did she drop off dinner?"

"Um, maybe seven-thirty after she finished working in the kitchen."

CJ made more notes and tapped the end of her pen on the pad. "I suppose that's it for now."

She hadn't completed the sentence when he popped up from the chair and started for the door.

"Of course, I'll need to speak to Kayla and verify she dropped off your dinner and you were here."

He stopped and stood rigid before turning to face her. "Do you really need to do that?"

CJ tilted her head. "Why would that be an issue? It seems you'd be eager for me to verify your story."

His gaze dropped to the floor. "Uh, well." He raised his eyes. "She spent the night in my cabin, but it was totally innocent."

"You two didn't sleep together, you mean?"

"We slept in the same bed, but we didn't have sex. I needed some company, and she offered to stay."

Disgusted, CJ completed her notes and turned to Ben. "Anything else on your end?"

"Nope. You've covered everything."

CJ stood and motioned to Evan. "We'll walk you out on our way to talk to Kayla."

Evan looked like he might puke.

TWENTY-EIGHT

Wednesday, September 14
Paradise Cove

Ben and CJ entered the crew quarters, and Kenny directed them to Kayla's cabin. "It's around the corner and down the hall. She's in the last one."

A young woman, about twenty years old, answered their knock. She was five-four with strawberry blond hair, hazel eyes, and a petite nose. "Uh, hello. Can I help you?"

CJ extended her hand. "Hey, Kayla. We haven't officially met, but I'm CJ, and this is Ben. Can we come in?"

"Um, sure." She backed away from the door and allowed them to enter the room. The windowless cabin included two single beds, with a nightstand between them, and two dressers. Someone had pushed a wire rack with hanging clothes into the corner.

Kayla pointed to a second young woman sitting on the bed farthest away. "This is Ryleigh. My roomie."

Ryleigh smiled, stood, and asked if she should leave.

"No, it would be best if we spoke to both of you," CJ said.

Ryleigh dropped back down, and Kayla joined her.

Kayla cleared her throat and said, "We don't have any chairs, but you—"

"That's okay. We only need a couple of minutes, so we'll stand."

Kayla swallowed hard and said, "Um, okay."

CJ unzipped her raincoat and pulled out the pad she'd been using for her notes. "Ben and I are trying to determine who killed Olivia and Anita. We're talking to people to gather information."

The young women nodded.

"It's important that you tell us anything you think might be helpful." She stared at Kayla, whose bottom lip was trembling. "Did you stay in the cabin last night with Evan?"

Her breathing became shallow and her eyes grew wet. She slowly nodded.

"What time did you go there?"

"I … um, I'm not sure. Maybe around 8:00 p.m."

"And you stayed all night?"

Tears rolled down Kayla's cheeks, and she swiped at them. "Yes," she said in a whisper.

"Evan said you slept in his bed, but nothing happened."

The young woman slumped over as her hands covered her face and her shoulder shook.

Ryleigh put her arms around her and said, "I told her it wasn't a good idea. The guy's a creep."

CJ dropped to a knee and delicately lifted Kayla's chin. "Tell me what happened."

She shook her head.

"Ryleigh, do you know what happened?"

Ryleigh leaned down and asked her friend if it was okay if she told them what she knew, and Kayla nodded. So, Ryleigh told CJ that earlier that day, Evan asked her if she would bring him dinner and sit with him while he ate. He said he was too upset to be with a lot of people. She told him she could deliver dinner, but wasn't allowed to be in the room with guests.

"So, then he asked Kayla?" CJ prompted.

Ryleigh nodded.

"Then what happened?"

Kayla continued to bawl, so her roommate spoke up. "When she got there, she sat at the table while he ate. Afterward, he asked her to stay and keep him company. She told me he was so sweet, and she felt sorry for him, so she agreed. They kissed a little and went to sleep."

"Okay, so no sex, then?"

Ryleigh whispered in her friend's ear and told her she needed to tell CJ what happened this morning.

Without looking up, Kayla mumbled, "We had sex."

"Tell her everything, Kayla."

The young woman raised her head. "I woke up really early and went to the bathroom. When I got back in bed, Evan started kissing me. He started touching me, and at first, I told him to stop, but ..."

"Did he force you to have sex with him?"

She shook her head. "It was my fault. I'm the one who went to his room and stayed the night." She laid her head on a pillow and cried.

Ryleigh motioned them out into the hallway. "The bastard planned it," she growled. "He propositioned me, and he even had condoms. Who has sex with a twenty-year-old less than two days after his wife is killed?" She glanced back at the closed door and, in a low voice, said, "Kayla has had little experience with boys and has kinda low self-esteem. She's beautiful but doesn't see it. He took advantage of that."

"Do you think he forced her to have sex?" CJ asked.

"My guess is yes, but I'm not sure she'll admit it." She sighed. "Please don't tell anyone else. It'll only hurt Kayla more, and Alan will fire her to top it all off. I told her to stay here when she returned and skip working breakfast, so he'll already be pissed."

CJ agreed and encouraged her to have Kayla reach out if she needed any help. It made sense now why Evan was sure to be seen at breakfast, but there had been no sign of Kayla.

TWENTY-NINE

Wednesday, September 14
Paradise Cove

CJ sat on a wooden bench outside the dining-room door as the water sprayed off the overhead canopy. The intensity of the rain had decreased from the prior night, but the wind continued to howl. Her eyes fixated on the forest, swaying back and forth.

Heat flushed through her, and she fantasized about arresting Evan for what he had done with Kayla. She avoided using the word hate, but the piece of shit had pushed it. Her eyes squeezed shut, and her mind drifted back to one of her first cases in Boston.

She crept down the dark hallway and pressed her ear to the door. Initially, silence filled the air until a male voice expressed his love to someone.

"People in love do this, baby," he said.

A female voice answered, "I'm not ready. Please stop."

"Come on! You can't do this to me," the man said.

The girl continued to protest until a loud slap sounded, followed by a piercing scream. She stepped back, drew her Glock, and splintered the door with the sole of her boot. Before the naked forty-year-old man could respond, she yanked him off the bed, and he landed face-first on the dingy gray carpet.

Her partner, an older officer, cuffed the man's hands behind his back. Only sixteen, the young girl sat wrapped in a bedspread, her eyes wide. While the man was being led away, CJ assisted the shaken victim in getting dressed and accompanied her into an ambulance to the hospital.

She despised sex crime cases. They challenged her. Not that they were more difficult to work on than other cases, but she struggled to contain herself with the perpetrators. She had to resist the urge to take the law into her own hands.

"CJ?" Ben asked. "Did you hear what I said?"

Her head snapped up to find her fiancé with a slack expression beside her. "Uh, yeah. Sorry."

Ben rubbed her shoulder. "I grabbed your camera," he said as he held up a key. "After we examine Anita again, I've asked Kenny and Walter to move her to the freezer with Olivia."

He held out the camera, and she took it, hoping he didn't notice her shaking hand. "I wanna take some more shots of the wound so we can compare it to our first victim. There's something about it that's familiar. I just can't place it."

"I'd like to determine which hand our killer used as well," Ben said. "Hopefully, it will help us narrow down our suspects." He peered up at the rain. "The weather's better, but with no communications, there's no way to know when it'll break for good. Remind me to check with Alan about the radios."

Kenny arrived, and they went to the storage room near the end of the walkway. He waited by the door as Ben and CJ disappeared inside. They flipped on the lights and cautiously unwrapped Anita's upper body. The one remaining eye was glassy and stared blankly at the ceiling. On his knees, Ben pulled on plastic gloves and ran a flashlight beam along the young woman's neck.

CJ snapped photos with her camera and cell phone. "Can you tell what hand our killer used?" she asked.

He pointed to the wound. "My guess is he's right-handed. The cut is deeper on this end and shallows up." He made a cutting motion.

She thumbed through the photos of Olivia's body and held it up. "It's difficult to compare since the bodies were in the water, but it appears to be the same in both."

Ben leaned back. "So, that confirms we have one perp. And if we assume he's right-handed, maybe that narrows it down." He sighed. "Unfortunately, that's the predominant hand of eighty percent of people."

CJ peered closer at a triangular wound on the right side of Anita's neck—a missing patch of skin. "Hmm." She scrolled through her photos. "Ben, we may have a signature. Look at this."

His brow furrowed as she pointed to the spot on Anita's neck. "Did our first body have the same mark?"

She nodded and held up her camera. The missing equilateral triangle piece of skin, maybe a half inch on each side, was present in the same location.

"Whoever did this couldn't have done it with the knife he used to kill them," he said. "He had to use some other tool to make a cut so precise and peel the skin layer away."

"How 'bout a scalpel?" she asked.

He slowly nodded. "That would do it."

Rubbing her chin with the back of her hand, she said, "Do you think he took the piece with him? You know, as a souvenir?"

"It's possible. Who knows what a sicko like this would do?" Ben wrapped the body back in the plastic and taped the edges closed. He called Kenny and informed him that Anita could be moved to the freezer. The young man ran to get Walter.

Ben and CJ followed Walter and Kenny to one of the two massive freezers in the fish processing area. They placed the wrapped body on the floor beside Olivia.

Walter used a padlock to secure the door and handed the key to Ben before he left. "That lock ain't real strong, but it's better than nothing," he said. "I can't believe anyone would want to steal a dead body."

"We've searched the buildings before, but I'd like to do it again," CJ said. "We were so focused on finding Anita, we didn't look as closely for other evidence."

"There has to be a spot where he killed the women," Ben said, nodding. "I wouldn't expect him to do it out in the open." He asked Kenny to go with them and started with Walter's maintenance shop at the end of the walkway.

They searched the shop while Walter watched with his arms folded, and then moved to the second storage shed. The room contained metal shelves holding various boxes.

"What's all this stuff, Kenny?" Ben asked.

"It's mostly extra equipment for the boats—life jackets, floats, and fish boxes with gear the guests leave. Lots of our guests come every year and leave their tackle here so they don't have to carry it back and forth."

CJ crawled on her knees when she said, "I think I found something."

Ben joined her and shined the light on the floor.

"These look like drops of blood," CJ said as she took photos. "I wish we had a way to test them."

"Kenny, can you see if Walter has another padlock?" Ben asked. "I'd like to lock this room."

A few minutes later, Kenny held up a small lock. "Walter took this one off the other storage shed where we had Anita's body. This is the only one he has left. He told me he had a box of new ones, but they're gone."

Ben glanced over at CJ, who frowned.

What the fuck were they looking for?

Sitting alone in his cabin, his mind raced with potential mistakes. Did he leave something behind that would incriminate him? He never used to worry about it in the past, as escaping was easy, but now he was trapped. He could take the path, go to the village, and steal a canoe. Or, once the weather broke, he could take one of the lodge's boats and run for it.

Okay, calm down. Let's not panic.

He sucked in a deep breath and released it. Like an old movie, his mind replayed each capture, confinement, murder, and disposal. When he captured the pretty little housewife, he wore gloves, and the rain would have washed away anything on his jacket that pointed to him. When he played with her and finally ended her life, he couldn't remember anything to be concerned about. Submerging the body in the rough water would have washed away any traces of evidence. He smiled, and a calmness came over him.

As he shut his eyes, the second movie rolled in his mind. He had been careful with the nosy bitch, but his breath caught suddenly. He recalled one thing that was different with her. She'd head-butted him when he leaned in, so Jeffrey could taunt her. His nose had bled. It wasn't bad, but did he leave any of himself behind?

Fuck!

He jumped up and paced as he cursed under his breath. All these years of evading those chasing him. He'd outsmarted them every time, even the intelligent detective in

Boston. Most of those after him were bumbling idiots, but not him. He was a match for him, almost.

Okay, okay. You can fix this.

He reached under the floorboard in his cabin as he worked to slow his breathing and gain control of himself. After opening his book of treasures, he traced the tip of his finger along the small patch of skin. A warm calm washed over him.

What's my plan?

A smile reappeared. He knew what to do.

THIRTY

Wednesday, September 14
Paradise Cove

CJ stood at the back dining room kitchen window and watched the sheets of rain come down. It picked up again after a brief lull and pounded the roof. The gusting wind forced its way into every crack, filling her nostrils with the salty smell. Movement at the end of the walkway caught her attention.

What are those guys doing?

Cal and Simon opened the maintenance shop door and peered inside before entering. After a few minutes, they reappeared and made their way to the storage shed door where they'd discovered the suspected blood. They stared at the padlock before grabbing it and pulling it. Unable to open the door, they entered the next storage room.

Ben joined her. "What are you watching?"

She frowned. "I'm not sure." She told him about Cal and Simon.

"Maybe they're looking for some equipment," he said. "Is Walter in his shop?"

"I think he's in the crew quarters having lunch. He and Kenny went in there at the same time we came in here."

As they talked, Cal and Simon emerged from the building and went to the fish processing area. They rounded the corner and disappeared.

"The only thing back there are the freezers," CJ whispered.

Less than a minute later, the men ran down the walkway and entered the crew quarters.

"You want me to go check on what they're doing?" Ben asked.

She shook her head. "No. I admit it's strange, but no need to do that."

"Excuse me."

Ben and CJ turned to find Stephanie behind them. She offered a faint smile as she fidgeted with a hand towel.

"Can we help you?" CJ asked.

"Um, well, I wanted to tell you about something that's been bothering me." She motioned them into the kitchen, away from the sparse number of guests having lunch. She peeked around the corner and cleared her throat. "I probably shouldn't be saying anything, but Alan lied to you."

CJ raised her eyebrows. "About what?"

The young woman glanced at the floor before looking at her. "Um, he has a handgun. He keeps it in his desk. I saw him with it."

"Are you sure?"

She nodded. "I think Alan keeps it in the office's desk's bottom drawer. I wasn't gonna say anything, but now that two women have died, I thought you needed to know. Please don't tell him I told you." She stepped past them and returned to the dining room.

CJ stared at Ben. "Why would he lie?"

"No clue, but there's one way to find out." He led CJ down the hallway and pounded on the office door.

After the sounds of a chair creaking, the door cracked open, and Alan faced them. "Can I help you?" he asked.

"We need to speak to you," Ben said as he pushed the door open and entered the office.

"Uh, I'm pretty busy right now. If you're asking me about the radio, Walter's working on it, and I haven't checked the ones on the boat yet."

"Actually, we have another question. I understand you have a pistol you didn't tell us about," Ben said.

The owner's mouth dropped open.

"Why did you lie to us?" Ben asked.

His face turned red before he said, "Who told you I had a weapon? I have no idea—"

Ben leaned close to him and cut him off. "It's not important how we know. The real question is, do you have one?"

The owner continued to deny he had a weapon, and Ben kept pressing him.

Finally, Alan exhaled and said, "Yeah. I have a Glock 19, but I didn't tell you in case I needed it to protect my wife and me." He turned and went to his desk. He inserted a key and pulled open the bottom drawer. His brow furrowed. "It's gone!" Frantically, he opened and closed the other drawers. "Where the hell is it?"

Ben wasn't sure if he was pulling a stunt or being truthful. "Are you certain that you locked the drawer?"

Alan nodded. "Yes, I locked it back in here this morning. I had it upstairs last night."

"Who else has the key?"

"No one." He held up a key ring. "I keep these keys in my pocket."

Ben pulled a flashlight from his back pocket and dropped to his knee. His eyes peered at the drawer. "Someone jimmied the lock," he said. "Who else knows about the gun?"

"Uh, I think just my wife and me. I'm careful not to flash it around since I make it a point to tell everyone no weapons."

They helped him search the rest of the office, but there was no gun.

CJ rubbed her temples as her mind screamed, *Great. So now our killer may have a Glock.*

———

Jamie sat huddled on the floor in the corner of the room. It should have been a relief being in the cabin with Rory and

Luka, but instead, she was dizzy, and her stomach was rock hard. *We have to leave here before the killer gets us.* Noah lay sprawled across the bed reading a James Patterson novel. *How the fuck can he read at a time like this?*

Her mind raced, and no matter how much she told herself she was safe, it didn't slow her heart rate or relieve the tightness in her chest. The face of her childhood friend, Becky, savagely murdered, was all she could see.

She squeezed her lids shut and recalled the summer day and the secret she'd told no one, not even Noah or her therapist. Everyone assumed the man who murdered Becky took her from her home, but the fact was he found her in the forest.

Jamie was forbidden to go into the woods, and so was her friend. There were too many ways to hurt themselves— plus wild animals and snakes. But like all kids, they ignored the rules, including on that day.

The secluded forest, with its tall trees, thick bushes, and silence, except for birds chirping, was their sanctuary. The place was their bliss, where no one bothered them, told them what to do, or scolded them.

They'd worked on their hideout all morning. Around lunchtime, Jamie went home to grab some snacks and left Becky behind. "You go, and I'll stay here and guard our fort," she said. Until that day, neither of them had been alone in the dense trees.

Tears ran down Jamie's cheeks. She'd kept another secret all these years … the worst secret of all.

She returned to their fort with a brown paper bag of goodies to find a man standing with an arm around Becky and his hand over her mouth. Her light brown eyes were fixed on Jamie in terror, and she whimpered.

The man had long, stringy black hair and was missing a front tooth. Grime covered his clothes. As he glared at her, he drew a finger across his throat. "Keep your fucking little mouth shut," he hissed. "Now go … git!"

Jamie raced back along the path as fast as she could, ignoring the limbs clawing at her. She hid in her bedroom, and when everyone scoured the neighborhood for Becky, she remained silent.

Why did I do that and not try to save my friend?

But Jamie knew why. She was afraid … chicken … a scaredy cat … a gutless coward.

When the police dogs found the body hours later, everyone assumed the killer dragged Becky into the woods and someone else made the crude hideout of branches, sticks, and leaves. Again, Jamie kept her mouth shut.

It all seemed so stupid now. At most, Jamie would have gotten whipped for disobeying, but lying by omission made sense to her at the time. For over twenty years, her lies had gnawed at her. She attempted to bury it and put it out of her mind, but reminders were everywhere—the park near their home, her husband's softball games, and any time she saw a child around ten years old.

I would deserve it if the killer got me.

"Baby, are you okay?" Noah asked, breaking her thoughts. "You're shaking, and you've been crying."

"Uh, yeah," she said. "I'm cold."

Noah folded the corner of the page in his book to mark his place, crawled off the bed, and dropped beside her. He kissed her cheek and wrapped his arms around her.

She leaned her head on his shoulder. *I don't deserve him … I deserve to die.*

THIRTY-ONE

Wednesday, September 14
Paradise Cove

CJ and Ben raced down the walkway to their cabin as the raindrops, mixed with sharp ice crystals, stung their faces. The wind remained lower, but now an eerie fog engulfed the lodge. They pushed through the door and shook the wetness off their jackets.

"This weather is unbelievable," CJ said. "Every time it looks like it's gonna break, it returns with a vengeance."

Ben handed her a towel to dry her face, and she used it to wipe the water from the pad she'd been using to capture her notes. Between the weather, lack of sleep, and the stress of trying to solve who killed two young women, she was exhausted. Her limbs were heavy, and she dropped on the edge of the bed and stared at her feet.

"Why don't you lie down for a bit," Ben said.

Tears filled her eyes and spilled down her cheeks. "I can't ... we can't," she said as her voice cracked. "Two people are dead, and we're no closer to catching whoever did it than when we started."

He sat beside her and draped his arm around her as she trembled. Like her, he was struggling, but he knew she was right. Neither of them could rest until they caught the killer. "How 'bout we take a hot shower and then sort through our suspects again?"

She dragged herself to her feet.

Ben pushed the dresser against the door and pulled the curtain across the window. He undressed her. "Go get the water going, and I'll join you."

A shower together was usually an enjoyable affair—a time to focus on each other. But not this time. They pulled their clothes back on within minutes and stared at the board with photos and names. They agreed to remove Evan from the list of suspects since he was in bed with Kayla at the time Anita was killed.

CJ shook her head, out of disgust and because of the lack of progress. "So, we still keep Alan and Walter on the list for now, right?" she asked.

"Yeah. For now, we can't rule them out." He pointed at the board. "We're gonna need to rethink the guests. I know most of them are well over sixty and a low probability, but we have to consider them."

"Especially Harley and his weirdo son, Junior," CJ said. "The father is a hothead, and the son, well, he looks unstable. I still haven't seen him say one word. He comes into the dining room and stares at his plate as he shovels his food in his mouth."

Ben huffed. "I guess he's used to not getting in a word with his loudmouth pop. There's another reason to consider them."

She furrowed her brow. "Why?"

"Kenny told me they're the only guests who don't follow the rules and go out back. Besides you and I, of course."

"He said he caught Junior prowling around in one of the buildings, and Walter ran him out of the shop."

CJ added a question mark to the father and son duo. "So that leaves us with the rest of the crew. Are we still safe to rule out the females?"

"Yeah. I think so, although I'd add a question mark beside Debra since she's Alan's wife. She may know more than she's letting on. We need to talk to her, but I don't see her as a suspect for the murders." She nibbled on her thumb. "That leaves us with Victor, Cal, and Simon, so we still have seven to weed through. I asked Kenny who on the crew was right-handed and he said everyone except Simon."

"I'm certain our killer is right-handed, so let's cross Simon off," Ben said.

CJ stared at the list. Finding their target would be a challenging and time-consuming task. "Okay, we'll need to interview more people. Maybe we should start with—"

A loud pounding on the door interrupted her, and she held her breath. Ben pulled the curtain back and then slid the dresser away.

Kenny hustled through the door with a strong gust of wind and spray of water. "Hey, guys. I need you to come to the shop and talk to Walter."

Ben and CJ looked at each other.

"Walter?" CJ asked.

The young man nodded. "He has some information you need to know. It may help you."

"Do you know what it is?" she asked.

Kenny glanced at the floor and shuffled his feet. "Umm, yeah." He looked at CJ. "He told me, but swore me to secrecy. But he's ready to tell you now."

"Wait. Why would Walter tell you?" Ben asked.

He shrugged. "I don't know. For some reason, he's always been nice to me. I'm the only one he ever talks to."

"Let's go," CJ said. "We can talk to Victor and Cal afterward."

They followed Kenny through a narrow gap between the cabins and the main lodge. It was a tight squeeze.

"Why are we going through here?" Ben asked.

"I'd rather not let Alan see us. It'd be better for Walter."

———

Walter sat on an overturned five-gallon bucket as they entered the shop. He tipped his head and told them to sit in two metal folding chairs where they had sat last time. Kenny climbed up on the end of the workbench.

"Kenny said you wanted to talk to us," CJ said.

Walter smirked. "Well, I didn't really want to, but the youngster convinced me I should." He fidgeted with his fingers, picking at the tip of one of his nails.

"We're ready when you are," CJ said.

The older man pulled off the forest green cap he always wore and ran his fingers through his dark brown hair. "Well, uh, I guess I best start at the beginning." He blew out a long breath and stared at her. "I'm here because of something I did twenty years ago. But I'm tired of running, and I ain't covering for Alan no more."

"Wait—"

Ben touched her arm, signaling she should wait and let him talk.

"I wasn't honest with you before. I served five years for armed robbery in the Clemons prison in Brazario, Texas, south of Houston. I tried to stay straight when I got out, but finding work wasn't easy." He pinched the bridge of his nose. "After a few months, I fell into my old ways and robbed a couple of liquor stores. It was easy money until one night, an owner of the store decided he'd had enough of people taking his money. He pulled a gun and ... I, uh ... shot him." He dropped his head and sat breathing heavily.

CJ watched as his chest heaved and asked, "Did the man die?"

He shook his head. "Thank God, no. I grabbed the cash and ran. I thought I'd killed him, but I found out on the news he was alive and going to recover." He returned his gaze to her. "I never meant to hurt anyone. The gun was to scare folks. With my prior conviction and that incident, I knew they'd lock me away for at least twenty years for aggravated robbery, so I ran. I wound up in Alaska and ultimately here."

"You know we gotta tell the authorities, right?" CJ asked.

"Yes, ma'am. I know. My only hope is helping you solve these murders will be taken into account."

"I tell you what. You help us, and we'll do what we can for you."

He bobbed his head. "Fair enough. I don't know who killed these last two young women, but they aren't the killer's first."

CJ squinted and then glanced at Ben.

Walter dug a photo from his jacket pocket and handed it to her. "That's Chantelle. She worked here last year on the kitchen crew. A sweetheart of a person—kind, considerate, and beautiful inside and out."

CJ frowned. "Alan mentioned to me that she was supposed to be coming here this year but didn't show up. He told me that's why he was short-handed."

"The bastard lied. He knew she wasn't coming back."

"How do you know?" she asked.

"Cause I was the one who found the poor thing floating in the water right outside my shop. I pulled Chantelle's body out and ran to get Alan."

"He came and told me to wrap her in plastic and hide her body in here. I did as I was told since … since … well,

Alan knows about my past. He told me to keep my mouth shut, and he'd handle it."

"How did he do that?"

He smirked. "Lied. Told the girl's parents she drowned and paid them ten thousand dollars."

"Did she drown?"

He pulled out his cell phone and scrolled to a photo. He passed it to CJ. "You tell me."

The pasty white face with glassy eyes stared blankly at her. Her long black hair was twisted and covered with slime. A deep reddish-black gash ran across her throat. CJ used her fingertips to enlarge the photo to see the wound, and a chill ran through her. The same signature as the last two women was evident.

"You took this?" she asked.

"Yep, I snapped it when I got the body on the deck. No one knows about it." He chewed on his lower lip. "I thought someday I'd need some insurance. I guess I was right."

"Wait. What did Alan tell the crew?"

"He said she ran off. Ridiculous, but that was his story."

"Why would anyone believe him?"

Walter shrugged. "Everyone's young and stupid, I guess. After I put the body in the shop, he had me pack her clothes in a duffle as part of his ruse. It made his lie more believable."

"What happened to the body?"

"Uh, Alan had it flown back to Ketchikan. He has a cousin who works for Ketchikan PD and he probably helped with the coverup."

"But why tell me he expected her back this season?"

"Hell, if I know. That's a stupid thing to say."

"Why would he cover up a murder?"

"I can't answer you there. Maybe cause Alan owes so much money on this place, he's afraid he'll lose his business."

Walter explained that Alan had struggled since buying Paradise Cove Lodge. First, he overpaid the former owner. Alan was so infatuated with having an Alaskan fishing lodge he coughed up way more than the place was worth. And the operating costs were higher than expected, and he couldn't fix much himself.

"That's why he added two weeks to the season—money. The former owner always ended the season in August." He stared at her before adding how Alan added cabin thirteen, which she and Ben now occupied. "He hired some guys out of Ketchikan to help him build it, and honestly, they didn't do a very good job."

"What do you mean?" she asked. "The cabin seems nice."

"Oh, it looks okay, but structurally it has issues. It's not connected to the rest of the primary structure."

CJ stared at Walter as he sat with his head hung. "Do you think Alan's capable of murder?" she asked. "Maybe he killed Chantelle?"

Walter frowned. "I don't think so, but he's got a temper and has messed around with some of the female crew before."

"What do you mean by messed around with?" she asked.

"Mostly flirting, but I know Debra caught him with a young woman in her cabin their first year here. She was mad as hell and forced him to fire her."

"I'd like a copy of this photo, but you can't text it without Wi-Fi."

He waved his hand. "Keep my phone. I probably ain't gonna be needing it. My code is 3481. My son's birthday."

"Thank you." She stared at the photo and then focused back on him. "If I confront Alan with this, he'll know it came from you."

He nodded. "Yeah, I'm sure he will. The only other person who knows the truth about Chantelle is Debra. I'd rather not piss him off, but you have to decide if it's necessary to stop all this killing." His fingers massaged his temples, and he blew out a long breath. "At this point, I figure I'm gonna have bigger issues."

CJ glanced at Ben, then said, "I'll do what I can to keep you out of it for now. Can you think of anyone who would kill someone?"

He shook his head. "Naw. Not really, but it's gotta be someone who's been here the last two years. Someone on the staff or a returning guest." He leaned toward her. "The same person has killed all three women from the look of things."

"Alan told us you were fixing the radio from the lodge. Any luck yet?" Ben asked.

"No, someone removed a part. And before you ask, someone also cut a piece from the cables connecting the boat radios to the battery. And the battery-powered radio I used to have here in the shop is gone."

He dropped his head. "I also didn't tell you everything about the satellite unit. It's true it's gone, but the wind didn't rip it off. The bolts holding it were removed."

"So, you think someone intentionally sabotaged all the communications?" CJ asked.

"I don't just think it, that's what happened."

She asked a few more questions, and Walter answered her. The information he provided was helpful and horrifying at the same time. She and Ben stood to leave.

"Thank you for providing us with this. We'll keep it to ourselves for now." They turned for the door, and CJ glanced back. "By the way, why'd you tell Kenny and agree to talk to us?"

He smiled, and his eyes grew wet. "The boy reminds me of my son, and I'm sick and tired of folks being hurt. I wanna help stop it, and whatever happens to me, happens."

THIRTY-TWO

Wednesday, September 14
Paradise Cove

Victor sat on the covered porch at the back of the crew quarters, staring at the deep green foliage behind the lodge. The torrential rains created a jagged gully, and muddy water rushed off the side of the mountain into the cove, causing a yellowish-brown sheen. The slope had several uprooted trees leaning haphazardly.

He pulled a tin of Skoal from his pocket and shoved a pinch of minty, smokeless tobacco behind his lower lip. His mind drifted back to his conversations with the detective and her fiancé. *What did I tell them?*

CJ confirmed what he already knew from observing her … she was smart as hell. He shifted his weight in the plastic chair and tilted his head back, resting it on the wall. He replayed the question-and-answer session in his mind.

Victor took pride in how quickly he could determine what someone wanted from how they spoke to him. He had to admit that finding safe answers to her rapid-fire questions was challenging.

She wanted to know about his background, and he told her he moved to Alaska ten years ago from Bridgeport, Connecticut. He worked in Ketchikan in various jobs until he got his captain's license and began leading fishing charters. The Paradise Cove Lodge hired him for full seasons to take guests out eight years ago.

He enjoyed his time here, and the money was good. It allowed him to work less during the offseason he spent in Ketchikan. Maybe he'd only tend bar a couple of days per week when he left this year.

The door to his left creaked.

"Oh, there you are," Cal said as he stepped onto the porch. He unclipped the strap, pulled a second plastic chair out of a metal rack, and slid it beside Victor. "That was interesting."

"Yeah. How'd it go for you?" Victor asked.

Cal blew out a breath, causing his lips to make a puttering sound. "Okay, I guess. I have nothing to hide, but having a detective ask you about yourself is freaky. You?"

"Same," Victor said. "She asked me about my life before I came here and a lot about Alan."

"That's what she asked me to. She's sharp, I'll give her that. When I told her I grew up on the East Coast, she

went right to New York." He laughed. "The damn girl recognized my accent. She peg you for Boston since you two
sound kinda the same?"

Victor snorted and said, "I didn't grow up in Boston."

Cal waved his hand. "Okay, northeastern Connecticut.
The same thing. Did she ask you about Chantelle?"

Victor nodded. "I told her we were close, and I was sad
she was gone."

"She ask you about her leaving?"

Victor stared at Cal before he frowned and answered.
"Uh, yeah. I just told her I missed her."

Cal chuckled. "Dude, you didn't tell her you two were
a couple, did you?"

"Well, we were. Chantelle was into—"

Cal touched his arm. "In your dreams, buddy. I was
here, remember?" He shook his head. "What is it with you
and women?" He tapped his knuckles on his temple. "You
gotta get over this delusion that women want you."

Victor's face turned red, and he gritted his teeth. "I'm
not fucking delusional. Why do you always give me shit?"

"Okay, okay. Relax."

They sat silently for several minutes before Cal asked,
"Did the detective ask you about where you were when the
two women were killed?"

"Of course."

"What'd you tell her?"

Victor lifted one shoulder into a half-shrug. "I told her
I was in my cabin."

"Yeah, me too," Cal said as he glanced at Victor. "Were you?"

"What?"

"Were you in your cabin?" Cal's lips curled into a smile.

Victor's eyebrows squished together, and he stared at him. "Umm, yeah."

"There's no way for her to know, so she has to take our word for it." Cal stood and secured the chair back in the rack. He glanced at Victor and said, "We both know neither of us were where we told her." He left the way he came.

Victor spat a long stream of tobacco juice into the water. Cal was his friend, but also an asshole. Maybe he'd embellished his relationship with Chantelle to CJ. *What the fuck was wrong with her for not wanting me?*

He knew he wasn't the best-looking guy, but women had rejected him all his life or just didn't acknowledge him. Kayla seemed interested in him initially, but then went and slept with that pompous jerk in cabin twelve. *I'm so tired of being alone and shafted by women.*

His fingers dug the sticky brown wad from his mouth and flipped it off the porch. It was time for him to confront the reality that his relationships would consist solely of one-night stands with intoxicated women he met at bars.

Victor stood and stretched. His thoughts went to a task he needed to complete in case the detective came back around. No one knew what he had, but he couldn't risk it being found. He put the chair away and headed for his cabin.

Evan paced the floor. He had received CJ's wrath over him sleeping with Kayla, but what was coming next? He'd been stupid, but his urges always got the better of him.

His pulse rate had slowed since CJ told him the young woman hadn't accused him of raping her. But it escalated when the thought of her changing her mind popped into his head. *Oh, God! That's all I need. It'll ruin me.*

This wasn't the first time he'd gotten himself into this situation. The same thing happened during spring break in Fort Lauderdale between his sophomore and junior years at UGA. He'd sweet-talked a young woman into comforting him after his girlfriend broke up with him and then forced her into sex.

He rubbed his hands together and paced faster. Forced was too strong a word. He hadn't made her have sex with him. He merely encouraged her, and she never said no. At least that's what he told the police officers. Thanks to a call from his father, they let him leave uncharged. He was sure the twenty-thousand-dollar check to the girl's parents also helped.

Damnit! Evan was enjoying all the sympathy from the other guests, but was worried sick they'd find out about Kayla. He told himself she wouldn't say anything. She was too embarrassed and wouldn't want Alan to know. But her damn roommate was avoiding him, and what if the guests noticed and started asking questions?

Evan spent the next thirty minutes riding an emotional roller coaster. Finally, he decided he'd deny the sex if the others found out. *She stayed in my room overnight to keep me company, but we never slept together.*

He headed to the bathroom and turned on the hot spray. A shower would relax him before he went to dinner. Worst case, he'd lock himself in the cabin until the weather broke. He sighed. He could ask his dad for advice if only his cell phone worked.

THIRTY-THREE

Wednesday, September 14
Paradise Cove

After meeting Walter and interviewing Victor and Cal, CJ and Ben splashed their way back to their cabin. She pulled a pillow behind her and propped herself up against the headboard. Ben rolled over and promptly fell asleep, leaving her with her notes.

Based on what Walter provided and what they had before, she scanned the names of those on her suspect list. She and Ben agreed that Walter wasn't the murderer. There's no way he'd have volunteered so much information otherwise.

She crossed off any of the guests that weren't at the lodge last year and stared at the remaining names—Rory,

Harley, his weird son, Junior, and Leo and Marie. After crossing off the old couple, three names remained. Her eyes drifted to a second sheet beside her and the crew list where she'd noted question marks—Alan, Victor, and Cal.

Which of you six is a killer?

CJ pushed her fingertips into a knot in her shoulder, and she rotated her head. She was making progress in narrowing her search, but the tingling in her chest remained. What if they were mistaken about Simon or Walter? They'd both been here last year.

She dropped the pad on the bed and squeezed her eyes shut. Her mind was cloudy, and her concentration dull from lack of sleep and food. Throw in the stress of dealing with the guests and finding their perp, and she was near a breaking point. *I sure could use a drink.*

She would have engaged in excess to escape in the past, but she knew she had to fight the urge. Then she would have brought a bottle from the den to her room and drunk the whole damn thing. Hit the self-destruct button, as Dr. Greedsy would say.

Her fingers punched in the code Walter provided for his phone, and she pulled up the photo of Chantelle lying on the walkway. She enlarged the wound and pulled up the same images for the other two women. The lacerations to the throat appeared identical, with the unmistakable triangular signature present. One person undoubtedly committed the killings of all three.

She closed the two phones. The manner of death seemed familiar, but she couldn't place it. *Where have I seen that exact signature before?* It was as if someone had removed a flap of skin. *A trophy?*

Ben stirred and rolled over. "Are you still staring at those notes?"

"A little."

He sat up and pulled her to him. "Liar, you've been at it the whole time."

She pressed her lips to his.

"What time is it?"

She glanced past him at the clock on the nightstand. "It's almost five."

Ben yawned and stretched. "We better hustle to the dining room soon. Then we need to finish our interviews." He ran his fingers through her hair. "After that, my darling, you need to get some sleep. I'm refreshed and will stand guard."

She hopped off the bed and headed to the bathroom. "Let me throw some water on my face, and I'll be ready."

Ben stood at the door and watched her. "Do you think we should confront Alan about last year?"

CJ exhaled. "I'm not sure. We both know he'll lie and then go after Walter." She squeezed past him and dropped onto the chair by the table. She wrestled her boots on and said, "At some point, we'll broach it with him, but maybe not yet."

He nodded. "Okay. At least the information lets us narrow the list. Who do we have left now?"

She recited the six names, and he grimaced. "What?" she asked.

"Rory. Do you really think he's capable of murder? He has his son here with him."

"I don't, but so far, excluding those who couldn't have done it is helping us whittle down our suspects. It's all about how we talk to him about it. We need to ask him for anything he might remember and not make it seem like we're accusing him."

As he pulled on his rain jacket, Ben asked, "If you had to bet on a person, who would it be?"

She tilted her head to the side and pursed her lips. "Victor or Junior, Harley's son. We still need to interview Junior but he gives me a weird feeling."

"Hmm."

"Who did you think I was going to say?"

He frowned. "I don't know. Maybe Alan."

"He's an ass for sure, and he's lying and may have been involved in a cover-up, but I don't think he's a killer."

"We know little about the others. Junior acts strange, I'll give you that, but why'd you say Victor?"

She told him how Kenny said Victor always chased after the girls, and they never gave him the time of day. He thought it enraged him, and he has a temper. CJ added how he'd leered at her and creeped her out in the fish processing area.

"Hmm. So, you think spurned advances may have set him off?"

"It's possible." She pulled her hood up, and a thought popped into her head. "I have a way we can get a response from Alan about Chantelle without telling him what we know."

As they burst through the door, approximately twenty guests were scattered throughout the den and dining room. Most sat silently, with dazed looks on their faces.

"Miss CJ, wanna play cards before dinner?" Luka asked as he smiled at her.

"Sure." She pointed to a table in front of the picture window. "How 'bout you grab the cards, and we'll sit over there?"

"You don't have to play with him if you don't want to," Rory said as he approached. "I know you're exhausted. The little man seems to be the only one getting any sleep."

"It's fine. I could use a distraction."

As she played Go Fish with Luka, she scanned the room. Everyone had arrived except Harley and his son. *Where the hell are they?*

"Do you have any nines?" Luka's small voice drew her attention back to the game.

"Uh, no."

They had just finished their second game when Bev announced dinner was being served. "We're having home-made pizza and Caesar salad tonight. The menu called for grilled rib eyes, but ..." She spread her arms, palms facing the window.

The long faces of the kitchen crew meandered around the tables, serving drinks.

Ryleigh approached CJ. "What can I get you to drink?" she asked.

"Water's fine."

The young woman leaned down and whispered, "I swapped tables with Steph. I don't wanna be near Evan."

CJ glanced over at the table and eyed Evan, who was sitting beside Leo. "I understand. How's Kayla?"

"She's still shaken up. I told her to stay in the crew's den tonight. The boys will watch over her."

Everyone was halfway through dinner when Harley burst through the back door, followed by Walter. Harley spied Alan on a stool by the kitchen bar and stomped toward him. "You need to tell your fucking crew to lay off Junior!"

Alan herded them into the hallway leading to his office. Everyone in the room listened as they yelled at each other. Ben and CJ stood and joined the three men in the hallway as the argument continued.

"Junior wasn't doing anything," Harley screamed, his face bright red. "He was only taking a walk."

"No, he wasn't. I caught him peeping in on Kayla," Walter said. He confronted Harley, standing nose-to-nose with his fists balled up.

"Cool it, guys!" Ben said as he pushed himself between the two men.

"Oh, just a little misunderstanding," Alan replied. "Harley, how 'bout you go have dinner, and we'll talk later? You too, Walter."

"It wasn't a misunderstanding," Walter snapped. "I saw the little pervert myself. He was gawking at Kayla through the window and rubbing his crotch." He stomped away and out the back door.

"I'll take my damn dinner to my room." Harley bumped Ben's shoulder as he returned to the kitchen, grabbed a tray with a pizza and a six-pack of beer, and stormed out the front door.

"Sorry 'bout that," Alan said to Ben and CJ. "Harley's had a little too much to drink."

Ben opened the office door and motioned for Alan to follow him. "Let's chat."

"Uh, okay. I guess I can chat now if it's import—"

"It's important," CJ said.

The owner ran his fingers through his hair and slid into his chair.

CJ sat on the edge of the desk and leaned close. "Remember when you and I were talking about your crew, and you mentioned you were short-handed this season?"

"Um, I think so."

Her eyes narrowed. "You said a girl named Chantelle didn't show up. Remember that?"

Alan's eyes darted from her to Ben and then to the floor. "I could have ... she told me she was coming back and—"

"She died last year!" CJ said in a raised voice.

"Uh, I must have misspoken," Alan said, struggling to find a response. Suddenly, his expression went tight. "Wait! Who told you that?"

CJ smirked. "That's none of your damn business. How did she die?"

He squirmed before he said, "She drowned."

"Really? That seems to happen a lot around here." She leaned so close she was almost touching him. "Was it the same kind of drowning as Olivia and Anita?"

Alan jumped up and grabbed her arm before Ben yanked his hand away and pushed him against the wall. "I'd be careful, Alan. The lady's about had enough of your shit, and so have I." He released him, took CJ's hand, and led her out of the office and through the back door.

Ben and CJ stood under the canopy over the fish processing area. Neither of them believed what Alan had told them. As he had done before, he skirted their questions and hid his secrets.

"I have this overwhelming urge to slap him every time I see him now," CJ said. "I understand wanting to protect your business, but three young women are dead, so you'd think he'd get it."

"I still think he's got something to do with it," Ben said. "He may not have wielded the knife, but he knows who did."

CJ stared at the stream of water rushing off the edge of the roof. The raindrops battered the wooden walkway and splashed her legs and boots. Her eyes focused on the dim light coming from the crew quarters. A loud crash coming from inside broke her trance. She and Ben bolted through the back door.

THIRTY-FOUR

Wednesday, September 14
Paradise Cove

Ben and CJ burst into the dining room as Harley and Rory struggled to their feet after flipping over one of the tables. The older man was swaying and cursing loudly. He took a wild swing at Rory, who ducked before lunging and sending both men back to the floor.

Jamie wrapped Luka in her arms and ran out the door. The other guests stayed back as the two men grappled on the floor, each trying to gain an advantage. Ben rushed forward, grabbed Rory, and yanked him backward. Both men slammed into the back of the couch. Ben pinned Rory's arm behind his back and held him.

CJ grabbed Harley and tried to contain him as he fought to break free. A flailing elbow landed square under her right eye. "Damnit! Cut this shit out," she said as she wrapped her arm around his throat and her legs around his waist.

Noah came to her aid and helped her roll Harley over onto his stomach. Both sat on him until he stopped struggling.

"I'm gonna kill that son of a bitch!" Harley screamed, his face crimson.

"I've had it with you!" Rory said. "I've listened to your bitching and moaning every year, but this year you're over the top. Ever since you started drinking again, you're out of control."

"Both of you need to calm down," Ben said. "I don't know what started this, but it's not helping anyone."

Rory's breathing slowed, and his body relaxed.

Ben pointed him to a chair. "Sit!"

CJ ran her fingertips across her throbbing cheek. She asked someone to find Walter and tell him to bring her some rope. A seventy-year-old man from cabin four hustled out the back door. Minutes later, Walter appeared and helped her tie Harley's hands behind his back and sit him against the wall.

"Stay there!" CJ said. She turned to the stunned onlookers. "Now, can someone tell me what the hell happened?"

"Uh, I'm not sure," Marie said. "Harley came back and started fussing about being stranded, and the next thing I know, they were fighting." She stepped closer. "Your eye's swollen."

"Yeah, it hurts, but I'll be fine." She exhaled and scanned the room. "This is a bad situation for everyone, but this kind of crap needs to stop. It's late, so everyone needs to go to their cabin." She glanced at Ben. "Where the hell is Alan?"

"I assume upstairs. I have no clue how he didn't hear all the commotion."

She shook her head and glared at Harley. His eyes were bloodshot, and the stench of alcohol on him made her almost gag. He was an asshole sober, but being drunk took him to a whole other level. "Walter, can you help Ben get this asshole back to his cabin?"

"Yes, ma'am," he said as he dragged Harley to his feet.

She leaned close to the drunk man, ignoring the toxic fumes. "You better not come out of your cabin for any reason, or I'll lock you in the storage room."

"But I—"

"There are no buts." She turned to Ben. "You know what. Put his ass in the storage room until morning."

"No!" Harley bellowed. "I'll stay in my room."

She jabbed a finger at him. "Fine, but I better not see you before morning."

Ben and Walter grabbed his arms and led the stumbling man out the door.

CJ approached Rory, who sat rubbing his arm. "What's Harley's backstory? Has he always been this volatile?"

Rory frowned. "No. I've known him for three years. He and I both used to come here in late July and we both moved to this week when Alan offered us a discount." He paused before pursing his lips. Three years ago, Harley never touched alcohol—he only drank sodas and water. He was loud, but not belligerent. We enjoyed being around each other and even did a half day together on *Delila's Dream* with Victor."

Rory continued by telling her that last year, Harley started drinking again. Apparently, his drinking cost him his first marriage, and he quit for a long time. He got remarried, and that's how Junior became his stepson.

"What changed?" CJ asked.

Rory shrugged. "I'm not sure, but I heard his second wife ran off with another man. She disappeared and left him with Junior. I do know he started drinking wine, entire bottles at a time, at dinner last season. Now, he's taking beer with him to his cabin and always appears to be drunk. I've been avoiding him, or trying to."

She told him to return to his cabin. As he left, almost everyone else followed. She dropped onto a loveseat in the corner and leaned her head back. She was alone except for Leo and Marie, who turned the table over and put the chairs back together.

"Let me check out your eye," Leo said as he and Marie approached.

CJ leaned forward. "My cheek stings, but I'll be okay."

"Let him take a look, dear," Marie said. "My husband is a retired doctor."

CJ turned her head so Leo could examine her. His long, slender fingers caressed a spot under her eye. "It doesn't appear you have an orbital bone fracture," he said as he smiled. "However, you'll have a lovely bruise and perhaps a black eye."

"Wonderful. Another shiner for my collection."

The older man patted her arm and asked his wife to bring some ice from the kitchen. He went to a recliner, sat, and leaned it back.

"I found a pack of frozen peas. Perfect for what we need," Marie said as she joined CJ on the loveseat. "This will be cold, but it'll help with the swelling. Lay your head back, and I'll handle the rest." Marie glanced at the clock. "We're gonna do twenty minutes, then give you a break, followed by another twenty minutes."

"Thanks, Marie. What kind of doctor was Leo?"

"He was an orthopedic surgeon at the UCHealth University of Colorado Hospital in Aurora. He specialized in the spine."

As CJ's face went numb, Marie told her about how she and Leo met. She was a nurse, and they immediately fell in love. They had been married for almost forty years and had two children who were married and lived in Denver.

"How's the eye?" Ben asked as he came through the door. He pulled a chair over in front of her and rubbed her knee.

"It's frozen at the moment," CJ said. "Did you get Harley settled down?"

"I did … told Junior to make sure he stayed put. By the time I left, Harley was sprawled out on the bed snoring."

"Okay, that's twenty minutes," Marie said as she removed the frozen peas wrapped in a hand towel. "I'm gonna swap this pack for a new one, and you and Ben can take it to your cabin."

She returned, handed Ben the replacement, and told him to reapply it in about fifteen minutes. The two couples donned their rain gear and hustled through the wind and rain for their cabins.

THIRTY-FIVE

Thursday, September 15
Paradise Cove

It was a little before 6:00 a.m. when Ben answered the knock on the door, and Kenny stepped into the cabin. The rain slowed to a mist, and while the waves still rocked the lodge, the wind lessened. The clouds loomed overhead but shifted from charcoal to steel gray.

"The weather's getting better," Ben said. "I assume there's nothing new to report?"

Kenny shook his head. "Nope. We still can't get any communication with the outside. Walter was hoping to repair one of the old radios, but he's not had any luck so far."

"What's going on?" CJ asked as she exited the bathroom.

"Oh, shit! What happened to your eye?"

She delicately touched her cheek. "I caught an elbow from Harley last night." She told him about the fight.

"Jeez, I'm sorry." He hesitated before saying, "Um, listen. I wanted to tell you guys about something."

CJ squinted. "What?"

"I was sitting in the crew's den near the window, and Victor left his cabin around midnight. He looked around like he was afraid someone would see him, and he was carrying something wrapped in a towel. It was strange, so I cracked the door open and watched him go to the end of the walkway by the footbridge. I think he tossed a gun into the water."

"He told us he didn't have a weapon," Ben said.

The young man shrugged. "I never knew he had one, but that's what it looked like."

CJ glanced at Ben. "Do you believe it was the one Alan claimed was missing from his office desk?"

"There's only one way to find out." He grabbed his jacket off the hook and slid it on. "How 'bout we go ask him?"

"Is it okay if you don't tell him I told you?" Kenny asked. "Victor sorta freaks me out, and I'd prefer not to wind up on his bad side."

Ben nodded. "We don't need to tell him. He'll never know as long as he didn't see you."

"I'm sure he didn't. His cabin is at the end next to Walter's, and he never came to the den."

"Okay, you go to the guest dining room and hang out there," Ben said. "Where is Victor?"

Kenny nodded. "I haven't seen him this morning. He's probably still in his cabin. It's the next to the last one on the left."

Victor cracked the door and stared at Ben and CJ. "You guys need something?"

"We need to talk to you again," Ben said as he pointed inside.

"Uh, sure." He stepped back and opened the door. "My place is small and a mess, but come in."

His cabin was no more than ten by twelve feet, with an unmade single bed, a narrow four-drawer dresser, and a rack for hanging clothes tucked in the corner. The lone window faced the walkway with a dingy white curtain. A plastic water bottle, used to spit tobacco juice in, sat half full on the top of the dresser.

"The only nice thing about these outside cabins is you don't have to share," he said.

CJ pointed to a door in the back. "What's back there?"

"That's the bathroom." He forced a laugh. "If you think this room is small, you ought to try squeezing in there." He leaned against the dresser and rubbed the side of his neck. "What can I help you with?"

"You told us you didn't have a weapon when we spoke before," Ben said.

"Uh, yeah, that's right."

"Are you sure?" CJ asked.

Victor dropped his head. "Yeah. I don't have one."

"Look at me," CJ said. "Have you ever had one?"

He lifted his head. "No. Not here at the lodge."

"Were you in your cabin last night?"

Victor furrowed his brow. "Uh, yeah. What's this all about?"

"You were outside last night and threw something in the water," Ben said.

He rubbed his chin. "I went out last night to check the footbridge but didn't throw anything in the water. Who told you that?"

"Doesn't matter," CJ said. "But I don't believe you."

He spread his arms. "What else can I say? I've never had a Glock." His face went white.

"A Glock?" she asked.

"Uh, I mean a weapon."

They pressed him a few more times, but he maintained his story.

"We'll find out if you're lying," CJ said as they left.

━━━━

Victor closed the door, went to the bathroom, and splashed water on his face. He stared at himself in the mirror. They knew he was lying. *Who in the fuck told them about the gun?*

He used a brown hand towel to dry his face and returned to the bedroom. As his mind recalled the prior night, he sat on the bed and rocked back and forth. He'd been careful to ensure no one was outside and all the lights in the cabins were dark. *Who wasn't asleep?*

A blast of wind forced air into the crack around his window and caused the curtain to gently sway. Only three people could have observed him at the end of the walkway. Walter would have a view from his shop window, but his lights weren't on. Alan's window in his upstairs apartment would provide a view, but it was too far away.

He stood and paced the short runway. The only other person was that nosy busybody, Kenny. Since CJ had asked him to help, he'd been playing mini-detective and stuck his nose in everything. *I bet the little bastard spied on me.* His fingers massaged his throbbing temples. Perhaps he never saw the gun. It was pitch black … wait! There was a light on the post near the footbridge. *Was it bright enough?*

Alan would have his ass if he found out Victor had a gun. Only a few people knew he had a weapon. He always made it clear to everyone that they were not allowed. He couldn't be sure, but only those who worked here a while would know.

In the end, he decided it didn't matter. He'd continue to deny he had a Glock and should be safe. Worst case, he'd get fired. They wouldn't be able to connect him to anything else.

CJ's threat of "we'll find out if you're lying" was hollow. The only way someone could do that was to search the bottom of the cove. There was a fat chance of that happening anytime soon. He slipped on his raincoat, opened the door, and raced for the crew's dining room. He needed to keep an eye on that sneaky little Kenny.

THIRTY-SIX

Thursday, September 15
Paradise Cove

Ben and CJ were walking towards the dining room when Ryleigh intercepted them. She asked if CJ had a few minutes before breakfast, as Kayla wanted to talk to her again.

CJ left Ben on a couch in the crew's den and followed Ryleigh to her cabin. Kayla sat on her unmade bed in the faintly lit room. Her eyes were damp, beet red, and swollen.

CJ slid onto the bed across from her. "I understand you want to talk to me again. How are you doing?"

There was a loud sniff, and Kayla said, "I'm doing okay, I guess." She bit her lip. "I don't really need to talk to you. I guess—"

"Talk to her," Ryleigh said as she dried her short, curly brown hair with a towel, giving her a porcupine look. "Please." She joined her roommate on the bed and took her hand. "You and I discussed this, and you know it's what you said you wanted." She hugged her and whispered, "It's scary, but it's the only way for you to move past this, and it's the right thing to do."

Kayla sat frozen until she offered a slight nod of her head.

"You can tell me anything," CJ said, her voice soft. "I'm happy to listen to whatever you have to say."

The young woman kept her head down as she told a different version of her night in Evan's cabin. She stayed overnight, and they fell asleep after some petting. It was the portion of her story about the early morning that changed.

She said she woke up when Evan kissed her neck and ran his hand under her T-shirt. The only thing she had on underneath was her underwear, and she told him to stop, but he wouldn't. He kept telling her it would be okay. She said she finally pushed him away, jumped up, and went into the bathroom.

"So, you never had sex?" CJ asked.

The young woman put her hands over her face and fell against her roommate's shoulder.

"Tell her the rest," Ryleigh said.

"I can't."

Ryleigh caressed her back. "Do you want me to tell her?"

After a couple of minutes, Kayla finally sat up, blew her nose, and shook her head. "No, I'll do it."

She cleared her throat and focused back on CJ. She said Evan opened the bathroom door while she was standing at the sink washing her face. He came up from behind, wrapped his arms around her, and started kissing her neck again. "I told him to stop," she said.

Tears erupted as her eyes drifted to the floor. "He picked me up and carried me back to the bed," she said as her voice cracked. "Before I knew it, he was on top of me and forced me … to have sex."

"So, you never consented like you told me before?"

"No. He kept saying it would be okay, and I kept saying no. In the end, he got what he wanted."

CJ's pulse raced. "I'm so sorry this happened to you. What he did was rape."

She nodded as tears rolled down her cheeks. "I'm ashamed of putting myself in that position. I was naïve and stupid. It's my fault."

Rather than agreeing with Kayla about how stupid it was to stay in a cabin with Evan, CJ said, "No, he raped you. You were trying to be kind, and he took advantage of you. This is on him, not you. You have nothing to be ashamed of."

"What happens now?" Ryleigh asked angrily. "His ass needs to pay."

"I'll help her file a report."

"Arrest him right now!" Ryleigh said, her face crimson and her fists clenched.

"I agree, but we need the local authorities for that."

"Aren't you a cop? Why can't you do it?"

"I don't have jurisdiction in Alaska, but I can make sure it happens." CJ moved beside Kayla and put her arm around her. She told her she should file a report so he couldn't hurt another woman and asked if she could do that for her.

"Do it, Kayla!" Ryleigh said. "I'll help you."

The young woman quietly nodded.

CJ knew it would be a 'he said, she said,' and often, these cases resulted in no charges or not-guilty verdicts. She expected Evan to deny that sex happened at all. No witnesses or evidence existed to challenge it. She hesitantly explained this to the young woman.

Ryleigh went to the dresser, pulled out a plastic bag, and handed it to her. "Here are the panties she was wearing. This will prove they had sex." She rejoined Kayla on the bed.

"But you mentioned to me before that he wore a condom, so there won't be any semen."

"I said he had them," Ryleigh said. "Tell her Kayla."

"He wasn't wearing one, but he didn't …" She clutched onto her roommate, who completed her sentence.

"Finish inside her."

Heat flowed through CJ's body as she fought to remain calm. "I'll keep this, and as soon as law enforcement arrives, we'll report it."

Kayla nodded and quietly said, "Okay."

CJ hugged her and whispered, "Good. Your roommate's right. He shouldn't get away with what he did, and you'll help others not go through this." She released her and stood. "Can I do anything else for you right now?"

"No. I'm not gonna go to work today. I don't want to see him."

"I think that's best," CJ said.

"I told Bev she was sick," Ryleigh said. "Steph and I can handle the tables, and I'll do my best not to slap the shit out of Evan. Kenny told me he'd keep an eye out here while I'm up front."

CJ hugged Kayla once more and left the room. She motioned Ben outside when she entered the den, and they stood under the canopy outside the back door to the dining room.

"What was that about?" he asked as his brow furrowed.

She told him the true story of Kayla's night with Evan.

After she finished, he exhaled. "What a son of a bitch." He asked if she wanted to go to his cabin, confront him, or lock his ass in the storage room.

"I have another idea," she said. "Let's not say anything. We'll let Evan think he's scot-free and surprise him when the local authorities arrive."

"Do you think he'll bother Kayla anymore?"

She shook her head. "He'll avoid her and hope she keeps her mouth shut until he can get as far away as possible." Her eyes were cold and sharp when she added, "If he does, then you can deal with him."

THIRTY-SEVEN

Thursday, September 15
Paradise Cove

She crawled off the bed and slipped on her boots. "You gotta be more careful, or we're gonna get caught. That damn detective is sharp." She turned to him. "Are you listening to me?"

"Yeah, yeah. You need to relax."

She poked her finger in his face. "Don't tell me what to do! I'm always the one who has to make sure your mistakes don't cost us."

He stretched his arms and groaned. "I could use some more sleep."

"Let me ask you something," she said with an edge in her voice. "Why did you kill that guest? Didn't you think that'd be a flashing neon sign saying here I am?"

"Come on. Why do you ask such stupid questions?" He hopped off the bed, rummaged through the dresser, and grabbed a pair of pants. As he slipped them on, he said, "You know damn well why." He pulled a shirt out of the drawer. "Besides, it's not my fault. I can't always control Jeffrey."

"You always say that, but you're the one using the knife." She went into the bathroom and closed the door.

He sat in a chair, pulled on his socks, and climbed back on the bed. His eyes closed, and his mind raced.

The rain stopped, and he ventured out to prowl the neighborhood. He wasn't looking for trouble or anyone, but there she was. Instantly, Jeffrey stirred awake, and he crossed the street.

The young woman was exquisite. She wore a pair of white slacks tailored to her form. The baby blue blouse she wore brought out the color of her eyes. Her silky blond hair curled around her perfect face.

He approached the spot where she stood and pretended to window shop. Far enough away not to be threatening, but close enough to hear her as she talked on her cell phone.

"I can't believe you won't be home tonight," the woman said. "I'm sick and tired of your bullshit and you standing me up. I'll go to the wedding alone. I tell you what, don't call me anymore, asshole!" She hit the end button. Her perfume was intoxicating, and he stole a quick glance.

She gazed down the street before she started walking away. He followed behind her, keeping his distance. When she reached the street corner, she stopped and glanced right and left. "Where the hell am I?" Wetness ran down her unblemished cheeks,

He slowed as he reached her and offered her a smile. "Are you okay?"

"No," she said as the tears erupted. "I'm lost and just broke up with my boyfriend."

"I'm sorry," he said in the most concerned voice he could muster. "Where are you trying to go?"

She told him she was meeting some girlfriends at Ricky's After Dark, an upscale bar. The taxi driver assured her this was the spot when he dropped her around the corner. "But obviously, the idiot didn't take me to the right place. I don't see any bars and the map on my phone doesn't show it."

The bar was only one street over and close, but he had another idea. He pointed back in the direction that he'd come. "It's back that way."

Her pale blue eyes peered past him. "Really? I thought that way was just a bunch of warehouses."

"Well, there are some, but two streets down, on the left, there's a street you can cut through. It'll drop you right out in front of Ricky's. It's not far at all."

The young woman frowned. "Maybe I need to call another cab." She peeked down at her heels. "These things aren't exactly the right shoes for a hike." She stared out at the cars. "Trouble is, this isn't a great place to hail a ride."

His pulse ramped up as a light breeze blew her vanilla scent past him. "I'm happy to walk with you if you'd like. It's no problem at all." His heart sank when he heard her following words.

"I see a taxi!" She waved her arms, and the driver slowed before passing. "Damnit! What happened?"

"His sign was off. He must be off duty."

She lifted her wrist and glanced at her watch. "I'm gonna be late. I need to call my friends and let them know. Thanks again. I'll be fine. I'm sure another cab will come by soon."

"Okay. Have a pleasant night." He turned and walked back the way he came.

Ten minutes later, he smiled from the shadows as the young woman approached him. She paused when she reached the street ... well, the alley ... and stared. "Shit! This can't be right."

After further consideration, the young woman started forward. He tapped on the metal door behind him, and she froze. Her eyes darted around frantically.

Her mouth dropped open when he stepped out, and she realized she had made a terrible mistake. She tried in vain to escape, but tripped and banged her knee into the hard surface of the street.

She crawled away from him and begged him to leave her alone. He yanked her up by the arm before punching her and sending her back to the ground. She was groggy, and he whisked her to his hideaway.

For two days, he enjoyed her company. Her, not so much. Her fear became sheer terror when he showed her the knife.

From that day forward, he knew the type of women Jeffrey preferred—damsels in distress.

"Are you fucking daydreaming again?" She startled him back to reality when she returned from the bathroom. "That's sick," she said as she pointed to his erection. "I never understood how killing a woman was such a turn-on for you."

"Leave me alone. At least I don't rape them like some psycho," he snapped.

She raised her eyebrows. "Wow! Like you're not." She kissed his cheek and started for the door.

THIRTY-EIGHT

Thursday, September 15
Paradise Cove

Jamie sat squeezed into the corner of the bathroom. She had wrapped herself in a blanket but still shivered uncontrollably. Her mind bounced between her past and present situation. She flinched with every creak, crack, and groan, and images of what could happen flashed through her mind.

"Sweetheart, you need to come out," Noah said as he kneeled in front of her. "You've been in here all night."

Her head shook swiftly as she gripped the blanket so hard her fingers turned white.

He leaned closer and caressed her cheek with his fingertips. "Please come out, and we'll get you something to eat."

She yanked away from him as his hand attempted to pull her up from where she had burrowed herself.

"Okay, we can wait until it's lighter outside," Noah said as he stood and closed the bathroom door behind him.

"She still won't come out?" Rory asked.

"No," Noah said as he sighed. "I've never seen her this scared. She's always been jumpy, but never like this." He motioned toward the door. "You and Luka may as well go to breakfast without us. While you're gone, I'll do my best to convince her to leave the bathroom longer than just for you guys to pee. I'm sorry we're being such a pain."

Rory nodded. "Don't worry about that. I wish we could help her somehow." He glanced at Luka standing beside him. "We'll go eat, return, and stay with her so you can go. Or we can bring you something back."

"I'll go later."

"Okay, push the dresser back when we leave." Rory zipped up his son's jacket and tightened the drawstrings on his hood. "Let's go, son."

They opened the door to steady wind and rain and raced for the dining room.

Noah dropped onto the bed and stared blankly at the ceiling. He had become more worried about Jamie's mental state than the murderer. Between him and Rory, he was confident they could fight off anyone, but Jamie needed help, and for more than just her fear a killer might grab her.

He recalled the many times she'd gone to counseling and the varied results. She'd be able to cope with her all-consuming paranoia and fears for a while, only to slip back into a dark place where she could not function. *There has to be more to it than the trauma from the murder of her childhood friend,* he thought. *But what?*

Over their six years of marriage, she had retold the story to him more times than he could remember. It always seemed the same, almost rehearsed. He knew it was a much more complicated situation than that. Something deep inside her she couldn't bring herself to say.

On more than one occasion, he had probed her with questions, hoping she'd divulge the secret she hid inside. But every time, all he got was, "That's everything," and pushing her resulted in anger. He rubbed his eyes. Maybe he was losing it himself and seeing something that wasn't there.

The ticking sound of the ice particles bouncing off the window grew louder. Noah climbed off the bed and pulled the curtains back. The dull gray light, combined with a fog, stared at him through the rain-streaked glass. He only hoped that time would speed up and they could leave this place.

Noah opened the door to Jamie's wide eyes and sat on the floor at her feet. "I thought I'd join you. The boys went to eat, and maybe you'll feel like going after they return." He smiled feebly at her.

"I need to stay here," she said in a low, coarse voice. "It's not safe outside."

He opened his mouth to argue, but thought better of it. Instead, he did something he had done while camping when they first started dating. He sang Jamie her favorite John Denver song, *Sunshine On My Shoulders.*

An hour later, a loud knock startled them. Noah jumped up and peered at Luka, waving to him in the window. "Honey, the boys are back. I need to let them in."

The man and his son hung their rain gear on the hooks.

"Is she feeling any better?" Rory asked.

"Not really," Noah said. "She still refuses to leave. If you guys need to get in there, I'm sure I can get her to at least move outside the door."

"No, we're fine. We may grab a shower later, but we can use your old room," Rory said. "Let's leave her where she's comfortable."

"Dad, can I give Miss Jamie this?" Luka asked, holding up a blueberry muffin and a plastic bottle of orange juice.

Rory glanced at Noah, who nodded. "Maybe this will help. She loves kids."

The two men watched as the boy crept to the bathroom door, opened it, and disappeared inside.

"I can go get him if you'd like," Rory said.

"No. Leave him. Who knows, maybe he can snap her out of it. If you're okay with it, I'll go eat and be back."

"Fine with me. Be careful."

Noah hustled through the fog engulfing the lodge. He entered the dining room to find about a dozen guests around the room, most of them sitting silently. He went to the counter, retrieved some lukewarm scrambled eggs, bacon, and toast, and sat across from Ben and CJ at his usual table.

"Jamie didn't want to join you?" CJ asked.

He told her Jamie was afraid to leave the room—to be more accurate, a corner in the bathroom. As he picked at the food on his plate and his eyes grew moist, he told them how he'd tried everything but couldn't reach her. "She hasn't eaten or slept much in days now."

For the next several minutes, Noah told Ben and CJ what had happened to Jamie when she was young and how it impacted her. Although years of counseling had provided some relief, there were moments when she descended into a deep darkness. This time, he hadn't been able to pull her out.

"It was one reason we moved in with Rory and Luka," he said. "Plus, he has Luka, and we both need a bit of help. When I left, the little guy was in with her. She's so passionate about the kids in her class, and I'm hoping he can cheer her up."

Noah pinched his temples with his fingertips. "I'm doing the best I can not to lose my shit with her. I've grown accustomed to the paranoia and how nervous she is all the time, but I'm damn sick and tired of walking on eggshells. I was about to explode, so when Rory suggested he'd watch Jamie while I came here, I jumped at it." He ran the palm of his hand down his face. "We gotta get out of here, or one of us is gonna lose it. Am I being a shitty husband?"

"No," CJ said. "You can love someone, but wanting to be happy yourself doesn't make you bad." She shrugged. "This situation is taking a toll on everyone."

They discussed when the storm would subside enough to allow someone to go for help or for help to arrive. Unfortunately, they had no new information because they couldn't fix any of the radios. The timing hinged on when they could take the risk of leaving the cove and traveling to a location with cell tower range.

Noah finished eating and put some food into a Styrofoam container to take back for Jamie. As he was about to leave, CJ asked him if it would help if she spoke to his wife.

"At this point, I have no clue what to do," he said. "I guess it can't hurt."

CJ told Ben she was going with Noah and would meet him back here so they could interview Harley and Junior.

———

CJ cracked the bathroom door open, and Jamie lifted her head. She still sat in the corner, wrapped in a blanket, but Luka had joined her. He had fallen asleep with his head lying on her shoulder. As CJ closed the door, he woke up and drowsily said hello.

"I'm sorry. I didn't know you were sleeping," CJ said.

He stirred and rubbed his eyes. "It's okay, I'm awake. Do you wanna come in too?"

"Uh, yeah. I wanted to check on Jamie, but I'll come back later."

Luka crawled out from under the blanket and stood. "It's okay. It can be your turn to keep Miss Jamie company.

My dad and I are gonna go take a shower." He squeezed past her and left them alone.

"Can I come in?" CJ asked.

"I guess, as long as you don't force me to leave here."

CJ raised her palms. "I just wanna talk and see how you're doing. That's all." She sat in front of Jamie and crossed her legs.

"Luka sure has taken to you," Jamie said in a low voice.

CJ smiled. "He has. He's a wonderful little guy."

"Do you and Ben want kids?"

"We've talked about it, and … yeah, we both do. The challenge for us is I'm thirty-three so we won't be able to wait long to try. Ben's six months younger, but age isn't an issue for men, anyway."

The young woman sniffed and adjusted in her corner. "Earlier, I told you Noah and I hoped to have kids." Tears streamed down her face. "We desperately want them, but I'm not able to get pregnant."

CJ patted her shoulder. "You can always adopt. There are so many children who need good homes. You two would be great parents—any child would be lucky to have you."

Jamie nodded and wiped her nose. "I guess."

They sat silent for several minutes before Jamie asked when someone would arrive to help them and when they could go home. CJ conveyed to her that there were no recent developments on the timeline. She slid closer to Jamie as she started crying. The room was silent except for the occasional sniff.

"Is there anything I can do to help?"

"Um, not really. I need to be away from this place." Jamie frowned. "I never really wanted to come here. I've been afraid of being out on the boat since we got here, and now this." She rubbed her forehead. "I only came because it's what Noah wanted."

CJ twisted her mouth. "Ben and I coming here was my idea, although he loves boats, the water, and fishing." Without saying Noah had explained the trauma from Jamie's early childhood, CJ asked Jamie more about her fears.

For several minutes, Jamie deflected, and CJ delicately pushed. Finally, the young woman mentioned why the thought of a murderer was so painful for her. Then she opened up and told CJ the version of the story she had told everyone—her husband, family, friends, and counselors.

CJ asked about her friend Becky's desire for solitude in the woods, feeling there was something missing.

"I ... I don't know."

"It seems odd since you said you two were close and always together. Yet that day you both chose to be alone."

Jamie lifted her head and stared at her. "You don't believe me, do you?"

CJ cleared her throat. "No, I don't. It makes little sense to me." She brushed the dark brown hair away from Jamie's cheek. "Another thing that doesn't fit is how afraid you are."

"Why? I told you, my friend—"

"I know you lost someone close to you at the hands of a wicked person, but ..." CJ paused as Jamie's lip began trembling. "But I think you were there with Becky and saw the man. You said it was on TV, but that's not true, is it?"

Jamie's head hung, and she whispered, "You're very good at your job." Over the next two minutes, she unloaded the secrets she'd buried for over twenty years as she bawled on CJ's shoulders.

THIRTY-NINE

Thursday, September 15
Paradise Cove

Victor sat on the bed in his cabin as his mind raced. He couldn't let the issue over the gun go. Who had told on him for having the Glock? He was convinced it had been Kenny. Alan or Walter would have already confronted him if they had seen him. Simon and Cal would have also said something, and the girls would have avoided him. *That little shit Kenny ratted on me!*

The more he thought about it, the angrier he got. He grabbed his raincoat, slipped it on, and bolted out the door. Moments later he entered the crew's den where Kenny sat on the couch beside Kayla.

"You fucking ran your mouth about me!" Victor said as he approached Kenny. "What did you say to that detective?"

"Uh, what are you talking about?" Kenny said, as he shifted his weight and spread his arms. "I'm not sure—"

Victor stepped closer and pointed his finger at him. "Don't screw with me. You know what I'm talking about."

Kenny shook his head. "Uh, I don't—"

"You told her I had a gun and threw it off the dock," Victor said, his eyes flaring. "Now I'm a suspect."

Kenny drew a deep breath and stood. "Well, I saw you that night, but I never said I thought you murdered anyone."

"You bastard!" Victor said as he shoved Kenny backward, causing him to flip over the back of the couch. Before Kenny was on his feet, Victor punched him, knocking him back to the floor.

"Stop it!" Kayla screamed. She jumped up and grabbed Victor's arm, but he pushed her away. As he turned back, Kenny tackled him, and both men went down. Victor wound up on top and rained blows down on the smaller man.

Simon and Cal burst into the room from the back porch, and Kayla pleaded with them to stop the fight. Victor told them to stay away, and neither man made a move. Instead, they stood silently and watched Victor pound Kenny with his fists.

"Assholes!" Kayla said as she raced barefoot out the door and across the deck to get Walter.

When Walter appeared, he pulled Victor off Kenny. "Cut this shit out!" He turned to Simon and Cal and told them to hold Victor. Reluctantly, they did as they were told.

Walter told Kayla to bring him a towel from the kitchen as he sat Kenny up. Blood oozed from his nose and mouth, and his right eye was already puffy. Walter unloaded a tirade on the other three men and told them to return to their cabins. "I've had it with all this bullshit!" he said as they left.

Kayla dropped to her knees and helped wipe the blood from Kenny's face. After the nosebleed slowed, she hopped up and grabbed some ice from the freezer. She wrapped it in a clean towel and placed it on his eye.

Twenty minutes later, the nosebleed finally stopped, but his right eye was swollen closed and turning black. Kenny sat in a chair with a wet cloth against his face.

"Wanna tell me what that was all about?" Walter asked.

Kenny sighed. "I told CJ about Victor having a gun and tossing it in the water."

"Where did he get a damn gun?"

"I don't know," Kenny said, shrugging.

The older man frowned. "All right, let's take you upfront. Alan needs to know what happened, and we need to get some gauze for your nose." He helped Kenny to his feet and told Kayla to go with them.

Walter led Kenny and Kayla through the back door and into the dining room. A dozen guests sat blankly staring out the picture window at the blowing rain and swaying trees on the mountain across from the lodge.

"Where's Alan?" Walter asked Bev, who was cleaning the last of the breakfast platters.

"Uh, I think he's in his office," she said, as she eyed Kenny. "What happened, sweetie?"

"I got into it with Victor," he mumbled.

Bev led him to a chair and brought him an ice pack. She motioned for Marie. "Can Leo take a look at Kenny's nose?"

Leo examined Kenny's nose with the tips of his fingers. "You have a broken nose, son. It's minor, and I can realign it, but it'll hurt. Unfortunately, I don't have a way to numb it."

Walter reached and took Kenny's hand. "Doc needs to straighten it. You squeeze my hand and scream if you want."

The young man nodded, and Leo aligned his nose in a few painful minutes. "Ice it for fifteen minutes several times a day and take acetaminophen if we have some. That'll help the eye, too. Be sure to elevate your head when you sleep to help with the swelling."

When Alan rounded the corner, Walter approached him. "You need to control your damn crew," he said. "Victor attacked Kenny. No one's paying attention to what's happening in the back. You can't keep your ass up-front and ignore your responsibilities."

"I don't need a lecture from you," Alan said in a high-pitched voice. "I'm doing my best to protect our guests and the crew."

"Really?" Walter said, smirking. "The way I see it, you've dumped the guests on Ben and CJ and ain't hardly been in the back." He stepped closer to Alan. "We've got crew members staying alone, wandering around, and doing God knows what."

"Are you accusing one of my staff of something?"

"I ain't accusing anyone of anything, but the fact is we've got two dead girls, and someone sure as hell did it." He poked Alan in the chest. "I hold you responsible."

Alan pushed his hand away. "You know, Walter, I've been good to you, especially with your history, and you repay me by stabbing me in the back."

The argument grew more heated until Ben, who was checking on Kenny, stepped between them. "That's enough, guys. We don't need more chaos. Everyone's under enough stress."

Walter huffed and left through the backdoor.

"Thanks, Ben," Alan said. "Walter's such a hothead, and—"

"He's right. I haven't seen you exert much effort in protecting anyone other than yourself and your wife."

Alan's eyes narrowed. "So now you're gonna lecture me, too?"

Ben shook his head. "I'm just stating the facts." He turned when CJ entered through the front door after meeting with Jamie.

"What's going on?" she asked.

"We can add another fight to our list," Ben said. "Victor and Kenny."

She frowned as she gazed at the young man with an ice pack covering most of his face. "What happened?"

Kenny told her how everything unfolded, including the gun part, which piqued Alan's interest.

"Victor had my Glock?" he asked.

The young man shrugged. "All I know is it was a pistol."

"Damnit!" Alan said as he stomped out the backdoor.

CJ stood as she dug her fingertips into the knot in the back of her neck. The strain of having everyone cooped up and a murderer among them was escalating and about to explode.

She pulled Ben aside and updated him on Jamie. He asked why, after all these years, Jamie had finally told someone her secrets about the death of her friend. Her only response was that perhaps she'd reached such a low point that she had to get it off her chest.

Ben glanced out at the heavier fog as it crept toward the lodge. "Let's go meet with Harley and Junior."

FORTY

Thursday, September 15
Paradise Cove

Junior closed the cabin door behind Ben and CJ and paced back and forth in front of the two double beds, running his fingers through his curly reddish-brown hair. His stomach quivered, and he tried to convince himself that nothing was wrong. But he knew they were on to him.

"Calm down," Harley said, as he rubbed his throbbing temples. The night of drinking had left him hungover and his stomach doing backflips.

"Easy for you to say! The cops aren't after you." Junior raced into the bathroom and slammed the door. He dropped against the wall. A tapping on the door drew his attention. "Go away. Leave me alone."

"Let's go grab some food. I need something to settle my gut."

"No! I don't wanna see anyone, and those damn detectives are probably there."

"Okay, suit yourself."

Junior listened until the door rattled shut, stood, and returned to the bedroom. He resumed his pacing and mumbled to himself. His sickness was going to cost him. He'd suffered with it as long as he could remember. He stretched out across the bed and squeezed his lids shut. Memories of his early days flooded back to him.

He was twelve years old when he first saw his new neighbor. She was a junior in high school and a swimmer. Her house was behind his, and she had a pool where she would swim laps. It was early Saturday morning when he pushed his face against the fence, and his eyes followed her as she swam—mesmerized by her beauty.

After she finished her swim, she stood in the bright sunshine, toweling off her slender, toned body. His eyes flared when she glanced around and removed her canary yellow bikini top. He moved further down the fence to get a closer view as she stretched out on the red cushion of a chaise lounge chair, letting the sun's fingers tickle her skin.

An hour later, the young woman climbed off the chair, wrapped her towel around herself, and went inside. He waited until the sliding glass door slid shut and carefully snuck across her yard along the hedges. His heart skipped a beat when the drapes in the window above him closed. Holding his breath, he stood and peered through a crack in the curtains. She was standing naked in her bathroom, brushing her long jet-black hair.

Junior's eyes popped open, and he struggled to slow his breathing. He swiped away the moisture on his forehead and sat up. Why did women like his exquisite neighbor torment him and get him in trouble? *Bitches!*

As his breathing slowed, and his muscles relaxed, he laid back and closed his eyes again.

He was only curious and spied on her for several weeks from outside her window. She never locked the door and, finally, his boldness lured him inside. His evasive abilities allowed him to slip into her home unnoticed, and he could get a better view from inside and sometimes snag a trophy. Eventually, he made a mistake.

He was crouched outside her bedroom door, watching her get dressed after her shower, when she saw him and screamed. His legs carried him as fast as they could, but bad luck caught up to him. Her father arrived home and chased him down before he could race away.

Yelling ... her father at his father, then his father at him. He conjured up some tears, but they afforded him no relief from either man. His father spanked him then sent him to his room, and he received a second spanking after his mother found his neighbor's panties in his blue jeans pocket.

He opened his eyes and gazed at the ceiling. His sickness only grew worse. When he was young, his father said he was only trying to learn—just being a boy. But as he grew older, he wasn't just an inquisitive child searching for answers about the opposite sex. His parents took him to doctors, but they were no help. Neither were the pills they provided him. Then he started getting more aggressive.

Junior pressed his fingertips into his forehead. His thoughts drifted back to his mid-twenties and a trip he'd taken with his friends to South Padre Island.

After a night of drinking in the bars, one of his friends picked up a girl and brought her back to the house they'd rented for the week. The girl's roommate was interested in him, but he told her he was too drunk and needed to go home.

He recalled lying in bed listening to the giggling in the next room until it turned into dirty talk and moans. After sneaking down the hall, he turned the knob and cracked the door. He ogled the intertwined bodies and admired how his friend skillfully handled the young woman once he was finished with her.

A thumping outside startled him, and the door opened to his stepfather. "I brought you a turkey on whole wheat sandwich and some kind of pasta salad." He offered Junior a brown paper bag. "The damn salad tasted like shit to me, but you'll probably like it."

Harley squinted and pointed to Junior's crotch. "What the hell is that? Have you been playing with yourself again?" Laughter erupted as he grabbed a towel and headed for the bathroom. "Damn, you're a piece of work. I'm gonna grab a shower."

Junior spread the contents of the paper bag out on the four-foot square table. He gobbled the sandwich and pasta down. His stepfather was right, he liked the macaroni salad. The bathroom door creaked, and Harley stepped out, fat and naked. Not the sight one wanted to see right after inhaling their lunch.

"You still freaking out over that detective grilling you?" Harley said, as he pulled on a pair of navy-blue boxers.

"I dunno. Maybe."

"She doesn't know shit." Harley sucked in his gut and shimmied into his camouflage pants.

"What if she looks up my record?"

Harley pulled a long-sleeve T-shirt over his head. "How's she gonna do that? The Wi-Fi's down, and so is the internet." The enormous man dug a Budweiser from the cooler and popped the tab. "Were you peeping at that girl?"

"Well, I—"

Harley chuckled. "That's a yes." He smacked his lips after a swig of his beer and said, "I can't understand why watching is better than doing."

Junior dropped his head and shrugged. "I don't know. I just like to do it."

"I mean, I've tried to help your sorry ass. I took you to the whorehouse, and you still couldn't close the deal." He flipped his hand at his stepson. "Aw, well. To each his own. Get me another beer."

Junior went to the cooler, pulled out another red, white, and blue can, and handed it to him.

"How many more I got in there?"

"Looks like seven."

Harley took a long drink, wiped his mouth, and stared at Junior. "Let me ask you something else. Were you gonna hurt Kayla?"

"No, I was only looking at her. I promise." He cleared his throat. "Now I have a question for you. What if Alan tells CJ about me peeping last year?"

Harley's solemn eyes stared at him. "He'll keep his mouth shut. He has too much to lose if he blabs."

FORTY-ONE

Thursday, September 15
Paradise Cove

Alan closed the apartment door, walked to the window overlooking the cove, and stood beside Debra. "This mess is turning into a total shit show. It gets worse by the hour."

"What are the two law enforcement officers doing?" she asked.

"Sticking their noses into everybody and everything. If this storm doesn't move on soon, there's no telling what they'll uncover." He turned and headed to the shelf where he kept his liquor.

He poured himself a tumbler of Jack Daniels Black and took a big gulp. "I just chewed Victor's ass out. Apparently, he's the one who stole my pistol."

"Really?" Debra asked. "How do you know?"

"Kenny told CJ he saw Victor with it before tossing it off the dock by the footbridge."

"Why the hell would he do that?"

"I'm not sure. He, of course, denies it, but I can tell he's lying." He added some more brown liquid to his glass and took another sip.

"You've been good to that one. I'm not sure why Victor would betray you."

"Yeah, I know. Victor's not stable and tends to go off the rails. He just got into a fight with Kenny and broke his nose."

"I'm not surprised. Everyone's losing it with what's happening and being locked in together."

Alan pushed a brown recliner closer to the window and dropped into it. He scanned the horizon and the black clouds building in the distance. A jagged flash of light crossed the sky, followed by a low rumble rattling the blinds. The storm was about to erupt again.

Debra climbed into his lap and kissed him on the forehead. "I suppose we had to know our secrets would spill out one day. The key is, what do we do about it?"

He rubbed his chin as sleet started bouncing off the glass, and the rain picked up. "That damn body floating up started all this mess."

"Do you think the detective has figured everything out yet and knows what you've done?"

"Nah, not yet, but she's a crafty one. Her eyes are always scanning, searching, and probing for answers."

"You need to play nice and make sure you're kept up to date on the investigation."

Alan stirred the ice cubes in his glass with his finger. "I'm trying, but it's difficult since they suspect me. Have they talked to you anymore?"

"No. We've spoken only once, and I told them I didn't know anything about who might murder anyone. I told them we've never had any problems."

"Did they ask about Chantelle?"

"Yeah, I told them she ran off. I acted clueless about any drowning or murder."

He groaned. "Unfortunately, they know now that she didn't just run off, which has made us both liars. I can't be certain, but I'm pretty sure Walter told them."

"Yet another one you've protected. Asshole."

Debra slid off his lap and headed toward their mini kitchen. She pulled out a bag of Tostitos and poured some cheese dip into a bowl. As she crunched on a chip, she asked, "Are you gonna be able to control this situation?"

Alan exhaled and took another gulp of his drink. He'd wondered the same thing himself. In the past, he'd always managed their secrets. But having a guest, a detective no less, find two dead bodies in the middle of this massive storm had thrown him off his game.

"Did you hear me?"

"Yeah, yeah. I'm not sure how to answer."

If only he had found the bodies, he could have covered up the murders before any guests got involved. Now, he could only deflect things and hope the weather broke soon. Once that happened, he could get the guests on their way home and deal with his cousin at the Ketchikan Police Department about the two dead women.

He regretted adding two weeks to the end of the season. It had been nothing but trouble, but he needed the money. His expenses for running the lodge were larger than he expected. The prior owner hadn't exactly lied, but he'd been far from forthcoming. Now, he had this tangled mess to unravel and this fucking storm. Both would be costly.

Debra sat in a chair next to him and offered him a snack. He shook his head and sipped more of his drink.

"I'll leave this here in case you change your mind," she said. "I'm going to take a shower. I told Bev I'd help her with dinner."

He nodded. "Good. It's come up that you've been a little scarce around the lodge. We need to put on a brave face and show we're not rattled."

His eyes followed her as she left the room. Another sudden flash drew his attention back to the window. He downed the last of his whiskey, reclined the chair, and closed his eyes.

The rumbling grew louder, and his mind went back to another time that the sky bellowed. It was the night he was with Chantelle in her cabin. He'd known he was in trouble the first time she stepped off the floatplane, and his insides quivered. She was stunningly beautiful with an infectious smile.

Debra had picked up on the fact that he lusted after the young woman. She read him the riot act that night and threatened him. "You better leave her alone, or I'll cut your nuts off." He loved his wife but often wondered what it would be like to be single, free to roam without her lurking in the shadows.

Throughout the season, he was strong and fought his urges. It had been no easy feat, especially the day he took the crew on the inner tubes behind the boat—play day, as the staff called it. Chantelle opted to sunbathe instead.

A shiver ran down his body as he recalled the black bikini she wore under her cutoff shorts and a white T-shirt. She peeled off the outer layer, and he almost lost control of the boat and himself. Debra had stayed at the lodge, allowing him to relish the view and get his cheap thrills when the young woman helped him drive.

That night, he lay in bed beside his snoring wife and pondered whether Chantelle was young and naïve or if she wanted him. He had to know, so he devised a ruse to do one-on-one performance reviews the last week of the season. *I'll meet each of you in your cabin and go over how you did this year.*

He slogged through the exercise with everyone, saving Chantelle for last. He arrived late and sat beside her in her cabin. Her honey-brown eyes sparkled as she stared at him. The apricot scent of her newly washed, long black hair intoxicated him more than the whiskey he'd consumed earlier.

The first time he pressed his lips to hers, she flinched but didn't reject him. As he pushed for more, she told him no and leaned away. He wrapped his arms around her and tried to convince her it was okay, but she squirmed from his grasp. When he grabbed her arm, the little bitch slapped him and ran outside.

"Why are you breathing so hard?" Debra asked, startling him.

"Uh, I was thinking about how I was gonna get out of this mess." He yanked the lever, sat upright, and popped up out of the chair. "This stress is killing me."

Her narrow eyes glared at him. "You were moaning."

Alan ran his fingers through his graying black hair. "I must have dozed off and was having a nightmare," he said as his thoughts screamed, *she knows you're lying.* He didn't need to hear her shit about his fantasies right now.

He pulled her to him, hugged her, and brushed his lips against her cheek. "Listen, we've got a few minutes before we're needed downstairs. Let's go to the back."

She tightened her fingers against his back as he pulled her head back and nibbled on her neck. "Mmm, I'd like that," she whispered.

He took her hand and started for the bedroom when a knock stopped them. "Hang on, sweetheart."

Bev stood in the doorway with her lips pinched together. "Sorry to bother you, but I have a problem."

"What's up?" Alan asked.

"I can't prepare dinner," she said. "The gas isn't working. I planned to bake ling cod, but I'm dead in the water without the oven."

"Hmm, it should be. The service recently filled the tanks."

He told Debra he needed to run, and followed Bev down the stairs.

FORTY-TWO

Thursday, September 15
Paradise Cove

The sky continued its steady drizzle as Ben and CJ entered the dining room. The rollers were still rocking the lodge, and menacing clouds loomed in the distance. Slowly, the coal black wall inched closer. Rumbles grew louder and the flashes brighter.

The guests filling the room created a low buzz. The brief improvement in the weather, albeit soon to be gone, translated to everyone's mood. Ben and CJ joined their usual tablemates, and Luka jumped up and hugged her.

"Did you take a nap, Miss CJ?" Luka asked.

"A short one. How 'bout you?"

He nodded as he climbed back into the chair.

They talked about the storm and if it was gone. Everyone tried to be optimistic, although the gloom on the horizon told them there was more to come. Even Jamie's spirits were better. She smiled when Luka asked if she would play Go Fish with him and CJ after eating.

Evan sat across the room beside Leo and seemed strangely happy for someone who'd lost their spouse only a few days ago. CJ gazed at Junior, sitting with his head down beside his stepfather. Harley's eyes were bloodshot, and he slurred his words while telling a tall tale about a two-hundred-pound halibut he caught last season.

"Excuse me, everyone," Alan said as he entered the room. "I'm sure we're all pleased that the weather is better. I have nothing new to report since I don't have communications, but we can hope the worst is behind us." He motioned to Bev, who was standing behind the counter. "I do have some unfortunate news."

Before he could continue, Harley piped up, "What's it now?"

Alan glared at him before continuing after clearing his throat. "As I was about to say, Bev could not cook a proper dinner for you tonight. We're having a problem with our gas system."

The room broke into grumbles and groans, and the concerned faces reappeared.

"What's the issue?" Rory asked.

Alan furrowed his brow. "Well, to be honest, I'm not sure. I've checked it but we seem to have had a leak."

"So, now we can't even eat," Harley said, shaking his head. "What the fuck else is gonna happen?"

With a forced smile, Alan mentioned, "We still have plenty of food, but it'll be limited to cold cuts and so on. Don't worry. No one will starve. Right, Bev?"

She spread her arms and smiled. "We'll have lots to eat, and I could still make a yummy ice cream pie for dessert. I'll have a delicious stew for you tomorrow night as I have a couple of crock pots and a portable generator I can use now that I know I need to improvise."

Ben glanced at CJ and pursed his lips. They both knew there was more to the story than their host had admitted. He leaned to her and whispered, "We need to see what really happened."

Stephanie, Ryleigh, and Kenny delivered platters to the tables and began retrieving drinks. Ryleigh steered clear of Evan, but he asked her how Kayla was feeling from across the table. She lost it and threw a glass of water at him.

"You're an asshole! You raped her, so how do you think she's feeling?"

Before she could hit him with the pitcher she had in her other hand, Ben jumped up and grabbed her. Ryleigh screamed and kicked, but he lifted her off the ground until she stopped fighting him.

"Take it easy, Ryleigh," he whispered in her ear. "He's not worth it."

Tears erupted as she hung her head. Ben eased her to the floor as Bev ran to her. The older woman wrapped her arm around Ryleigh and led her out the back door toward the crew quarters.

"I don't know what I said to upset the poor girl," Evan said as every guest stared at him.

"Shut up, asshole!" Stephanie snapped.

"Okay, everyone needs to calm down," Alan said. "Kenny, please take Steph to the back, and I'll have Debra serve the dessert." He nodded, took Stephanie's hand, and hurried out the door.

Ben and CJ waited until everyone resumed eating and walked over to Alan.

"Everyone's nerves are frayed," said Alan. "Sorry for the disruption."

"Yeah, adding a rape to two murders is unsettling," CJ said, smirking.

Alan frowned at her as he crossed his arms.

"We wanna look at the gas tanks," Ben said.

Alan narrowed his eyes. "Why? I told you what happened. The tanks leaked."

"The reason it happened is what interests me," Ben said.

"Suit yourself." The owner turned, and they followed him out the back door and down the walkway to the gas storage area.

Walter was lying on his back using a wrench, as Victor, Simon, and Cal watched him.

"Walter, what caused the leak?" CJ asked.

"Someone tampered with the valve," Walter replied.

"Who the hell would do that?" Harley asked, as he and Junior joined the group.

"Why are you guys out here?" Alan asked in a raised voice. "We don't need the whole damn lodge out here gawking while Walter works."

Harley jabbed his finger at him. "I have a right to know what's going on!"

Ben squatted beside Walter. "Is there any way to fix the problem?"

The maintenance man peered up at him. "Not without some parts, and I ain't got them. We're stuck until I can retrieve what I need from Ketchikan. Plus, the gas is gone." He pointed to a metal collar. "Whoever did this closed the valve to stop the gas flow and cut this piece, probably with a hacksaw. Once this is done, you can turn the knob back open, and poof, the gas leaks out."

He almost had to laugh. Hidden under this logical conversation was fear, panic, and uncomfortableness. How could someone commit this act without being noticed? Right smack under their damn noses.

It had proved to be a simple task. He'd done it in less than five minutes while everyone was at breakfast. As soon as he knew the morning cooking was done, he closed the valve and clipped the collar. What surprised him was how fast the tanks drained themselves.

His eyes scanned the group standing in the spitting rain—seven other men and the pain-in-the-ass detective, the niece of his arch nemesis. Perhaps she wasn't as bright as he thought, and not like her uncle who was a match for his skills.

He glanced at the treetops on the mountain behind the lodge. They'd stopped swaying and only shivered in the mild breeze. The drizzle gave way to a mist. However, the light gray sky would soon turn black, but not because of nightfall.

According to the weather report on the handheld radio he had hidden under the floorboards in his cabin, a massive surprise was coming. His body tingled. Terror would arrive with it.

FORTY-THREE

Thursday, September 15
Paradise Cove

Ben and CJ returned to the dining room to find that most guests had returned to their cabins. They joined Noah and Jamie in the chairs by the broad picture window.

"Wow, everyone cleared out pretty fast," CJ said. "I can't believe that Luka passed on playing cards."

"Yeah," Noah said. "The outburst with Evan dampened the mood, and Rory convinced his son they would play in the room."

Jamie smiled and said, "I told the little guy I'd join them soon." She gazed through the glass. "Do you think those black clouds are coming here?"

"It's tough to tell," Ben said. "The wind direction's hard to read since it's dropped, but I guess it will."

"Will those big waves come back?" Jamie asked, as her eyes glistened under the overhead track lights.

"Maybe, but we should be fine. Hopefully, we'll just get more rain, and it'll blow through," Ben replied.

Before she left with her husband, Jamie pulled CJ aside and thanked her for her help earlier. She couldn't explain why, but telling CJ about her secrets had relieved her. After all these years, she'd also finally told Noah. They hugged, and then all four returned to their cabins.

———

CJ pushed her hood back and turned to Ben. "I'm not sure Jamie caught it, but you didn't sound too convincing about the weather. You think we're gonna get hit with another bad storm, don't you?"

"I attempted to reassure her, but you're right, we're gonna be pounded again. This may be the worst part yet."

She stared at the page as he drew a sketch and explained what he'd seen on the radar before he lost his connection to the app. The drawings showed a series of storms, broken with periods of relative calm. She pointed to the last item he'd drawn. "What does that mean?"

Ben cleared his throat and chewed on his lip. "I may be mistaken since the information is old, but if not, we'll get one last whopper before the storm departs for good."

She slowly nodded. They discussed what else they could do to protect the guests and crew. The weather only added to the fears about the murderer among them. Her stomach quivered as she tried to convince herself it would all be okay.

"Are you all right?" Ben asked.

"Not really, but no one is, so I'll deal with it."

Pulling her to him, he wrapped her in his arms. "Why don't you lay down for a minute? You've not had much sleep. I can keep watch."

"No. I wanna go over our notes again. It's frustrating not being able to nail down our perp." She turned and went into the bathroom.

A low rumbling outside grew louder, and Ben peered out the window. Suddenly, he yanked the door open and raced out. "Oh, shit!"

CJ heard him and hustled out the door behind him. He stood on the end of the dock, staring at Harley and his stepson in one of the Jetcraft behind the lodge. Ben waved him back, but the heavyset man drove toward the narrow passage between the lodge and the shore.

"Harley, turn the damn boat around! You can't leave. The water's too rough!" Ben shouted.

He stayed his course straight ahead. As he neared, Ben grabbed a rope dangling from the side and Harley eased back on the throttle. Ben pulled the craft against the dock and wound the rope around his wrist.,

"Let go, damnit! Junior and I are outta here. I ain't waiting until we're both murdered."

"I'm telling you, this boat cannot stand the waves out there. It'll capsize!" Ben yelled.

CJ's heart rate ramped up at the word capsize, and the vision of Grannie's strained face as she issued her warning came flooding back. *Waves ... an overturned boat ... Ben struggling in the water ... a dead body ...*

Harley continued to argue. He yelled that being out on the water was a lower risk than sitting on his ass in the lodge. "You better let go of that fucking rope!"

Ben kept trying to persuade him he needed a vessel at least three times larger to have a chance. "The seas will be impassable once you leave the cove."

Harley's glossy eyes gazed at the horizon. "The damn weather's better. I can make it," he said, slurring.

Pointing at the looming black wall, Ben said, "What the hell do you think that is? It's a monster coming straight at us. You might as well be in a dinghy."

The two men argued back and forth until CJ grabbed her fiancé's arm. "Let his stupid ass go. If he wants to commit suicide, let him," she huffed.

"I can't do that," Ben said as he shook his head. "I'd basically be murdering him. He's drunk and not thinking clearly." He turned back to the red-faced man. "Come on now. Let's turn this thing around. Please."

Victor and Cal thumped up behind Ben and CJ and yelled at Harley to return the boat to the slip. The older man's eyes darted between them. He smirked and then jammed the throttle forward, causing the craft to lurch.

The force yanked Ben off the walkway, causing his head to slam into one of the wooden dock posts.

"Ben!" CJ screamed as she leaped into the ice-cold water.

Harley's boat smashed into the neighboring posts before he backed it up and resumed his path out of the cove.

Cal splashed in behind CJ and fought to get Ben's head above water. Within seconds, he was treading, holding Ben. Victor gave up trying to get Harley to return, dropped to his stomach, grabbed CJ's water-logged raincoat, and dragged her to safety.

"Victor, please get Ben," CJ said.

Rory appeared, and with his help, they laid Ben on his back on the dock. Victor made sure he was breathing and stared at the large bump on Ben's forehead.

"We need Leo," Cal said as he raced down the walkway.

CJ sprawled herself across Ben's chest as her tears dripped, pleading with God not to take away the man she loved. She offered anything if he'd be okay.

"Shit!" Victor said. "Those two idiots are in the water." He pointed to the hull of the upside-down boat fifty yards from the lodge. Harley and his stepson's arms thrashed as they bobbed like two orange corks with the rollers.

"At least they had on their life jackets. As soon as we get Ben settled inside, I'll get the larger boat and go get those two dumbasses," Victor said. "I have half a mind to let them stay out there until they float back."

"You wanna move him now?" Rory asked.

"Not until Leo examines him. I don't think he broke anything, but we need to be sure it's safe to move him again." Victor pointed toward the back of the lodge. "How 'bout you go get Walter, so we have more help."

Victor put his hands on his knees and leaned down. He tried to console CJ as she shivered intensely, but she refused to leave her fiancé. His eyes caught movement at the other end of the walkway. "Here comes Cal with the doc."

FORTY-FOUR

Thursday, September 15
Paradise Cove

CJ tenderly ran her fingertips across Ben's forehead as she lay beside him. She avoided the dark red, soon-to-be-black lump above his right eye. "Can I get you some more water?"

"I'm good for now," he said in a low groggy tone. "I don't wanna have to pee again." He winced as he struggled to adjust himself on the pillows under his head.

"Okay, let me know when you change your mind, and I'll get it for you," she said, brushing her lips on his temple. "You're supposed to rest and not do a lot of moving around."

Leo had examined Ben after the crew helped her get him into the cabin. Based on his observations, he believed Ben had a borderline moderate head injury. It would likely be minor except for the brief loss of consciousness. In layman's terms, it was a concussion. He told them headaches, dizziness, and sensitivity to noise and light were common. If Ben's condition grew worse, nausea and a more significant disorientation might appear.

Leo left after handing CJ a list of handwritten notes—not overly legible—and a bottle of Tylenol. His instructions were to come get him if any new symptoms developed.

The pecking of ice crystals intermittently sounded on the rattling windows as the monster, as Ben called it, approached. The roaring wind caused the cabin to rock, creak, and groan.

CJ fixed her eyes on the hanging light above the table as it swayed. "The storm's getting bad again." *When is this gonna end?*

"Do you think we should make some rounds and make sure everyone is secure?" he asked.

"I think everyone's okay. Besides, you're not going anywhere until you're steadier on your feet. You damn near fell going to the bathroom."

She flicked off the light beside the bed, leaving the room faintly lit by the bathroom light. Leo had advised her that Ben should remain awake for a while so she could monitor him. "Let him rest, but not totally," is what he'd said. *Whatever the hell that means,* she thought.

CJ was happy they had a doctor on the premises, but wondered how much he knew about head injuries. His answers to some of her questions had seemed nonchalant. *What if Ben has internal bleeding?*

Her mind drifted to Grannie's warning, and a shiver ran through her. She hoped the images that flashed before when she held the old woman's hands were past them. Her breath caught when she thought about how close they'd come to Ben being the dead body in the water.

Even though Ben lay right beside her, a sudden loneliness gripped her. He couldn't help ensure people's safety or uncover the identity of the three young women's killer any time soon. Like so many times before, she was now on her own. It rested on her to safeguard both of them and everyone else. *Maybe finding the killer can wait until help arrives.*

Water splashing outside drew her to the window. It was pitch black, so she used the flashlight, and her heart skipped a beat. Waves of water were crashing over the boat slip out front and sloshing against the wall. The angry wind blowing straight at them, and the high tide meant more water and more danger.

She stepped closer, scanning down the walkway, and her foot squished on the carpet. *Shit! We've got water coming in around the door.*

She sprang backward when a chunk of the wooden boat slip slammed against the window, and the glass shattered. "Ben, we gotta get you up and out of here!"

Doing her best to remain calm as the wind and rain roared into the cabin, she slid his rain boots on and helped him wobble to his feet. He took two steps and collapsed against her, knocking them both to the wet floor.

The room heaved and groaned as a massive wave surged. A loud crack erupted and a gap between the walls in the corner appeared. *What if this whole place slides into the water? Ben can't walk, much less swim.*

"Fuck! This damn add-on room is breaking away." She slipped her hands under Ben's armpits and dragged him back to his feet, only to have him fall again. Her eyes stared at the water pouring down the wall and flooding the floor. "Stay here, Ben. We need help."

She scrambled from underneath him, ran to the door, and opened it to find a chaos of wooden posts and planks. Drawing a deep breath, she climbed through the open window, cutting her palm on a jagged piece of glass. Racing three doors down, she pounded on the door until Rory appeared.

"Our cabin is about to break away," CJ said as she pointed to the end of the walkway. "I need help to get Ben out."

Rory and Noah chased her back, and working together, they got Ben on his feet. Getting him through the window was challenging, but after two failed attempts, they scurried down the walkway and into cabin ten.

"Let's see that hand," Rory said.

CJ dropped a duffle bag to the floor with some of her and Ben's clothes, her note pad, and camera, and lifted her hand as blood dripped to the floor.

"You need a couple of stitches." He told Noah to wrap her hand in a towel as he opened the door to a blast of wind and fought his way to Leo in cabin one.

Minutes later, Leo used a needle and thread from an emergency kit to put six stitches along the edge of CJ's hand just above the little finger as she gritted her teeth. "I'm sorry. I know this hurts, but all I have to numb your hand is the spray, and it's not very effective," he said.

"I'm good. Just do it."

Leo had just finished wrapping her hand with gauze when the lights suddenly flickered and darkness engulfed the entire lodge. The only light came from the periodic flashes across the sky. The power had vanished, making it impossible to discern what or who was approaching.

———

CJ and Rory returned to the cabin after investigating the cause of the power outage. Walter showed them how someone had sabotaged the two generators serving the lodge. Not only was there no communication and no gas, but now there was no electricity.

CJ shook the water from her jacket and approached Ben, who was asleep on the queen bed. "How's he doing?" she asked Jamie.

"He's still disorientated and has a headache. Doc told me it was okay for him to sleep, so I let him."

Dropping to a knee beside him, CJ brushed her fingertips along his chin. Her chest was tight, as if someone had turned the handle on a vise and clamped down.

"What should we do?" Jamie asked. "I'm afraid the waves are gonna come in here with us."

CJ stared at Ben as her new roommates chatted behind her. She was lost in her thoughts about the one thing that now concerned her. How was she to care for Ben? When Rory touched her shoulder, she rejoined reality.

"Do you think everyone needs to go onshore?" he asked.

"Uh, no. Moving a group of over thirty in the dark is too dangerous. Besides, the mountain will be too treacherous, with no protection. I'm sure there's water everywhere and there may be mudslides."

He cleared his throat. "We can't stay here in the cabin. The boat slips are all breaking apart, and it's only a matter of time before we don't have a way to leave. Plus, I assume more windows are gonna get busted."

She stood and rubbed her face with both hands. Walking to the window, she pulled back the curtains. Sheets of water were slamming against the glass. *It's getting worse, not better.* Without turning, she said, "Okay, let's go to the main dining room. It's safer there, and we can brace the tables against the picture window in case it shatters."

Blowing out a long breath, she turned and stared at Rory. "I'll need help. We gotta move Ben, as he can't walk." She wanted to say to hell with them, but instead she said, "After he's settled, we'll need to go door-to-door and get the others."

He nodded and motioned to Noah. "We can carry Ben, and you can help Jamie and Luka."

CJ went to the bed and tenderly kissed Ben on the cheek. "Honey, we need to move to the main lodge. It's not safe here."

His eyes fluttered open and blinked, trying to focus. He groaned as he tried to sit up with her help, but collapsed backward.

"Let the guys carry you," she said.

The two men slid Ben to the edge of the bed and got him to his feet. After getting his raincoat on, they picked him up.

"We need to walk as close to the lodge as we can," Rory said as he glanced at Noah. "Brace your shoulder on the wall as you go."

CJ turned the knob, and the wind slammed the door against the wall, and a deluge of water hit her. Her heart raced. Rory and Noah moved down the walkway. CJ carried Luka as Jamie clung to her, crying hysterically. They entered the den with slow movements and flickering flashlights and carefully positioned Ben on one of the couches.

"This glass is thicker, so it should hold up better," Rory said, as he pointed to the picture window. "Plus, there's no boat slips in front of it. I don't think the patio will break apart."

He crossed the room to where CJ sat with Ben. "Whaddya think? Should we move the tables?"

She scanned the window with her flashlight. "No. Let's leave them. If we lose the window, we'll move to the crew quarters. It'll be cramped but offers more safety as it's somewhat blocked from the wind."

Realizing he was waiting for her to decide the next steps, she cleared her throat. "Let's grab some trash bags and get everyone else. They can throw their towels, blankets, and flashlights in the bags to keep them dry. We'll have to make do without mattresses."

By midnight, the den and dining area was full of guests. Three more cabin windows had broken from the flying debris, so while cramped together, everyone remained safe.

CJ climbed the stairs behind the beam of her flashlight and banged on the door of the owner's apartment. Two minutes passed before the latch clicked and Alan appeared.

"Hey, I was just about to come down," he said.

She pursed her lips. "I wanted you to know we've moved all the guests into the main area. The cabins aren't safe. We've lost four windows so far from flying debris. You need to go check on the crew. The generators are gone, and Walter told me he can't fix them until he has the right parts. Someone sabotaged them."

Alan squinted. "I was asleep and all the racket woke me up. That's when I realized the power was out. I assumed the weather caused it."

She glared at him. *Is he this clueless or just does not give a shit?* "And you'll check on the crew? I'm staying with Ben. You may not know this, but Harley attempted to leave in one of the boats, and Ben got injured."

"Uh, I didn't know that. Where's the boat?"

"Really? That's what you're worried about?" she asked, enraged.

"Well, um, no. I was talking about Harley."

Liar! "He and Junior flipped the damn Jetcraft, but Victor got them out. They're downstairs." She stared at him and asked him about checking on the crew in the back again.

"Do you think it's necessary to check on the crew now, or is it okay to do it first thing in the morning?"

"I'd do it now, Alan," she said sharply. "Walter said the buildings weren't damaged yet, and he's moved everyone into the main room, but you're the one who's responsible." She waited for a response that never came. "Oh, and one more thing, I busted the lock on the storage closet in the hallway and got the cases of bottled water out. Without power, I assume the pumps won't work so there's no water. Since we also won't have bathrooms, I've told the men to go outside by the covered back area, and we'll have to figure out something for the women once it's daylight." When again, he just stood looking at her, she thought, *No 'that's a good idea, thanks,' or even a 'go fuck yourself.'*

Before turning to go, she asked if he had a mattress she could use for Ben. She wanted to get him into the small room off the den so he could rest. Moving one from the cabins wouldn't be safe since it would act as a sail in the high winds.

"Uh, yeah. I've got an extra double one we can bring down. I'll get it ready if you can send someone to help me."

As she angrily descended the stairs, she told herself she should worry about just Ben and herself. After all, he'd got injured while trying to prevent someone else from killing themselves. She didn't believe Alan when he said he was about to come down. The bastard had answered the door just wearing sweatpants. He'd planned to stay holed up with Debra in his apartment. If the owner didn't care enough to get off his ass, why should she?

PART THREE

THE MAN WITH THE SCAR

FORTY-FIVE

Friday, September 16
Paradise Cove

CJ sat on the floor in the dim light of a battery-powered miniature lantern. Ben lay stretched out on the mattress Alan had sent down. The musty smell of the blanket covering him mixed with the salt lingering in the air from the sea spray and filled her nostrils.

The lodge bobbed as the relentless wind roared, and the waves thundered against the structure. With every massive gust, the building creaked and shuddered as if protesting about being punished.

The sitting room muffled the voices of the other guests in the den. Some sat in chairs or lounged on the floor on pallets they'd made from blankets. At least CJ could keep Ben in a quieter area.

Her heart fluttered. What would she do if the place came apart like their cabin? How would she move Ben? Surely, Rory and Noah would remember that they were tucked away and would come to help. She hoped they would.

CJ pressed her back against the wall and stared blankly at a map of Alaska. *Who would have expected a dream trip with someone you love would turn into such a nightmare?* She had a hollowness in her chest and was exhausted, but couldn't sleep.

An old demon crept into her thoughts—guilt. Despite Grannie's warning, she'd still decided to come here. She bore the responsibility for why they were in this mess and for Ben's injury. As much as she tried to convince herself this wasn't the case, the little voice in her head told her otherwise.

Doctor Greedsy's words echoed in her mind. *What happens when things go awry?* She tried to focus on how things would be after they survived the ordeal. But what if they didn't or if Ben died? Who knows how bad his head injury was? His disorientation had gotten worse. *What if* … She couldn't finish the thought.

She squeezed her eyes shut, trying to will herself to think optimistically, but all she saw was the image of her older sister lying in the hospital bed. Tubes and gadgets surrounded her until she surrendered and joined their parents. Death seemed to follow CJ and take those she loved the most.

Why is the world so cruel? Her job left no room to believe there was anything good in it. She regularly went to Mass and prayed, yet evil still surrounded her. People committed the most heinous acts against each other. *Why?*

She thought of Olivia, Anita, and Chantelle. Three young women had lost their lives here for no apparent reason, except they had met the same deranged person. Solving the case should be high on her list, but she struggled with the motivation to do so. Besides, why should she risk her and Ben's lives when it wasn't her responsibility? And even if she wanted to solve the damn case, she only had limited clues and resources. There was no forensics, technical support, or the ability to complete a simple task like searching online.

She prided herself on her work, but this case seemed way over her head. After all, it wasn't her job … But it was a shitty excuse, and she knew it. Protecting others was part of her. Another wave of guilt swept over her.

CJ picked up the clear bottle with the red and gold emblem she'd taken from the shelf in the den—Smirnoff No. 21 Vodka. Her fingers twisted off the cap, and she lifted it to her nose. The faint odor of alcohol tickled her nostrils. *Maybe I should have a drink to numb this pain.*

She lowered the bottle and peered at it in her shaking hand. This was her test. She could succumb to her old ways of using excess to escape. The choice lay before her … prove Greedsy was right that she wasn't ready to stand on her own or prove the therapist wrong. After a long exhale, she tightened the cap and sat the temptation aside. She stretched out on the floor beside Ben and draped her arm over him. She couldn't give in. He depended on her, and she needed a clear head to remain calm and strong, no matter how overwhelmed she felt.

The movement of the door caught her attention. Marie peeked in through the crack, her face a shadow in the faint light.

"CJ, is everything okay?" Marie whispered.

"Uh, yes. Well, I think so."

The older woman entered and sat down beside her. "You need to eat something." Her wrinkled hands offered her a plate. "I made you a turkey sandwich. I'll grab you a bottle of water."

Accepting the food, CJ said, "I'm not too hungry. I wanted to make sure Ben was drinking, so I have some water."

"How's he doing?"

CJ's bottom lip trembled as she fought not to cry. "I'm not sure. Initially, he had a bad headache and felt dizzy, but recently, he's become disoriented. He can't walk on his own."

"The rest will help. I'm pleased you have this spot away from the others." Marie reached out and caressed her cheek. "He'll be okay."

Looking at Ben, CJ said, "I keep telling myself that, but then my mind goes elsewhere. What if …" She fell against Marie's shoulder and lost her battle of holding back her tears.

Marie smiled as she wiped her eyes after five minutes of bawling. "How about you take a break and I look after Ben? It would be good for you to stretch your legs."

"Thanks, but I should care for him. He'll wake up any minute and might need something."

"Did you forget I was a nurse? Taking care of people is what I do." Marie patted her arm and pointed toward the door. "Now, go and take a break." She handed her the plate with the untouched sandwich. "You can stand at the counter in the back and eat."

CJ nodded gently. "Okay. By the way, do you know what time it is? I turned off my cell phone to save the battery, and Ben's watch is under the blanket."

"It's almost four-thirty. It'll be daylight in a couple of hours."

She stood and told Marie she'd be back soon.

———

CJ stood at the kitchen counter behind the dining room, staring at the blackness. She nibbled a few bites of her sandwich and drank a bottle of water.

Behind her, most guests were sleeping or, more accurately, fitfully dozing. The constant shaking of the lodge prevented anyone from relaxing. More than once, cries of alarm erupted when a tremendous gust rattled the picture window.

CJ turned and surveyed the room, lit by three battery-powered lanterns in the corners. She watched Luka curled up on Jamie's lap in a two-seater loveseat. Neither had their eyes closed, and both flinched every time the room shuddered. Jamie offered her a tight smile.

The tension in the young woman's face sent a stabbing pain through her. CJ had almost convinced herself she was right not to help any further with identifying the murderer, as she had been focused on the guests as generic, faceless people. *I need to watch mine and Ben's backs and let everyone fend for themselves.* But among the assholes were some truly exceptional individuals. Her stomach flip-flopped, and she dropped her sandwich in the trash bin. She returned to gazing out the window.

The first signs of daylight approached, and she could make out the shape of the crew quarters down the walkway. *Did Alan make sure they were safe?* Like the guests, it was difficult to not feel a sense of concern for them.

"Miss CJ," a small voice said behind her. She turned to find Luka standing, staring up at her.

She squatted, and he threw himself against her.

"I'm trying not to be, but I'm scared," he said as his voice cracked.

She squeezed him and told him it would be okay. The storm would leave soon, and someone would come to rescue them.

"But what if the bad man gets me?"

CJ leaned back and looked at him. Tears ran down his cheeks, and his bottom lip quivered. "He won't get you. You're safe in here."

"But he might be in here with us."

Her chest throbbed. "Your daddy won't let anyone hurt you."

He gripped her tighter and said, "But he's not a policeman like you. Will you make sure no one hurts me?"

His words hit the mark, and the fog in her brain lifted for some odd reason. She had to ignore the distractions, discomforts, and negative thoughts. "I promise I won't let anyone harm you."

"My daddy, too? Oh, and Miss Jamie. She tries not to cry around me, but I can tell she's scared like me."

CJ nodded and gave him a warm smile. "No one else will get hurt."

"Will you make sure someone will come help us?"

"I will."

Luka hugged her and told her he would go tell Jamie that she promised everything would be okay.

Her eyes followed him, and she spurred herself to fulfill her promise. She had to protect Ben and the others and get help here. And, until it arrived, she had to find the killer among them. She scanned the room and then gazed toward the back. *Whoever and wherever you are, I'm gonna find you.*

FORTY-SIX

Friday, September 16
Paradise Cove

"Which one of you is a cold-blooded killer?" CJ whispered as she flipped through her scribbled notes she'd saved in the bag she brought from her room. She glanced at Ben, who was still sleeping beside her in the sitting room. Her thoughts bounced between solving the case and being concerned for him.

Returning her attention to her pad, she told herself, *Let's start fresh from the beginning.*

Whoever killed the three women was the same.

The perp was at the lodge for the last two years.

Alan, Walter, Victor, Simon, and Cal fit the time period, but she crossed Walter and Simon off. She and Ben had cleared them. So, for the crew, she was left with Alan, Victor, and Cal.

Wait! She flipped the sheets on her pad. There was something else Walter had mentioned. Kenny was here fishing in the final week of last year. That's the week Chantelle died. Her pulse picked up. *Why did he tell me this was his first year? Damnit!*

She added his name to the list and an asterisk with a question mark. Her gut told her he wasn't the murderer, and she slowly drew a line through his name.

For the guests, she scribbled down Harley, Junior, Rory, Leo, and the two men in cabin five for the guests who matched the timeframe. But three of the men were over seventy and not likely to be able to subdue the victims. That left three guests as possible culprits: Harley, Junior, and Rory.

It can't be Rory, can it? Would he leave his son alone while he chased down a young woman? In all the chaos, it occurred to her she hadn't interviewed him. She stared at the six names. *Okay, let's calm down. You gotta work through it.*

Ben stirred, and she waited for him to wake up. Instead, he rolled over and went still again. It would be a boost if he woke up, and his mind was clear. Not only for the sake of his health, but for her mental state. Plus, he could help her sort out this mess. The fingers of loneliness clawed at her, so she took a break. She stood and crept through the door.

"Rory," she said as he glanced up at her. She motioned him over and held out her pad. "Can you help me with something, please?"

"Sure. Whatcha need?"

"Can you remember the guests who were here the final week of last season?"

He took the pad, furrowed his brow, and scanned the room. She watched as he used his left hand to jot down the names she already had. Her tension eased a little. *Rory's not right-handed. He can't be the killer.*

"By the way, CJ," Rory said. "Thanks for being so patient and kind with Luka. My wife and I got divorced last year, and it's been really tough for him. It's why I brought him with me."

"No problem. He's a great kid." CJ thanked him, went to the kitchen, and grabbed two bottles of water. She stood at the back window as the sky grew brighter. Daylight was coming.

The raging wind became a breeze, and the rain was now a drizzle. Debris littered the back walkway—boards, pieces of the roof, and trash. Several of the boats had broken free and sat mangled against the shore.

She hustled to the front window. The walkway was gone, but the deck in front of the dining room remained. Despite a few planks being torn away, it had survived the wind's onslaught. As she surveyed the horizon, a surge of adrenaline went through her. The clouds, once black, were now a light gray. The rollers continued to rock the building but were not as high.

CJ twisted the knob and entered the sitting room. Ben remained asleep on his side. Sighing, she took her place on the floor next to him. She flipped to the sheet where she'd written her list and crossed off Rory. *Minor progress, but it's better than nothing*, she thought.

After reviewing her notes again and rehashing conversations, she made two groups. Those who were her primary suspects and those secondary. *If only we knew whose blood was on the floor in the storage room and had DNA.*

Her top three candidates for the murderer were Alan, Victor, and Junior. The others seemed less likely to her for various reasons. She wrote the first name on a clean sheet.

Alan.

The owner of the lodge was hiding something. He'd lied about Chantelle's death and paid off her parents, although he'd argue it was out of compassion for their loss. *Yeah, right.*

He'd made an effort to divert attention from the actual cause of Olivia's death, even though it was evident she had not drowned. Hell, his first response to Anita's death was "the poor thing drowned." And then there was the gun he said he never had until Victor stole it.

She recalled what Walter told her. Debra caught him with one of the female crew the first year they owned the place. Could Alan have propositioned the others and killed them when they rejected him? As special forces, he was capable and skilled with a knife. But would he sabotage his own lodge?

Her fingers pinched the bridge of her nose and then rubbed her temples. CJ exhaled and wrote a second name.

Victor.

The licensed boat captain was more of a mystery. If Kenny was right, he'd stolen a Glock and thrown it in the water, but the victims weren't killed using a gun. Victor was delusional about women and appeared to have some sort of grudge against them, but would he kill over it? Perhaps he was an incel—involuntarily celibate with resentment of those who aren't. He definitely appeared hostile at times. Could Victor have made moves on the women and lost it when they rejected him? Like Alan, he could have committed the crimes.

She shivered as she recalled how he leered at her while she watched the crew clean their fish. She wrote down one more name.

Junior.

She couldn't get past his unusual behaviors and the fact Walter had caught him peeping at Kayla. When she spoke to him, he was evasive and nervous. Something lingered in the air, but what was it?

CJ had two names left on her list: Harley and Cal. Harley because he'd been drunk all week and was a hothead. And Cal, due to her lack of knowledge about him. He was cooperative and appeared forthcoming when they spoke, but something was off when she interviewed him. His body language was guarded, and his eyes never held contact with hers.

The key was finding which of the five people was the perp without Ben. She needed help, but who could she trust? After checking to ensure Ben was breathing for about the tenth time, she slipped out of the room.

"Listen, I need some help," she said to Rory after pulling him into the corner. "Without Ben, I wanted to see if you would step in?"

"Uh, I guess," he said, "but I have Luka to consider."

"Understood. If you're willing, we can ask Jamie to watch him. I'll need Marie's help with Ben."

He chewed on his lip and then nodded. "Okay, what do you need?"

She leaned close and said, "I need you to keep a close eye on Junior. If he leaves this room, follow him."

"Okay," he said, nodding. "That sounds easy enough."

She pointed toward the outside. "The storm ripped off the walkway to his cabin, so he can only go out back."

"What am I watching for?"

"Just where he goes. Say near the storage shed or around any of the women."

After she had got Rory onboard, she approached Marie and asked, "Would you help me again with Ben? I may need to step out occasionally."

"Absolutely," the older woman said. "I'd be happy to. It'll give me a much-needed distraction."

CJ thanked her, returned to the back kitchen window, and stared at the dense green foliage on the mountain as the lights came up. Several trees had been uprooted and lay haphazardly. The pounding rain had created a wide gully with water gushing into the cove, turning the surface a dark brown.

All I need to do now is figure out how to keep an eye on Alan and Victor at the same time.

"I think our storm may be over," Alan said, startling her when he approached from behind.

"Uh, I hope so," she said. "Have you gone out back to see how the crew fared last night?"

He scowled. "Not yet. It's still early, and Debra and I just woke up."

Must be nice to sleep through a storm and not worry about thirty other people, she thought. She pointed out the window. "The buildings look okay. There's a lot of clutter from the front walkway and roof."

He frowned and shook his head. "Yeah, I know. The damn storm's gonna cost me a fortune. It's the end of the season, and the cost to get a crew in here will be at least double." He exhaled before he asked, "How's Ben doing?"

"He's asleep, so I'm not sure." She forced a smile. "Speaking of that, I need to go check on him." She wheeled around and headed to the sitting room. Her thoughts screamed one word … *Asshole!*

CHAPTER

FORTY-SEVEN

Friday, September 16
Paradise Cove

CJ closed the sitting-room door and entered the den area. The fragrance of dirty socks and body odor almost gagged her. The area was filled with empty water bottles, paper plates, and trash.

She cleared her throat, drawing attention to herself. "Since it's stopped raining and not as windy, how 'bout we open the front and back doors? Let's get some fresh air in here. Jeez, this place stinks."

Rory seconded her motion, and soon cool, crisp air permeated the space. The guest's faces were strained, and everyone was bleary-eyed. The lack of sleep and the stress of the situation had taken its toll. CJ went to the kitchen and grabbed a trash bag to collect the litter. As she turned, Luka met her.

"Can I help?" he asked. "I'm a good picker-upper."

"Sure," she said, smiling. After handing Luka the bag, she suggested to the room that they fold and put away the blankets until the evening.

"Who the fuck made you the boss?" Harley growled. "I may want to take a nap—"

"Shut up, Harley!" Rory said, glaring at him.

The older man's eyes narrowed, but he kept quiet.

"Has anyone seen Alan?" CJ asked. "Did he go out back?"

"He went back upstairs," Rory said.

"Damnit! I asked him to check on the others," CJ said as she shook her head. *The damn guy is worthless.* She started for the back door when Noah stopped her.

"Uh, would you mind talking to Jamie before you go? She's upset again, and I can't calm her down. You seem to have a way with her."

She nodded and found the young woman on the loveseat in the corner. She had her knees pulled up and her forehead pressed against them. Her shoulders quivered as she sobbed.

CJ sat beside her and slipped her arm around her. "What's going on?"

"I have to get outta here," Jamie mumbled. "I can't take it anymore."

For several minutes, CJ tried to get her to relax. Finally, Jamie sat up, blew out a long breath, and wiped her eyes.

Hoping to distract her, CJ asked if she'd inventory the food and list what they had left. "Can you do that for me?"

"I guess so. Noah can help me." She stood, took her husband's hand, and walked toward the kitchen.

"That's why you never bring a damn woman with you," Harley said, as he smirked.

Noah broke free from his wife and was on him in a flash. He lunged, and both men went to the floor. Before Noah could pummel him, several of the men separated them.

"What's wrong with you two?" CJ asked in a harsh tone. "We're all stuck here together, and you two fighting isn't helping."

She stepped nose-to-nose with Harley, who smelled like a brewery. "And you, keep your damn trap shut." He opened his mouth, but before he could respond, she warned, "One more word, and I'll lock you in the storage room. I'm sure these guys will happily help. You've created enough chaos." She shoved him in the chest, and he landed backward in a recliner. "Now sit!"

After she dealt with the lodge loudmouth, she read Noah the riot act and told him to stay away from Harley as she would deal with him.

"All right, I'm sorry."

Her chest heaved as she scanned the room. "Anyone else have any issues or questions?" she asked as her eyes flared, daring someone to speak up.

Silence.

"I'm going to check on the crew," she said as she turned to Rory. "You're in charge until I get back."

Evan had slipped out of the den and made his way to the crew quarters. He had to talk to Kayla and make sure she kept her mouth shut about their night together. Ryleigh's accusation in front of the entire group had freaked him out.

That stupid little bitch better not cross me, he thought. *She has no clue who she's dealing with. But what if she keeps up with the story that I raped her?* He told himself it would never stick, but an accusation like that could damage his reputation.

He approached the crew quarters and lucked out when he saw Kayla sitting beside Kenny on the couch in the crew den. He needed her alone so he could talk some sense into her. Pulling the door open, he said, "Uh, sorry to bother you, guys, but CJ needs to see you, Kenny."

The young man glanced at the wide-eyed Kayla. "Will you be okay? I won't be gone long."

She stood. "I'll go back to my room."

As Kenny left, she started picking up some magazines from the couch. When she turned, Evan stood blocking her path to the hallway to her cabin.

"I need to talk to you," he said softly. "I only need a couple of minutes."

"I have nothing to say to you." She tried to push past him, but he grabbed her arm.

"You best think twice before you spread lies about me," Evan said. "You and I both know you wanted me." His eyes bore into hers.

She yanked her arm, but his grip held tight. "Let me go!"

Evan leaned close. His eyes were icy. "I'm an important man, and you're gonna do what I tell you." He told her she was to keep her mouth shut or he would make her pay.

When he told Kayla she was a whore, her eyes flared, and she slapped him with her free hand. She twisted and momentarily broke free before he grabbed her again. He threw her on the couch like she was a rag doll and loomed over her.

"I'll make you pay, you little—"

"What the fuck's going on here?" Walter said. He'd entered without Evan noticing and approached with his fists clenched.

"Uh, I was just seeing how Kayla was doing. She's not been feeling—"

"Bullshit!" the older man said as he stepped closer. "You were threatening her."

Before Evan could react, Walter slammed a fist into his stomach and put him in a headlock. Evan struggled, but Walter clamped down hard, cutting off his air. "Here's how this is gonna go. After I whip your ass, I'm locking you up, and when the police arrive, they're gonna arrest you."

Evan spewed a string of curse words, and a second vicious punch landed, dropping him to his knees. Walter struck him several more times until blood trickled from Evan's nose and mouth.

Satisfied, Walter yanked him up by the collar and dragged him out onto the walkway. He was about to toss him into a storage room when CJ and Kenny arrived.

"What's going on, Walter?" CJ asked.

"This piece of shit was threatening Kayla, so I'm gonna put him in here." He tipped his head to the storage room.

"He broke my ribs," Evan whined.

"Yeah, he may have slipped and fallen," Walter said as he forced a laugh.

"He's a fucking liar! He hit me, and I'm gonna sue." Evan twisted his head and looked at CJ. "Don't let him put me in there."

CJ glanced at Kayla, who was standing in the doorway. "Did you see what happened?"

"Like Walter said, the asshole fell. I never saw anyone throw a punch." She turned and left with Kenny.

CJ squatted beside the red-faced man. She reached out and pressed her fingertips into Evan's side, which caused him to yelp. "I tell you what. Walter's going to take you back up front so the doctor can check you out. You'll stay there, or I'll let him lock your ass up."

"What about him assaulting me?!"

She shrugged. "According to an eyewitness, there wasn't any assault." She stood and told Walter to take him to the den.

He frowned, but nodded.

CJ's gaze stayed fixed on the two men as Walter dragged Evan up the walkway. She scanned the area. Broken pieces of wood littered the area and floated in the water. The storm had ripped away portions of the lodge's roof. Their cabin leaned toward the shore and appeared ready to fall any minute. *I guess we'll lose the rest of our clothes. At least I saved a few of them, plus my notes and camera.*

Her gaze shifted to the mountain, where the trees gently swayed. A lone eagle sat perched on the top of a cedar that had snapped off at the halfway point. The scene reminded her of something one might see after a hurricane. She stared up at the gray sky. Rubbing a knot in her shoulder from the night spent sitting against the wall, she asked herself, *Is the storm finally gone?*

CJ wasn't sure how much more of the bad weather and chaos among the guests and crew she could handle. A sudden tightness gripped her chest as she thought of Ben, who still hadn't woken up. *I need to get him to a hospital. If someone doesn't arrive soon to help …*

Her eyes caught a movement in the upstairs window. Alan stood staring at her with a vacant look on his face. She knew what she had to do.

FORTY-EIGHT

Friday, September 16
Paradise Cove

CJ pushed open the door to the maintenance shop and found Walter sitting in a folding metal chair after delivering Evan. "I need your help."

He scrutinized her. "With what?"

"I have to get far enough out into the cove to reach a cell tower so I can send a text message."

Walter twisted his mouth before saying, "The damn water's still too rough. It'd be risky as hell to take a boat out. You'll have to get into the Sumner Straight to find a signal."

She stared at him. "I have no choice. Will you help me get a boat ready?"

"You can't go out by yourself. One, it'd be nuts to be alone, and two, you ain't experienced enough."

They argued back and forth for several minutes. Walter gave her every reason she couldn't go, and CJ held firm that she was going with or without his help. Finally, he shook his head and told her to wait as he left.

Five minutes later, Victor trailed Walter through the door.

"I told Victor what you're up to, and he agrees with me. You ain't got no business being out on the water. But you're a damn headstrong woman, so we've agreed he'll take you."

CJ's pulse ramped up. She wasn't sure going out with one of her top suspects was smart. "I'm fine going by myself. Besides, as you said, it's dangerous, so why should two people risk their lives?"

"You ain't able to do it," Walter said sharply. "Tell her, Victor!"

"The storm has churned up the water. While it looks better from here, believe me, once you round the corner of the island, it will be bad," Victor said. Realizing CJ wasn't backing down, he pointed out the window to the large boat tied behind the crew quarters. "The only chance anyone has is to take *Delila's Dream*."

"Then that's what I'll do," she said sternly.

The two men stared at each other, and Victor shrugged. "I'll take you. I'm the only certified captain with even close to the experience needed to make it."

Her mind ran through a tally of what could go wrong. The boat might capsize, stranding her in the angry waves, or Victor was the murderer, and she'd be at his mercy. But if she didn't go, Ben might die.

She pulled Walter aside and questioned him about the safety of going with Victor. He furrowed his brow and told her it should be fine. He was an excellent captain with loads of experience. Frustrated that he wasn't realizing her concern, she turned back to Victor.

"Let's go," she said as her chest went tight.

He told her he'd need an hour to prepare the craft, and they'd leave at noon. "I wouldn't tell Alan," he said. "He's gonna be royally pissed about us going out."

She nodded and turned for the door. "I'll keep it quiet."

As she returned to the lodge, she ignored the alarm bells ringing in her head. She was taking a considerable risk, but told herself she had no choice.

———

A few minutes before noon, CJ pressed her lips to Ben's forehead and whispered that she loved him. Marie assured her she'd take care of him until she returned. CJ hadn't told her what she was planning. She only told her she needed to handle something.

Minutes later, CJ stood on the edge of the dock as Victor explained the twenty-six-foot boat wouldn't start. After investigating, it appeared someone had sabotaged the vessel by cutting the wiring.

"We're not gonna be able to go. The other boats are too small."

"Are any of the others working?" she asked.

"Well, yes. Most have the same issue as the big boat, but I've looked and one appears to function okay. The problem is, it's only a twenty-one-footer and not able to take the pounding of the waves."

Walter approached, and Victor showed him the gnarled mess underneath the console. He agreed that there was no way to repair it anytime soon. CJ pondered about why someone had left one boat in working condition. Was it Victor?

She rubbed at the ever-present knot at the base of her neck. "We have to try."

"Please don't do this, CJ," Walter said. "It's too damn risky."

Rubbing at her chin, she stared at Victor. "I have to find a cell signal. If you don't take me, I'll go alone."

The two men glanced at each other.

The younger man cleared his throat. "All right, I'll take you."

He led her to a twenty-one-foot Jetcraft tied to the dock in an end slip. After double-checking things, he motioned for her to join him, and she climbed over the railing. They donned life jackets, and Victor told her to sit in the seat and hang on to the ropes he'd strung along the railing. He asked her again if she was sure she wanted to do this.

"Yes," she said as visions of how she might die rolled through her mind. The image of her losing Ben won out. She was going. She had to.

Victor turned the key, and the engine roared to life. As he pulled back on the throttle, the vessel crept backward until it cleared the corner of the crew building. The breeze, lower but still stiff, attempted to spin them toward the shore, but Victor eased the controls forward, and they moved along the side of the lodge.

"Victor, you turn that damn boat around!" Alan screamed from the dock in front of the lodge. His face was crimson as he frantically waved his arms.

Victor smirked, flipped him off, and increased their speed. The sky turned a darker gray, and the drizzle turned to rain as if the storm knew what they were doing. Tiny ice pellets splattered on the windshield, and the salty tang of the sea air mixed with CJ's tension, almost suffocating her.

"Stay tucked behind the top and hang on," Victor said. "Brace your feet and push yourself against the seat."

The boat crashed, jolted, and smashed against the waves approaching them head-on. The force threw CJ to the floor multiple times. Loud creaks and groans erupted from the vessel as it strained to hold together. Victor stood behind the wheel, dodging logs, kelp, and debris, fighting to stay on course.

As they neared where the island ended, the wind caught the bow and spun the boat sideways. A wave of water sprayed across the side. Wrestling the wheel, Victor regained control.

"We may reach a signal in another two hundred yards or so," he said over the howling wind. "We can't go much further."

CJ dug her cell phone out of the watertight glove box, concentrating on not dropping it in the foot of water on the floor. Nothing.

"Do you have your text ready?" Victor yelled. "Make it short."

"I do," she yelled back. "It's only a few words, and I have a couple of photos." Her heart pounded as she stared at the rollers, now higher than the boat. She expected the water to engulf them every time they dipped to the bottom of one.

"Try now!" Victor yelled.

As she hung on with one hand, she glanced at the display. Still nothing.

"We gotta turn back!"

"Wait! I just got a bar." She stood and slammed against the side of the metal bar connecting to the top. "I have two bars." Her thumb pressed the blue send arrow. Failed.

"Damnit!"

Another wave hit them and almost flipped them over.

"We gotta go back," Victor said.

"Give me just another minute." She deleted the photos, hit send again, and the text went through.

Releasing the bar so she could use both hands, she prepared a second text with her first photo and sent it. She repeated the process and got the second photo to send.

A wave hit them as she reached and jammed her cell phone back in the glove box, and she stumbled backward and over the side. She grabbed the rope and hung on, screaming for Victor to help her. He glanced at her and remained behind the wheel.

"Victor! Help me!"

Still, he remained where he was as the icy waters soaked her clothes and pricked her skin.

As Victor swung the bow around, she threw a leg over the side and landed in the ponded water in the bottom of the boat.

"Are you okay?" he asked.

"Hell no! I damn near drowned. Why didn't you help me?" she asked angrily.

"I couldn't let go of the wheel, or we'd flip," he said as he turned them for the lodge. "Sit back in the seat, and I'll get us outta here."

Several guests stared out the den picture window as they neared the lodge. Alan stood on the dock, still angry. He raced through the door as they passed the side of the lodge.

Walter, Simon, Kenny, and Cal were waiting on the back dock as Victor slowed the boat and moved toward the slip. Walter grabbed the side of the boat and helped Victor ease it into position. After tying it up, Victor hopped out. CJ rejected his offered hand, and she climbed out by herself.

"Look. I'm sorry I didn't help you. If I—"

"You were fucking trying to drown me," CJ snapped as she glared at him. "If I hadn't grabbed the rope, that's what would have happened."

Victor tried to explain again, but she ignored him. He was telling Walter what happened when Alan stormed up. Harley, Junior, and Rory trailed him.

"You're fired!" Alan said as he jabbed his finger into Victor's chest. "You risked one of my boats and guest on some joy ride."

"Joy ride?!" Victor's face went crimson, and his eyes flared. "What the fuck do you think we were doing?"

Pointing at CJ, he said, "She needed to reach a signal to call for help." He shoved the owner in the chest and balled up his fists. "You haven't done a damn thing to protect anyone."

As Alan stepped toward Victor, Walter blocked him. "Cut this crap out. At least Victor was trying to help. He's right. You haven't done shit."

Alan glared at him. "You're fired, too."

Walter snorted. "And I hope you know you can go fuck yourself." He wheeled around, grabbed Victor's arm, and led him away. The rest of the crew followed.

CJ, shivering in her soaked clothes, shook her head at Alan. "You're a piece of work."

Rory touched her arm and told her she needed to get on some dry clothes. "Come on, let's go."

FORTY-NINE

Friday, September 16
Paradise Cove

He needed a plan. Well, he had one, but was it good enough? The damn detective was becoming a real pain in the ass, just like her uncle, Detective Harry O'Hara. When he first met her, he believed she wasn't clever enough to find him, but now he was unsure.

His lips curled into a crooked smile. Imagine how stupid she'd feel if she realized she was within arm's reach of him several times. She could have easily snagged him. Of course, he could have also slid his knife along her smooth neck and added her to his conquests. It would be so cool to kill a detective.

Nibbling on his thumb, he wondered where he was on her list. *Maybe I'm not on her radar*, he thought. Wishful thinking. She wasn't her mentor, but she was sharp. Like one of the eagles perched on a limb above, he was confident her sparkling emerald green eyes could see her prey from a distance.

The boat.

His heart had beat faster when she climbed onto the Jetcraft he had readied for a quick getaway. Trekking through the woods and stealing a handmade canoe from the village wasn't appealing, especially with the rough seas.

Evidence.

What did she and her sidekick boyfriend have on him? If nothing, he could stay put, blend in with the others, and be safe. Hmm. What if the damn feds showed up instead of the incompetent local authorities?

Who had the detective texted? The FBI? They'd know him even with his new hair color and beard, and they had his DNA. Did she have any contacts at the bureau? *Shit!*

As sweat trickled down the back of his neck, his mind bounced between "I'm okay" and "they'll catch me this time." Specks danced before his eyes like the ice crystals splattering on the glass.

His thoughts wandered back to Boston and his last kill before fleeing to Alaska. Jeffrey wasn't satisfied after evading the old detective in his warehouse lair and leaving the luscious Marilyn alive. The evil one caused him to fuck up and leave a piece of himself behind when he hastily snatched another victim. The tiny nick of his finger had left his blood at the scene. *Damnit!* He would have cleaned up if her two burly brothers hadn't returned before he raced away.

Blood.

Did he leave his blood behind again in the storage room? He'd been over it numerous times and couldn't be sure. Something had to be in the room, or the nosy detective wouldn't have locked it. Maybe he could start a fire and burn the building down.

His breathing escalated, but the air wasn't reaching his lungs. It felt like someone was smothering him with a pillow. Another horrifying thought popped into his mind.

Bodies.

He convinced himself that there was none of him present on the bodies. The thrashing washing machine of the sea should have taken care of that. But what if he was wrong? What if he left a shred of himself on them? After all, he had left his mark, his autograph. Why did Jeffrey always insist on signing his victims? *Oh, God.*

He stood from the dark corner of his room and paced, hoping to determine his plan. What he'd do to escape justice once again from an O'Hara. He couldn't survive in prison with its stale air, cramped quarters, and loss of freedom.

A creak of the floorboard echoed like an alarm bell, and the weight of impending doom pressed down on him. His heart pounded so hard he thought it might burst out of his chest. He had to regain control of himself. *Don't freak out. If they find out I did it, they will tie me up and shove me in a room.*

As his breathing slowed, he thought of Alaska, the perfect place to hide, but could he stay? He had a plan to extract himself from this mess, but he needed a second opinion. After grabbing his jacket and slipping it on, he trudged out the door.

FIFTY

Friday, September 16
Paradise Cove

CJ sat cross-legged on the floor next to Ben. It took several hours, but she was warming up after spending time in the water. She longed for power to take a hot shower, but settled for borrowing a pair of sweats from Debra.

As she stared at Ben, who slept peacefully, she reflected on her excursion with Victor out into the teeth of the storm. The weather had improved and now appeared to be reduced to short bursts, much like a toddler throwing a tantrum. *Was it leaving for good, and if so, when would someone respond to her texts?*

A chill ran through her. Not from the earlier frigid water, but from the thought of her messages not getting through. Her cell phone showed they made it, but what if they hadn't? She decided she had to pretend that help was still days away. Hope for the best, prepare for the worst.

When had she returned, Marie told her Ben had stirred some but had not woken up. She tenderly caressed her fingertips on his forehead. He wasn't hot, and she hoped that meant he didn't have a fever.

A light tapping on the door distracted CJ, and the door cracked open. Rory stuck his head into the room. "I'm sorry to bother you, but do you have a minute?"

She nodded and followed him out. "What's up?" she asked.

"We're gonna have a food problem if help doesn't arrive soon. The stuff in the fridge won't last much longer." He frowned. "As you know, we're limited to what we can cook without gas and power. The wood stove isn't much help, and neither is the grill."

CJ rubbed her eyes and sighed. "Let's go take a look."

They went to the kitchen and reviewed what food remained in the refrigerator.

"You're right," she said. "Nothing's gonna be kept cold in there." Her thoughts went to Alan and his lack of doing anything for anyone but himself and his wife.

She motioned for Rory to follow her to the walk-in freezer with the processed fish. Opening it, she peered in.

"It's not running, but the frozen fish is still firm." When the flashlight beam crossed the bottom shelf, she pointed to some bags of ice.

"Let's take a couple of fish coolers from the boat, put everything salvageable in there, and toss some ice on it." A wave of dizziness flooded over her, causing her to sway.

Rory grabbed her arm and steadied her. "Are you okay? You've not eaten or slept much, and it's catching up with you."

She bent over, hands on knees, and sucked in several deep breaths before standing. "I'll be fine. Do you think Noah can help you with the food?"

"Sure. I can grab him and get Jamie to help." He stared at her as she dropped onto a bench by the back door.

"I'm gonna sit here for a bit," she said. "I need some fresh air."

Rory told her he'd have Marie check on Ben and reluctantly returned inside.

CJ sat gazing across the back of the desolate lodge area. The scene reminded her of something out of a low-grade horror movie where everyone is hunkered down, waiting for the killer to strike. She almost expected a deranged lunatic wielding a knife to sprint toward her at any minute.

As the drizzle transformed into a mist, it contributed to the eerie atmosphere of the quickly fading daylight. While the rainwater continued its race down the gullies and splashed into the cove, the trees on the mountain shimmied. The air was crisp and there was a clean fragrance with hints of spruce.

Her fingers kneaded at a sore spot above her right knee. Another bruise, no doubt from being battered against the side of the boat by the sea. So much for a relaxing holiday.

She needed to go back to work in Charleston to rest up. As she rotated her neck, she reached into her jacket pocket and pulled out a folded piece of paper with the names of her suspects and those crossed off for one reason or another. The muscles in her neck tightened as if strong fingers grabbed her. There had to be something she'd missed that would help her sort out the murderer's identity.

Okay, what are you missing?

Of her top three suspects, Alan, Junior, and Victor, the only new thing was Victor's failure to help her when she was tossed overboard. If Ben was awake, she could ask him if his story of being unable to release the wheel was valid. *Of course, if Victor wanted to kill me, he had a perfect chance to do it,* she thought. She was certain she'd get an earful from her fiancé for being out on the water alone with him.

She stared at the remaining names on her list and mentally ran through her facts for each one. Her eyes scanned up and down the sheet until she stopped and focused on one name. Her breath caught, and her heart pounded.

Wait! When I interviewed him, he commented on the wound to Chantelle's neck. How would he know unless he saw her when Walter pulled her out or someone told him? Or he killed her. She exhaled and mumbled, "How in the hell didn't I catch that sooner?"

CJ jumped up and thumped down the walkway as the mist spritzed her face. She stopped at the end of the wooden boards and banged on the door. "Walter!"

The latch clicked, and the fifty-five-year-old maintenance man appeared. "What's wrong?"

She pushed past him. "Who else knew the truth about Chantelle?"

He closed the door and followed. "What do you mean?" he asked as he squinted.

"About her murder? Specifically, the wounds on her neck?"

"Uh, just Alan."

"Are you positive?"

He nodded. "That's it. After I told him, he had me wrap her body in plastic and concocted the drowning story."

"So, none of the guys on the crew would know? Maybe they saw her body?"

Walter shrugged. "I don't see how. Debra and the crew went out fishing that day and weren't here. I think everyone went. I stayed back like I always do. The only ones I saw around here were Alan and I."

"Would Alan have told anyone?"

"No way. He'd never do that. He was too concerned about hiding the details."

CJ stared at him as she chewed on her lip. She had to trust someone. "Listen, I need your help. I'm pretty sure I know who the killer is." Clearing her throat, she asked, "If I need your help to apprehend him, will you do it?"

He nodded. "If you need me, I'll be there."

CJ thanked him and hurried back to the lodge through the dim light. It would soon be pitch black except for the sparse solar-powered artificial lights, glowing less and less without the sun. She was sure she knew the identity of the murderer. Now, all she had to do was prove it, and make sure he'd used his knife for the last time.

As she reached for the back door handle, she stopped in her tracks. She suddenly remembered where she'd seen the triangular signature before. It was in the last case her uncle worked before retiring from the Boston PD. A ruthless serial killer who terrorized the upper east coast. "No, it couldn't be," she mumbled. "Is The Butcher here in Alaska?"

FIFTY-ONE

Friday, September 16
Paradise Cove

It was nearing midnight as CJ stood in the corner of a second-floor window overlooking the back walkway. Her position gave her a view of the owner's apartment door and the crew quarters. The only problem was the darkness.

Her fingers tightened on the flashlight, and she longed for her Glock. Ben, who would have been by her side, still lay motionless in the sitting room under Marie's watch. CJ was alone. Her only hope was Walter, and her mind calculated about how to utilize him if she needed him.

Rory had kept an eye on Junior, and though she was reluctant, she asked Noah to relieve him. The other suspect—really the one at the top of her list—was hers to handle. Her fingers slipped into her jacket pocket, and she double-checked her only means of protection—a fillet knife Walter had provided her.

CJ was trained in hand-to-hand combat, but a knife fight terrified her. If it came to that, she would be at a disadvantage. Her adversary was skilled, cunning, and ruthless with a blade.

Her thoughts took her back to the chilly April night in Boston when she'd faced a man clutching a knife. She recalled the flash of silver as he lunged at her. The deafening roar of her pistol when she wounded him before he could drive the shaft deep.

This time, there would be no thunder.

No projectile to stop her perp.

This time, the upper hand belonged to a man who would kill her without remorse.

A shiver ran down her, and her racing heartbeat caused a stabbing pain in her chest. She braced herself against the wall and struggled to block self-doubt from working its way into her thoughts.

Her wait was brief as a flickering beam near the crew quarters caught her attention. As quickly as it appeared, it vanished. She leaned close to the glass, peering into blackness. *Had she imagined the light?*

She stood in silence except for her ragged breaths. Waiting. Watching.

A sudden flash appeared on the walkway below her and disappeared under the canopy. She chewed on her bottom lip. *Where is he going? The only thing back there are the freezers.* Suddenly, she realized where he was headed. *Shit! There's no way for me to reach Walter.*

As she climbed down the stairs leading to the back door, a creak caused her to stop and hold her breath. Without the wind roaring and rattling the structure, every noise was amplified in the eerie silence.

Continuing her decline, she reached the landing in front of the door. Her fingers caressed the knob and twisted it as she prayed the latch didn't click. A slight relief passed through her as the door eased open without signaling her approach.

She crept forward with the unlit flashlight in one hand and the knife in the other. Her mind scrambled with how to approach this situation. If she could surprise him, perhaps he wouldn't fight. He might just give up. *Fat chance,* she thought.

A low screeching noise sounded to her right. Or was it scratching?

Scrrritch, scrrritch … scrrritch, scrrritch.

She squinted, trying to see what was making the metallic noise.

"I'll flip on the light," a male voice said, "so we can see how much more we need to cut."

The circular beam of light shined on the silver handle of the freezer and illuminated the hands of someone holding a hacksaw. *There's two of them and they're trying to remove the lock,* CJ thought. *The bodies are inside.*

The beam moved to the right, and a face appeared.

Bev. But who is with her?

She stood frozen until Bev made a final thrust and pulled the lock from the door handle. The second person pointed and Bev entered the walk-in. CJ crept closer. Silently, she prayed the wooden boards underneath her feet wouldn't squeak and reveal her presence. Whoever the man was with Bev turned on a miniature battery-powered lantern and sat it on the deck just outside the door. Then, he entered the frosty cavern with his back to CJ. The person was about her height, but the jacket concealed his head.

Who the hell is that?

"You're gonna have to help me," the male voice said. "I need to unwrap and strip her before we toss the body over."

She realized they wanted to put the dead bodies of Olivia and Anita back in their watery grave to destroy any evidence. CJ moved closer until she was within fifteen feet of the freezer's entrance. She readied herself as she tried to control her breathing. Her mind raced through her options, but none were suitable. It was too late to get Walter. One person was difficult, but two? Maybe she had time to get help.

She started to turn and go back for Rory when the back of a person emerged. Bent over, the person was dragging Olivia's naked body out of her temporary morgue. The flashlight beam from the second person in the freezer emerged and hit the person's face. *Cal. As I expected.*

As he dragged the body closer to the edge of the dock, CJ knew it was now or never. She couldn't let him dispose of the bodies. As she sucked in a deep breath, her fingers punched the button on her flashlight, and she aimed it at his face.

"Cal! What the hell are you doing?"

He yanked his hands away and faced her. Dull eyes gazed at her as his mouth dropped open. Then he smirked. "Get the fuck out of here!" he said as his hand went to his side.

Before he could pull his knife, she dropped her flashlight and sprinted forward. She lunged into him, propelling them to the unforgiving wooden boards of the deck. He pushed off, rolled over, and stood over her.

"You stupid bitch!" he sneered in the faint light as he unsnapped the sheath holding his knife. "Do you really think you—"

The sole of CJ's Timberline boot landed square in the groin, resulting in a satisfying groan. Cal stumbled backward into the side of the freezer and back to the ground.

Before he recovered, she grabbed the stunned man and wrapped an arm around his neck. She yanked his arm behind him with her other hand and pressed her weight down as he squirmed trying to break free.

A sudden movement to her right caused her to turn to find Bev emerging from the freezer. Her expression was a strange mixture of confusion and bitterness. "Oh my God!" she said. "Thank goodness you got here. Cal was forcing me to help him move the bodies of these poor, poor women." She sniffed. "He had a knife and told me he'd kill me." She covered her face with her hands and fell to her knees.

CJ glanced at the rope a few feet away, barely visible in the beam of her dropped flashlight. "Bev, bring me that rope!" CJ screamed. "I need to tie—"

The momentary distraction provided Cal with the advantage he needed. His free elbow flung back, smashing CJ in the face, and causing her to lose her grip. Cal jumped up and raced down the walkway into the darkness.

CJ wobbled to her feet, shook her head, and grabbed the flashlight. She bolted after Cal. "Oh, hell no!" she yelled. "You're mine."

FIFTY-TWO

Saturday, September 17
Paradise Cove

CJ sprinted after Cal, attempting to shine the flashlight ahead to prevent slipping on the slick wooden boards. Her hours on her exercise bike, she'd nicknamed the Punisher, and in the gym paid off. She caught Cal before he could reach the footbridge, dove, and slammed into him from behind knocking both to the deck.

Cal swung his fist, but she ducked it and returned a fist of her own, catching him in his jaw. Another satisfying groan escaped from him as he scrambled to get to his feet. CJ grabbed one of his ankles and twisted it, sending him back to the walkway. He kicked free and again struggled to his feet.

"You fucking bitch!"

She lunged from her knees and shoved him backward. He hobbled on his injured ankle before turning for the footbridge. After two steps, a loud thud sent him to the wooden boards again.

Walter flipped on his flashlight, stepped forward, and pressed the edge of the boat paddle against Cal's throat. "Stay down, asshole!"

Walter stared at him before dropping his gaze to CJ. "You all right? You're bleeding."

"I'm fine. I caught an elbow, but—"

Cal squirmed, but Walter added pressure, causing the younger man to yelp. "I told you to stay down! I knew you were up to no good when I watched you sneaking around." He pulled a ball of rope from his jacket pocket and soon had Cal's hands tied behind his back as he screamed obscenities.

Walter shined the light on CJ's face. "You have a broken nose?"

"Nah, I think he busted my lip. It'll be okay after some ice."

He flashed the light back on Cal. "Whaddya wanna do with him?"

"We need to lock him up somewhere until the authorities arrive."

The older man's lips curled. "I got just the place." He grabbed Cal's jacket collar and dragged him down the walkway toward his shop. Twice Cal tried to get to his feet and each time, Walter's vicious stomp stopped him.

CJ followed with the flashlight, gently touching a rag to her throbbing nose.

Walter stopped in front of a metal door. "This room is about the same size as the prison cell you'll be in soon."

"You can't put me in there," Cal spat.

"I can, and I will." With one smooth motion, Walter flung him into the dark space. He slammed the door and slid the latch closed. "Watch him, and I'll be back," he said as he opened the shop door.

Minutes later, he added a padlock. "I managed to find a couple more locks. This one should hold him." He held out a key to CJ.

"I'll stay and guard the door," she said.

"No. You need to have the doctor check you out." He unfolded a metal chair and placed it against the wall. "It's nice out tonight now that the wind and rain have stopped. I'm happy to be outside in the fresh air."

She hesitated, staring at the door. "He can't get out, can he?"

"Nope. The room's empty, and there are no windows. He can't claw his way out, and he ain't getting past me." He frowned. "By the way, that was stupid as hell," he said. "You're lucky it was Bev and not another man."

Walter was right. It was an incredibly dumb thing to do. "Thank you for helping me," she said in a low voice.

"No problem," he said. "You said you needed my help, so I was watching." He winked at her. "Add this to my good deeds tab. It's gotta help my case, right?"

She smiled and then grimaced as pain radiated from her lip. "Yeah, I won't forget it. I need to get Olivia wrapped back up and, in the freezer, check on Bev, and search Cal's cabin. After that, I'll see Leo."

She turned and jogged up the walkway.

———

CJ dumped the contents of Cal's top dresser drawer on the unmade bed in his cabin and sorted through it with her gloved hands. Nothing but clothes—T-shirts, underwear, and socks. The second and third drawers contained jeans, fishing pants, and long-sleeved shirts. There was nothing taped underneath the drawers.

A search of the bathroom, barely large enough to turn around in, yielded nothing but the typical items one would expect for a man. She returned to the room and crawled around on her hands and knees. Nothing under the bed, and no signs of any hidden areas under the floorboards. "Not a damn thing," she murmured.

She reached for the doorknob as she scanned the room one last time. There was one spot she hadn't checked. After pulling the dresser from the wall, she dropped to her knees and peered at the dusty spot underneath. She ran her fingertips along a faint line until she touched a screw, then tapped with her knuckles. *Something's off.*

CJ popped to her feet and swung the door open. Walter sat in his metal chair about thirty feet away. "Walter, do you have a screwdriver?

"Uh, yeah," he said. "I've got a bunch of them in my shop." He started to leave his chair until CJ motioned him to stay. She didn't want to leave Cal unguarded even for a second.

"I'll find one," she said as she crossed the walkway, pulled his shop door open, and disappeared inside. Two minutes later, she smiled at him as she returned to Cal's cabin holding up a two-foot-long pry bar. "This'll work better."

On one knee, she jammed the metal bar into the crack in the floor and yanked backward. A loud pop sounded when a wooden panel broke loose from the screw holding it in place. Using her flashlight, she peeked inside—a hand-held battery-powered radio, a yellow cloth bag, a leather case, and a three-inch notebook closed with a zipper. She carefully removed them and placed them on the floor.

CJ's fingers twisted the knob on the handheld, and after a brief crackling sound, a weather channel tuned in. "Son of a bitch, he knew about the storm the whole time," she whispered.

She picked up the cloth bag and opened it to find a Polaroid camera and two boxes of film. She aimed the camera at the vacant hole in the floor and squeezed the red button. A soft whirring sound followed a low click, and a photograph slid out.

Next, she untied the string on the leather case, flipped it open, and stared at five knives and two scalpels. All were razor sharp, and one slot was empty, but Cal had one knife with him when she caught him at the freezer.

CJ nibbled at her bottom lip as she peered at the last item. Carefully, she slid the zipper around and opened the notebook. Her eyes went wide as she turned the pages, and photographs of various young women tied to chairs with their throats slashed appeared. Each photo had a person's first name, presumably who was in the photo, and a location. On the opposite page was a self-locking plastic bag with a triangular piece of skin. The last three women were Chantelle, Olivia, and Anita. "Oh, shit," she mumbled. "Cal kept a murder book."

FIFTY-THREE

Saturday, September 17
Paradise Cove

Leo gently pulled CJ's bottom lip back and examined the inside. "You'll have a swollen lip, but I don't think you need any stitches," he said. "Keep ice on it and be careful when you eat."

CJ grabbed some ice from the cooler, dropped it in a baggie, and held it to her jaw as she checked on Ben. She entered the dim sitting room to find Marie lying on the floor beside her fiancé.

"Anything new?"

"Well, he woke up for a bit, and I got him to drink some water, but he dozed back off."

CJ's heart bumped. "How was he?"

"He was groggy but not as disoriented." Marie reached and took her hand. "He's getting better." She held the lantern closer. "What happened to you?"

"I caught the man who murdered Olivia and Anita—at least, I think I did."

Marie's eyes went wide. "Oh, my! Who was it?"

CJ told her what happened and that she'd brief everyone in the morning. She asked the nurse to keep it confidential until she informed the group. "Leo knows, but he's the only guest so far."

Marie pursed her lips and asked, "He can't escape, can he?"

"No, I don't think so. Walter is standing guard, and I'll relieve him after I get some rest."

Marie hugged her and slipped out of the room. CJ stretched out on the pallet and stared at the ceiling. Adrenaline pulsed through her, and though she was physically exhausted, she knew sleep wasn't coming. *I gotta get the word out and get someone here soon.*

It was 5:35 a.m. when she stood and left the room. After exchanging places with Marie again, she exited the back door and trudged down the walkway as the early stages of dawn approached. Walter was sitting in his chair.

As she approached, he crushed a cigarette under his foot and stood.

"Is everything okay?" she asked.

"Yep. Cal gave up banging on the door and screaming like a banshee. Ain't seen anyone else." His lips curved into a smile. "I see you got a fat lip. Doc check it?"

"Yeah. He told me I didn't need stitches. Do you need a break?"

He shook his head. "I'm good. Maybe after everyone wakes up, I'll grab some coffee, assuming we have enough fuel left to run the small generator." He chuckled. "I can live without food, but I need my caffeine."

She scanned the lightening sky and the rustling trees on the mountain. "I need to reach a signal to send another text."

Walter peered at the water, which still rolled but was nowhere near as bad. "I'm sure Victor would take you out again. The storm has moved on, and the sea's calming." He noticed her staring at the Jetcraft and before she could respond, he said, "He needs to take you. It's not safe enough for you to go alone. Besides, can you even drive a boat?"

CJ frowned. "I can. I've driven a boat in the Boston harbor and Charleston several times. I'm no pro but I'm capable."

"Neither of those places are Alaska, CJ." He leaned close and patted her arm. "You're a damn determined woman, but here one wrong read of a wave or the wind can flip your boat or dump your ass overboard."

She stood rigid, staring at him.

He sighed before asking, "I assume you wanna go now?"

She nodded. "It's almost daylight, and I'd like to tell everyone help is on the way. I hope to receive a return text when I can reach a signal."

"Hang on." Walter started for Victor's cabin door but the Jetcraft's engine roar stopped him before he made it. He raced back and watched as she pulled away.

CJ steered the boat through the debris trapped in the cove, past the lodge, and pushed the throttle forward. The rollers, now less than half the size they were, moved toward her as she neared the end of the island. The fingers of the sun wiggled above the horizon as she bounced with the waves until she reached the spot where she found a signal before.

CJ left her seat and held her cell phone up as she clung to the railing. A chime sounded, and she punched the green and white icon. Multiple messages appeared, and she scrolled to the one from Wally Gauge, the FBI Special Agent who covered southeast Alaska.

Her eyes scanned it, and her heart rate escalated as a chill ran down her spine. A name screamed at her. *The Butcher.*

"I need to get back!" she said out loud.

She dropped in the seat, pushed the throttle forward and turned the boat around. As she bounced toward the lodge, she stared at the last line in the text. *What does that mean?*

FIFTY-FOUR

Saturday, September 17
Paradise Cove

At 7:30 a.m., CJ slowed the boat as she approached the front dock. Numerous people emerged from the confines of the lodge, basking in the weather. The water's surface sparkled under the early morning sunshine and pale blue sky. The wind and rain were gone. Two otters played along the edge of the mangled walkway.

Victor caught the rope minutes later as CJ pulled the Jetcraft alongside the platform. He swapped places with her and pointed to a man sitting in a chair against the wall as the bodies parted. Ben's groggy eyes focused on her, and his lips curled.

"Ben!" CJ said as she rushed and wrapped her arms around him. "How are you feeling?"

He cleared his throat. "Better. I'm still a little fuzzy, but the fresh air is helping."

"He got himself out here," Marie said as she beamed.

Debra stuck her head out the door and told everyone that breakfast was ready. Bev had prepared scrambled eggs, bacon, and toast using an electric skillet and the toaster with the help of the portable generator. "The girls are cooking more food, so eat up."

After the guests and crew gathered inside, CJ announced that the person responsible for Olivia and Anita's deaths had been apprehended. Most were shocked that it was Cal but relieved. Even Harley congratulated her.

Everyone grabbed breakfast and found places to sit. Some sat inside, while others found spots on the front dock. The mood was bright with the change in the weather and CJ's announcement. No one seemed too worried about when help would arrive.

CJ explained the events of Cal's capture to Ben as they ate. He scolded her for taking such a risk, but admitted he would probably have done the same thing in her place.

Alan waved her to the corner of the room. He told her he had no idea that Cal was capable of murder. She read his face as he talked and didn't believe him.

"I do have a question for you," she said as she scanned the people on the dock and in the room. "Does Cal have a—"

Her heart rate bumped when her eyes settled on Walter near the counter, pouring himself a cup of coffee. She rushed toward him. "Walter, who's guarding Cal?"

"I'm heading right back. I just wanted to grab—"

It occurred to her who was missing as she raced for the back door. The last part of the text message about a sister made sense now. *Cal has a sister and she's here.*

Bursting onto the walkway, CJ saw Debra pounding on the storage room lock with a hammer. The older woman's eyes bulged at the sight of her, and she rapidly swung, trying to break the door free.

As CJ neared, Debra dropped the hammer and faced her. She pulled a Glock from her belt and aimed it at her. "Stop right there!"

CJ stopped within twenty feet of the sneering woman.

"Here's what's gonna happen. You're gonna give me the key to the door, and Cal and I are taking the boat."

"You're Cal's sister," CJ said.

Debra's face twisted, and she nodded. "Outstanding, detective. And my little brother and I are leaving."

"That's why you and your husband have been so secretive. You were protecting Cal."

"Ding, ding, ding. Aren't we a smart little lady?"

"But why?"

"Isn't it obvious? My brother has a problem." Debra's eyes flared. "He has a monster inside him, and sometimes he can't control him. We call him Jeffrey, after our older brother."

"What?"

"Jeffrey was evil and got himself killed after he raped a woman."

"Who killed him?"

Debra smirked. "Our father. Oh, he said it was an intruder, but we all knew the old man stabbed him and lied to the cops."

CJ's eyes searched for an opening as the older woman prattled on about her younger brother. She was too far away to rush the woman. As Walter and Rory thumped up behind her, she raised a hand, signaling them to stay back.

Debra babbled on about her and Cal's childhood. How their parents treated them, especially Cal. The only positive thing her father taught her brother was how to be a butcher in the family's shop.

"Why didn't someone get him help?"

"Well, we tried that after he sliced up some little slut from high school. But it was clear that wasn't going to help. I told Cal to trick them into believing he was fine, and it worked. They let him walk." She glanced at the lock. "Listen, I'd love to chat more, but it's time for us to leave. You've called for help, and we need to be long gone before it arrives."

"Why did Cal kill Olivia and Anita?" CJ asked, hoping to stall her.

Debra sighed. "Well, if you must know, Jeffrey has a soft spot for weak women. Pitiful creatures, like Olivia, or those who put themselves in vulnerable positions. You know, damsels in distress. As for Anita, she got her throat cut because she was nosy. She saw my brother stalking Olivia. So, I tipped him off and told him she needed to go."

CJ stared at her as her mind raced. This woman was as crazy as her brother. It was clear she pulled his strings. *Stall.* "Why did you two come here?"

Debra's eyes grew dark. "That, my dear, is your uncle's fault. We loved Boston, but your uncle was getting too close, so we fled to a place where we wouldn't be noticed."

CJ's focus went past the older woman's shoulder. Victor had crept up from behind and was no more than ten feet away. "Wait! Alan told me you lived in North Carolina before coming here."

"A simple lie, my dear." She flipped her free hand. "Enough! Unlock the damn door, and we'll be—"

Victor lunged and grabbed Debra, and they fell to the wooden deck, each struggling over the Glock. As CJ rushed forward, a blast echoed across the cove. She pulled Victor up. He had a small crimson stain on his white T-shirt.

"Oh, shit!" he yelled as he yanked his shirt up, revealing no sign of a wound.

CJ was already on her knees, pressing her hands to Debra's abdomen as the woman shivered and moaned. "Hang on, Debra," she said as she pulled the older woman's shirt up and replaced her palms as blood oozed between her fingers. "Walter, get Leo. Hurry!"

Debra's breathing grew more ragged until she took one last gasp and then went still. Leo arrived with Walter moments later, and moved CJ away as he examined the fallen woman. A shake of his head confirmed what CJ knew. Cal's sister was dead.

"I'll have Simon and Kenny move her to the freezer with the others," Walter said. "I'm sorry I almost fucked up. I never imagined the two were related, and I only planned to be gone a few minutes."

"It's fine," CJ responded quietly. "How 'bout you go eat and take a break? I'll stand guard."

Walter nodded and backed away.

CJ turned to a still visibly shaken Victor, who offered her the pistol. She took it and said, "You told me you didn't steal Alan's Glock, and it appears you were correct. What did you throw in the water?"

He gazed at his feet. "I had another one that I tossed."

"Why?"

"I was afraid I'd get in trouble if Alan found out I had it. I knew he'd eventually search our cabins for his missing Glock."

CJ nodded and lowered herself into the metal chair, hoping help would arrive soon.

FIFTY-FIVE

Saturday, September 17
Paradise Cove

The white Cessna 208 Caravan seaplane with a blue and yellow stripe circled the lodge and lined up for its approach. The guests and crew littering the dock and back walkway waved their arms and cheered.

CJ turned the guard duties over to Walter and raced toward the front of the lodge. She arrived as the plane glided to a stop near the edge of the wooden platform. The pilot, a man in his mid-thirties with a scruffy beard, popped open the door and stepped out.

The first passenger emerged, a man in his mid-forties wearing a navy-blue jacket with gold FBI lettering. As he stepped onto the dock, she recognized the short, stocky frame of FBI Special Agent Wally Gauge.

Wally offered her his hand. "It's great to see you again, but I wish it were under different circumstances." He glanced back and motioned to a husky man. "And you know this fellow."

CJ stepped forward and shook hands with Sitka Police Chief Freddie Richardson. Two additional FBI agents joined them. Wally told her that a second plane with agents was en route, and three other floatplanes would arrive for the guests. CJ told the men that Cal was being held in a storage room in the back and how his sister, Debra, was killed during a struggle. They followed her as she led them through the lodge and down the walkway.

Walter nervously stood as they approached.

"This is Walter," she said. "He's been a tremendous help to me in apprehending and guarding the person responsible for the two murders."

She reached, patted the older man on the shoulder, and glanced at Wally. "I'd like to discuss him with you once we get the prisoner squared away."

CJ dug into her pocket, pulled out the key, and unlocked the door. Cal was huddled in the back of the storage room when the doors swung open. The two agents handcuffed him and brought him out.

"As you noted from my text, that's Callum McAlister," Wally said. "Better known as The Butcher. The FBI has chased him for several years for multiple murders in the northeast." He reached over and pulled Cal's jacket up, exposing his back. A long, jagged scar ran from his beltline to the middle of his back.

CJ's blood ran cold. *The man with the scar.*

"His dad gave him this." He released the jacket and turned to her. "A few years later, he repaid the old man and his mother by slitting their throats. Boston PD couldn't pin it on him even though they knew he did it."

Wally told the two agents to take the prisoner up to the front, away from the guests, and wait until the next plane arrived. After that, they'd be transported to Sitka for a flight to FBI headquarters in Quantico, Virginia.

CJ showed Wally and Freddie the freezer with Olivia, Anita, and Debra's bodies and the apparent blood stains in the storage room beside the maintenance shop. She also showed him what she found in Cal's cabin, including the notebook with the photographs and Cal's souvenirs. Wally told her the forensics crew would process these areas when they arrived.

"We also have a paramedic on board the next plane," Wally said. "How's your fiancé?"

"He's better, but I'll be happy to get him checked out. He took a nasty whack to the head, trying to keep one of the guests from running off during the storm." She pointed toward the front. "Come on, and I'll introduce you."

CJ stared at the second floatplane as it approached the dock. The first man off she recognized as FBI Special Agent Robert Patterson. Behind him was the man who'd raised her after her parents died when she was eleven, her uncle, retired Boston detective Harry O'Hara.

Harry hugged her. "Robert called me and told me you'd done what he and I couldn't. Cracked the last case I worked on. Where's The Butcher?"

She led the two men to Alan's office and pushed open the door.

Cal's cold, dark eyes stared at the man in his sixties with salt and pepper hair. "Detective Harry O'Hara," he said, smirking. "We finally meet in the flesh. Too bad you couldn't catch me."

"And it's too bad for you my niece here did," Harry said with a wry smile as he closed the door. He turned to Robert. "He's all yours."

"I gave Special Agent Gauge the murder book with nine young women in it. How many people has he supposedly murdered?" CJ asked.

"He's connected to three through forensics and an eyewitness," Harry said. "He's suspected of at least six others, but only based on his location and MO. Plus, the ones here."

CJ pulled Harry and Robert aside and explained her concerns about Alan, Evan, and Junior. She also noted her suspicions against Victor, although she quickly pointed out how helpful and cooperative he'd been. Last, she discussed Walter's past issues.

"We'll investigate them all," Robert said. "Come on, Harry, help me out."

She watched them go through the back door and went to find her fiancé.

Ben sat on a chair on the deck as the paramedic finished examining him. The young woman jotted notes in a notebook, smiled, and told him he had a concussion but could fly to Sitka. A doctor was on standby to assess him before he would be cleared to return home.

Ben and CJ waved to the last of three planes carrying the guests and stood alone on the edge of the dock. They had said their goodbyes and exchanged numbers with Noah and Jamie, Leo and Marie, and Rory. CJ promised Luka that she'd email him a copy of the photo the two of them took in front of the floatplane.

"Grannie's vision was accurate," Ben said.

"Yes. She was right."

FBI Special Agent Robert Patterson approached Ben and CJ. "We have a plan."

He explained the FBI would take Callum with them, and he would be charged with multiple murders. Besides the evidence the FBI already had, plus what was being collected by the forensics team, there would be a solid case to put him away for life.

"The techs have told me it is blood in the storage room," Patterson said. "We believe that's where Callum killed the women. But we struck gold with what you found in his cabin. The photos with the pieces of skin he took from his victims as souvenirs is the solid evidence we've needed. If we can obtain DNA, he'll go down for twelve murders."

CJ rubbed her chin and shook her head.

"There's another twist. Callum is adamant that the owner, Alan, knew about Chantelle. In fact, he says he encouraged her murder. It seems he and the young woman had some sort of run-in."

"So, what happens to him?"

Robert pointed at the visibly shaken owner being led onto the dock in handcuffs. "He's going with us and will be charged. The prosecutor will sort out the details." He glanced at his pad. "As for the man who raped the young woman, Chief Richardson has arrested him and is taking him to Sitka. He'll fight the charge, but the soiled underwear destroys his 'no sex' argument, and the victim and her roommate have both said they'll testify nothing was consensual."

CJ chewed on her bottom lip. "It'll be a tough case to win."

He nodded as he scanned his notes. "The chief knows Victor due to two complaints for sexual misconduct in Sitka three years ago. It appears he didn't like it when the two young women spurned his advances. In the end, no charges were brought as the women decided not to press it and Victor never got physical. As for Debra's death, with your statement and the others who saw what happened, I'm ruling it an accident."

"And what about Walter?" she asked. "His armed robbery was twenty years ago."

"I'll have an agent escort him back to Texas. I'm unsure about the statute of limitations there, and your testimony will be helpful. In the end, he may not be charged or at least not go to prison. Would you agree with that?"

She nodded. "Yes, under the circumstances, I would. He probably saved my life."

They finished by discussing Junior. No charges appeared to be warranted, but Robert told CJ the young man had prior convictions for stalking, breaking and entering, petty theft, and, in his words, being a "pervert."

"The guy is on probation, so his peeping on a young woman here may land him in jail. I'll personally make that report." Robert stared at her and said, "Did I cover everyone?"

She nodded and sighed. "Yes, I think so."

A strange grin spread across his face. "Hell of a vacation."

Robert told CJ they'd work with the proper jurisdictions and keep her posted. She would be needed to testify in each case. "Are you ready to go home?" he asked.

She sighed. "Yes, we are. Assuming Ben's okay to fly back. We need to return to Ketchikan to catch our flight unless we can change and leave from Sitka."

He smiled. "We can do better than that. We'll take you two back to Sitka and fly you back with Harry on our private jet when Ben's cleared for a long-haul flight. It's the least we can do." He thanked them and returned to the back of the lodge.

"I'm ready to be back in Charleston," Ben said as they stared at an otter floating on his back as he crunched on an oyster shell.

"Me too," she said, slipping her arm around him. "There's something else I'm ready to do when we get back."

Ben furrowed his brow. "What's that?"

"Marry you."

———

CJ peered out the window two days later as the plane banked on its final approach into Charleston. The lights on the Arthur Ravenel Jr. bridge twinkled above the dark waters of the Cooper River.

The Harvest Moon from six days earlier remained two-thirds full and hung over the horizon, casting a white stripe across the water's surface.

Her cell phone chimed, and she glanced at the text message from her captain.

Welcome home. Call me ASAP. We have a fresh case.

Friday, December 9
Wando, South Carolina

CJ sat in the Adirondack chair on her uncle Harry's back deck and pulled the blanket over herself. The sun dipped below the horizon as the sky turned a pale orange with strands of yellow. The seagulls scurried to find their resting place for the night.

As the faint rotten egg odor from the marsh filled her nostrils, she reflected on her time at the Paradise Cove Lodge and the recent court proceedings where she served as a witness. The trip was a disaster—an unexpected major storm and numerous crimes and criminals. *How could so much chaos exist in such a beautiful place? And how do I manage to find evil everywhere I go?*

Cal, or as she knew him now, Callum, would face the rest of his miserable life in prison without the possibility of parole for the murder of twelve young women. Based on the evidence, a jury of his peers had found him guilty within less than two hours of deliberation. If anyone deserved the death penalty, it was Callum. Too bad none of the jurisdictions where he murdered his victims had it.

Alan faced five years in jail for his role covering up the murder of Chantelle. Based on everything he did and ignored, it should have been more. *Sometimes, justice falls short.*

FBI Special Agent Patterson's call to his counterparts in Texas resulted in Junior being deemed to have violated his probation. He was fined four thousand dollars and sentenced to one year in jail for voyeurism.

In the case that surprised her the most, an Alaskan jury convicted Evan of the first-degree rape of Kayla. The young woman fearlessly took the stand, and her words brought most of the people in the box to tears. Evan's father's money, power, and high-priced mouthpiece couldn't save him this time. He would spend twenty years behind bars.

Walter escaped jail due to questions over the statute of limitations and his testimony, in which he showed genuine remorse. CJ's words helped him, and in a true shocker, the victim whom he shot all those years ago spoke on his behalf. It seems the man chose to forgive Walter instead of remaining bitter. In the end, even the prosecutor who sought an attempted murder conviction was satisfied with the outcome.

"Here's your hot tea," Harry said as he strolled through the back door. "Oh, look. Your pelican is back." As he slid into a chair beside her, he pointed to the oddly shaped bird perched on a post in the middle of the marsh. "I don't see him too much. He must know you're here."

The clicking of the spoon in his mug as he stirred the honey into his tea echoed in the early evening silence. "Boy, it's been an adjustment not to have an evening beer. Bethany is adamant that I cut down, and I'm sure she's right."

"She is, and I'm happy she's keeping a close eye on you. How long have you two been dating now?" CJ asked.

"Well, let's see," he said, furrowing his brow. "I guess it's been almost seven months."

"And where do you see this going?" she asked, chuckling.

"Well, I was gonna wait until after your wedding, but if you must know." He reached into his pocket, pulled out a small box, and flipped the top open. "I'm gonna ask her to marry me next weekend when I take her to Hilton Head."

CJ almost spat out the sip of hot tea in her mouth. "Really?" She hopped up and hugged him. "I think that's wonderful, and the ring is perfect."

The man who raised her beamed as he talked about Bethany and how much she added to his life. He joked about how it was a no-brainer. "It's smart to marry a much younger woman and a nurse when you're an old fart with a bum ticker."

She settled under her blanket, and they sat silently until he asked her about the next day's ceremony. "Speaking of marriage, are you ready for tomorrow?"

She nodded and smiled. "I am. A bit nervous, I guess, but excited."

His eyes glistened under the faint glow of the porch light. "Well, I couldn't be happier. Ben is a good man, and he balances you out." He cleared his throat. "Who would have thought you'd marry a southern boy?"

They discussed the ceremony, and how Sam and her mother had handled everything. CJ's younger sidekick had given up on the colossal wedding and resigned herself to every detail of the event. All CJ needed to do was show up, which was fine with her.

"Is Ben okay being married by Father Sullivan with only a few of us there?"

"Yeah. He's happy it's the short version without a full Mass. It'll be short, sweet, and then off to Poogan's Courtyard."

"I wish you and Ben were taking a real honeymoon," Harry said. "Three days on Kiawah Island isn't much."

"We'll take a longer one later, but after our last trip, three days after a short drive works for both of us. Besides, The Sanctuary is beautiful, and our villa overlooks the water."

A soft ping drew her attention, and she pulled her cell phone from her pocket. She read the text message from Ben and smiled.

I just wanted to say goodnight and how much I love you. I can't wait to be your husband. See you tomorrow.

THE END

A LETTER FROM JOHN

A ginormous, heartfelt thank you for reading *The Last Cabin*. I'm honored so many have joined me on this journey. If you enjoyed it and want to keep up with my future releases, please sign up on my website using the link below. Your email will never be shared, and you can unsubscribe anytime.

www.johndealbks.com

Whenever I write a new book, I think of you, the reader … what you'd like to read … how you'd like to spend time with the characters I create, and their paths. While the books in my CJ O'Hara Crime Thrillers series all include crimes, I vary the mystery, suspense, and thrills for variety. Using multiple points of view, I provide you with a view through the character's eyes. I'd love to hear your ideas for future books and appreciate your feedback. Please contact me directly through any of the channels at the end of this letter or via email: johndealbks@gmail.com.

If you enjoyed my book, and if it's not too much to ask, please take a moment and leave me a review and maybe recommend *The Last Cabin* to someone else. Reviews and personal recommendations are invaluable to authors and help others discover new authors or titles. As someone who has only been writing a short while, it means the world to me and inspires me to keep writing.

Thank you for being so supportive, and I hope to keep you entertained with my next book. See you soon!

All the best,

John

CONNECT WITH ME!

www.facebook.com/JohnDealBooks

www.instagram.com/johndealbks

www.twitter.com/JohnDealBks

Follow John on Amazon:
https://www.amazon.com/author/j-deal-books

Follow John on BookBub:
https://www.bookbub.com/authors/john-deal

ACKNOWLEDGMENTS

This book would not have been possible without the inspiration from the people and places that make up the Lowcountry and Alaska. These are two of my favorite locations on the planet. Throughout my books, I often draw on my time spent there and the unique people I've met. Most of the locations, landmarks, streets, and restaurants are real.

If you get the chance to visit either place, I highly recommend it. Some of my favorite spots in the Charleston area include Poogan's Porch, the Boathouse at Breach Inlet, Vickery's, The Wreck of the Richard and Charlene, Coconut Joe's, Henry's on the Market, and Dunleavy's Pub. And you can't go wrong with Annabelle's or the Sourdough Bar on Front Street in Ketchikan.

It takes a team effort to produce a book. I owe a giant thank you to all those who have helped me turn my manuscript into a finished work. Beta readers, editors, proofreaders, and designers are an author's best friend. A special shout-out goes to Joanne Lane and Danna Mathias.

Finally, I thank my wife, Lisa, and family for their continued support.

Detective CJ O'Hara's life is full of demons...

Drowning in guilt over the death of her family, the Charleston Police Department's newest cop has more than crime on her plate. But serial killers don't take mental health leave, and as the body counts rise, CJ's instincts and sanity are pushed to their limits.

From cold-blooded killers, to Southern superstitions, and poisonous plants, CJ quickly discovers Charleston's murder cases are anything but ordinary — and they all hit just a little too close to home.

A must-read for crime fiction and mystery fans, the *CJ O'Hara Thrillers* series is a fast-paced collection featuring shocking plots, a gritty female lead, and twisted antagonists.

ABOUT THE AUTHOR

John grew up near Nashville, Tennessee, and now lives in the California Bay Area. His love for the South Carolina Lowcountry stems from the time he spent living in a beach house outside Charleston. This portion of his life inspires his writing and many of his characters. Besides books, he loves spending time with his family, especially his two grandkids, and going to the mountains, the beach, and fishing in Alaska.

Discover more about John Deal on his website.
www.johndealbks.com

Connect with John online.
www.facebook.com/JohnDealBooks
www.instagram.com/johndealbks
www.twitter.com/JohnDealBks

Made in the USA
Monee, IL
16 April 2025